Through Your Eyes

Through Your Eyes

Avril Sabine

Cracked Acorn Productions
Australia

Through Your Eyes

Published by

Cracked Acorn Productions

PO Box 1365

Gympie, Queensland 4570

Australia

978-1-925131-02-4 (Kindle)

978-1-925617-47-4 (EPUB)

978-1-925131-77-2 (Print)

978-1-925941-30-2 (Printed In Australia)

Genre: Young Adult Contemporary

Cover design by Caitlyn Petersen

To my long-suffering kids. It can't be that time, I'm sure I just sat down at the computer!

A girl, a boy in a coma and a diary. How far would you be willing to go to save the life of a stranger?

Life seems determined to throw one problem after another at sixteen-year-old Brenna. She feels like her life is disintegrating before her eyes and has no idea how to sort it out. Her best friend lives in another state, her parents are constantly arguing, her younger sister keeps prying into her things and she wants to break up with her boyfriend without it causing her more problems at school. The only person she has to talk to about everything is a boy in a coma. And she's terrified he might never wake.

*

This story was written by an Australian author using Australian spelling.

Chapter One

Brenna Reardon's fingers tightened on the note when a gust of wind tore at her. She wrapped her arms around herself, pulling her jacket close as the cold breeze strengthened. The action caused the straps of her school backpack to pull against her shoulders. It looked like spring would be late coming to Brisbane this year. She guessed she'd know in a fortnight.

Maybe spring would have Travis thinking about beaches instead of motorbikes. She mentally shook her head. Who was she kidding? There wasn't much chance of that.

She sped up, wanting to get out of the wind. As she entered the hospital a child ran into her. Brenna barely managed to jump out of the way of a flying drink, but the crumpled note was knocked from her hand. An irate mother dragged away the wailing child while Brenna stared at her note soaking in the dark brown liquid. It uncrumpled as the liquid soaked into it and the ink made artistic squiggles across the paper. Brenna bit back the scream of frustration that wanted to escape.

She closed her eyes with a sigh. Her day wasn't going to plan. But lately, none of them had. Some days she wished she could step out of her life and into someone else's. Just for a few moments.

"You all right, honey?"

Brenna opened her eyes to stare into the concerned face of a cleaner, who plopped her mop on the spreading mess. She nodded. "Yeah, I'm just…" she stopped and gestured towards the elevators. "Visiting." She started to move away then glanced back. "Thanks." She dredged up a smile.

The cleaner nodded and returned the smile, her mop moving back and forth over the mess. The soaked paper was irretrievable.

Brenna's steps slowed. She frowned as she tried to recall the details Adrian had scrawled. They hadn't been much clearer to read before their drowning. Maybe she should text Adrian and ask him which room Travis was in. She pulled her phone from her jacket pocket then thought of how low she was on credit. As usual. Maybe she'd try and find him first. Tucking her phone away she headed for the elevators.

Several minutes later she entered a room, coming to a complete halt when she saw the patient in the bed was hooked up to machinery. Clearly the wrong room. She'd give it one more try to find the correct room before she asked Adrian for directions again. Turning to leave the room, she nearly ran into a nurse.

"Well, this is a nice change. I was beginning to think poor Zach wasn't going to get any visitors." The nurse hurried past her and picked up the chart hanging at the foot of the bed.

Brenna hovered not far from the doorway, uncertain what to do. Should she leave? Did the nurse expect her to stay? She watched as the nurse took his blood pressure and temperature and recorded them in the chart.

The nurse strode towards her with a friendly smile. "All done. You can have him back. I put magazines in the top drawer a couple of days ago. Another patient left them behind. You could read them to him. There are a lot of studies that show the sound of a person's voice, or even music, helps coma patients. It's rare for them to remember what's said, but a few recall being spoken to."

Brenna's gaze darted from the nurse to the patient, wondering what she should say. She had to say something. The nurse clearly waited for a comment. "Thank you." It was all she could think of, but it must have been enough because the nurse smiled again.

"You're welcome." The nurse briskly left the room.

Brenna hesitated, her gaze drawn to the doorway. Would the nurse ask her why she was leaving already? It wasn't like she had any experience with hospitals. She didn't have a clue how things were done. Maybe she'd wait a few minutes and then leave. She stepped close to the bed and looked down at the man lying there. Her mouth dropped open when she saw how young he was. Only a couple of years older than her. His dark brown hair spread out around his head on the pillow, his skin was pale and tubes and leads were attached to him.

"Why don't you have any visitors?" Brenna frowned. And how had he ended up in a coma? She really should try and find Travis' room. He was expecting her. She checked the time on her phone. Maybe a few minutes wouldn't hurt. It wasn't like he'd be alone. Adrian was sure to be with him. She sighed.

She had to be honest with herself. The real reason she didn't want to face Travis was because she had to find a way to break up with him. A way that wouldn't cause problems for her at school. She'd never been good at confrontations. Telling someone you wanted to end it while they were in hospital with a concussion and a broken arm, from coming off a motorbike, wasn't the time or place.

She continued to stare at the young man, wondering who he was and how he'd ended up in hospital. And where were his friends? His family? She glanced towards the drawers beside his bed, shifting from one foot to the other. "Well…ahh… maybe I'll read one of those magazines to you," she looked at the name above his bed, "Zach."

She opened the drawer, pulled them out and laughed wryly as she turned to him. "How ironic. I really hope this isn't your usual choice of magazines. You can't imagine how sick I am of motorbikes. Dirt bikes in particular." She dropped the three magazines on top of the drawers. "Sick of them has got to be an understatement. There's been times I've wanted to dismantle Travis' motorbike." She frowned. Did he hear? Understand? Or was her voice only a background noise? She turned to the drawer, looking for something else. There was a large, hard cover notebook and a card. She pulled the card out first and skimmed through the words, expecting a sympathy card she could sit on his bedside drawers. She stared at the card, then read it again. It still said the same.

"What a bitch. Seriously, if you like this Tracey I think you're an idiot." She groaned. "Not that I can talk. That was such a tactless comment. A good thing you're in a coma and won't remember what I've said." She closed her eyes with another groan. "I'm gonna shut up now before I choke on my foot." With a deep breath she opened her eyes to stare at the card. "Or maybe I better stick to reading things to you." Her gaze was momentarily drawn to Zach, perfectly still in the bed. What was it like in a coma? Was it like dreaming? Or was it nothingness? A shiver went through her and she quickly drew her attention away from that uncomfortable thought.

She cleared her throat. "Dear Zach, I'm sorry to hear about your parents and the car accident. I did try and visit you a few times, but you know how I feel about hospitals. I spent more than enough time in them when I was a kid. I know this probably isn't the best time to do this, but we did decide to keep things honest between us. I hope you get well, but I'm sure you'll understand when I say things between us are over. All the best, Tracey."

Brenna closed the card and slid it in the drawer. She wasn't certain what to say. Did you comfort a person who couldn't hear you? It felt wrong not to say something. "I'm sorry she ditched you. But maybe you're better off without her. I mean, a person who's going to run at the first sign of trouble isn't worth worrying about. And to break up with you through a card is cruel." Brenna sighed. "Not that I can talk. Seriously, there has to be a nicer way to break up with someone than that." If only she could figure it out. At least she now knew how not to do it. After another glance at Zach, she stared at the open drawer in front of her. "Let's see if you've got anything else I can read you. Something better than motorbike magazines and cards from ex-girlfriends."

Brenna reached into the drawer and pulled out the large notebook. It didn't quite shut and when she flicked through the pages she saw photos, drawings and bits and pieces stuck in amongst the pages of writing. She closed the book and hugged it to her as she stared at Zach. She was so tempted. It was wrong. Beyond wrong. There was no way she could do that to him. Unless…

She opened the book again and took a quick look at the first page. It wasn't just a journal, with basic notes. It was far more detailed than that. Brenna slowly closed the diary and slid it back in the drawer. Her hand rested on it a moment before she drew away, picking up one of the magazines with a grimace. Before she had a chance to open the magazine, her phone rang. She read the display. It was Travis.

"Hi."

"Where are you? School was out ages ago. I thought you'd be here by now."

Brenna bit back the words that wanted to spill at his tone of anger and impatience. "What's your floor and room number?"

"You're lost, aren't you? Where are you? I'll send Adrian to find you."

"I'm not lost. I just…" she started to explain but decided to simplify. "I lost the note Adrian gave me." Holding her phone to her ear with her shoulder, she grabbed a pen she'd spotted in the drawer and scrawled the direction on her wrist. "Thanks."

"Hurry up. They'll have me discharged with the amount of time you're taking."

"Okay." She glared at the phone when Travis disconnected. She tried to remind herself he must be in pain. Not to mention he hated sitting around doing nothing. She brought her thoughts to a sudden halt as she realised she was making excuses for him again. As soon as she slid her phone in her pocket and the magazines in the drawer, she turned to Zach.

"I guess I'll…" her voice trailed off. What? See him later? Visit again? She didn't even know him. "I hope you get well soon." She strode to the door and stopped to look back at him. Why had no one visited him? She forced herself to step into the corridor, but couldn't resist one last glance back at Zach. She couldn't stand here all day. She had to find Travis. Sliding up the sleeve of her jacket, she looked at the directions. She'd got part of the number correct at least.

She knew she should hurry, but her steps slowed the further she went from Zach's room. Everyone knew you shouldn't run through a busy hospital. She knew it was a lame excuse the moment she thought it. There was no way she could justify the ten minutes it took her to reach Travis' room other than procrastination.

She paused in the doorway and took a deep breath. The two boys in the room were busy talking and didn't notice her. Brenna stared at Travis and wondered, for probably the twentieth time that day, what on earth she was doing with a boyfriend like him. Okay, sure, he was absolutely gorgeous, in the grade above her, and his best friend, Adrian, who'd been kept back a year at school, was eighteen with a car and licence. So yeah, she knew some of the reasons she'd been drawn to him. But it wasn't enough to make her stick around. She needed to find the right opportunity to end things. And okay, she was occasionally tactless and sometimes spoke without thinking, but even she knew now wasn't the right time.

Both the boys were nearly six foot tall, but where Adrian was slim enough to be called gangly, Travis had broader shoulders and a solid build. They were blond and blue eyed. Adrian's hair was baby fine and impossible to do anything with while Travis' hair was thick with a slight wave that looked good even after he ran his fingers through it. That was another thing that annoyed Brenna. Her hair was a reddish brown and no matter what she tried to do with it, nothing worked. She usually resorted to leaving it hang straight and kept it at shoulder length.

Who was she kidding? Everything was starting to annoy her about Travis. They never managed time alone. He spent more time with his motorbike than her. And he expected her to go with him to his uncle's property where he and Adrian kept their dirt bikes. At nearly three hours a round trip from Brisbane, there went most of the day. Their conversation suddenly sank in.

Brenna stepped into the room. "Are you crazy? You fractured your arm. You have to wear the cast for six weeks."

Travis looked at her. "About time you made it. And a fracture isn't a break. Five weeks will be plenty for it to heal."

"Then why does the doctor want you in the cast for six weeks?"

Travis shrugged. "I've been planning this camping trip all year. I'm not about to let a fracture get in the way."

Adrian nodded in agreement. "Yeah, you can't go camping with a cast on."

"I doubt a doctor would remove the cast for your convenience," Brenna said.

Travis stared at the cast for a moment. "I'm sure I can figure some way to get rid of it."

Adrian gestured towards the cast. "We could try bolt cutters. You'd think they'd be able to cut through a cast if they can cut chain links."

Brenna looked in disbelief at the two of them as they discussed the best way to remove the cast early. Why on earth had she agreed to visit him today? She slid her phone out of her pocket and checked the time. "I've got to go or I'll be late home."

"You just got here. Adrian can drop you home once the doctor says I can go."

"I'm surprised you don't check yourself out."

"I considered it." Travis grinned. "But he hasn't

given me a script for painkillers yet. I'm not about to leave without that."

"I'll see you at school on Monday." Brenna turned to leave before she said something she shouldn't.

"Bren!"

She kept her back to him, hesitating. "What?" She barely managed to keep the impatience from her voice.

"I thought we were doing something tomorrow."

She turned to face him, her brain frantically trying to come up with an excuse. "I'm sorry." Nearly giving up, an excuse came to her. "My parents grounded me this weekend because my room was a mess." Knowing he expected it, she dashed across the room, forced a smile, gave him a quick kiss and retreated before he could argue. "I'll see you Monday." She hurried from the room.

When she reached the bus shelter she reminded herself it would have to be soon. Monday. She'd end things Monday. She wrapped her arms around herself as she checked the bus timetable. Fifteen minutes. A glance showed her the warm spot against the shelter wall was taken. Spring couldn't arrive soon enough.

On the bus trip home, Brenna pulled out a couple of her schoolbooks to start on her homework. If the bus was running on time, she'd be home before her parents, but if not she could say she'd been at the library doing her homework. It always paid to have an excuse ready when you weren't where you were meant to be. And it beat trying to think up one on the spot.

Chapter Two

By the time Brenna arrived home, she was late. She ran across the front lawn and onto the concrete verandah that started halfway across the front of the house and curved around to the left, ending just before the kitchen. The concrete was painted mission brown to match the guttering on the single gable roof of the lowset fibro house.

Brenna eased the front door open and closed it quietly behind her. She stood there a moment, trying to figure out what to do. When she heard the raised voices coming from the direction of the kitchen she knew she hadn't been missed. If she was quick, she could be in her bedroom working on her homework before anyone looked for her. She hurried out of the lounge room through a timber archway and snuck down the hall past the closed door of her sister's room and into her own, freezing at the noise behind her.

"Where were you?"

Brenna nearly sagged in relief at hearing her sister's voice. She turned to face her. "None of your business." Danielle had dark brown hair cut fashionably short and blue eyes the same shade as Brenna's.

"I bet Mum wouldn't say the same."

Brenna glared at her sister before she muttered, "Okay. Fine." Her eyes narrowed. "What do you want?"

"Your nail polish. The new one. I want to borrow it."

"And you won't mention I was late."

Danielle mimed zipping her lips.

Brenna hesitated. She'd only ever used it once. She eyed her sister a moment longer before she turned and rummaged in her duchess drawer until she found the correct one amongst the jumble of makeup, jewellery and nail polish. She held it out to her sister. "You better give it back after you've used it. And only once. You're not using the entire bottle."

Danielle grinned as she grabbed the bottle. "Thanks." She dashed from the doorway, heading towards her room.

Brenna sat at her desk and tried to focus on her schoolwork. The shouting kept breaking her concentration. She sighed and dropped her head into her hands, her elbows resting on her desk. Didn't they care everyone could hear? Danielle and herself and, more than likely, the neighbours. She pushed her schoolbook aside and flipped open her laptop. Within minutes she was doing a search on coma patients.

A noise at her open bedroom door brought her head up. Her mum, Sandra, stared at her a moment. She had blue eyes and dark brown hair cut in short layers. "Dinner in ten." She continued past Brenna's room.

The only area past her room was the bathroom she shared with her sister. She tried to recall if she'd hung her towel up properly that morning. When her mum strode past her doorway again, moments later, she guessed nothing had been out of place. She sighed in relief. The last thing she wanted was an argument with her mum when she was in a mood. That only led to grounding and she didn't want to make her earlier excuse a reality. The sound of her dad's car starting up made her groan. Just what she needed. Another silent meal. Neither her nor Danielle would be game to say a word.

Rather than think about it, she turned to her screen and continued to read the comments made by recovered coma patients and their families. She grinned as she read one of the comments. 'I couldn't believe it when the first thing my brother said when he woke up was can't you ever shut up? I screamed. I don't know if it was in fright or joy. Maybe both. He didn't recall a single word, just the constant sound of my voice.'

Glancing at the time on the bottom of her screen, Brenna closed the lid and rose from her seat. She hoped that was true. Then Zach wouldn't know what an idiot she was. Brenna walked down the hallway, turning into the lounge room before she reached her parent's room. She stepped through the second archway that led from the lounge room and across the postage stamp sized hall that her dad's study, the second verandah entrance and the kitchen led off.

The study had once been a single long bedroom that ran the length of the hall and kitchen to the back of the house. Years ago her parents had divided it into a study and laundry since the house only had an old laundry tub that had been in a lean to, in the backyard. This meant the study had no window and you always needed to use the light. Her mum had complained but her dad had shrugged and said it was one of the downfalls of living in a house from the 1930s, but at least they weren't too far from the city centre. And real estate was all about location.

Brenna slid into her seat at the old wooden table, not meeting her mum's gaze and ignoring her sister. Moving her steak out of the way, she pushed her mixed vegetables into her mashed potato before she had a mouthful. She swirled her fork through the mash to blend them better, her mind still on coma patient stories.

"Must you do that Brenna? Stop playing with your food."

"I'm not-"

"Brenna."

She snapped her mouth shut and glared at her food. She wanted to say she hadn't been playing with her food. It wasn't fair. Just because they were fighting again, or was that still, why did she have to get in trouble?

The rest of the meal was silent. The only sound was cutlery against ceramic plates. Danielle pushed away from the table first, carrying her dishes to the sink.

"Have a shower, Dani. Don't leave it until the last minute."

"That's what I planned on doing." Danielle paused at the table, resting her hands flat on the surface. "Can I go into the city tomorrow? There's a whole group of us. We want to go to the Myer Centre. We're thinking of doing some window shopping and seeing a movie after lunch."

"Who's going?"

Brenna carted her dishes to the sink and rinsed them off, tuning out her sister's rambling answer. When she reached the kitchen door, her mum called out.

"Brenna."

She turned back towards the kitchen. "Yeah, I know. Shower."

"Don't get smart with me, Brenna."

She opened her mouth to argue, then closed it when she saw her mum's expression. What was the point? She turned around and stalked to her room. She hadn't said anything different to what Danielle had said. It wasn't fair. She grabbed her flannel pyjamas from her bottom duchess drawer and headed for the bathroom. She slammed the door, muttering under her breath about favoured younger sisters and the unfairness of life, fuming the entire time. When she finished in the bathroom she stopped, hand on the door. She leaned forward, resting her head on the cream coloured timber. What did she have to complain about? At least she wasn't in a coma, alone in a hospital. Where were Zach's friends and family? There had to be someone. No one was completely alone in the world. If it was her in the hospital even Danielle would visit. And Danielle would never be nominated for a 'best sister in the world' award.

She pushed away from the door and headed to her room. She stopped in her doorway. "Dani! Get out of my room."

Danielle looked up from where she sat at Brenna's desk. "Shh. Mum'll be in here yelling. Why are you reading about comas?"

"None of your business."

"I'll mention it to Mum."

"See if I care." Brenna continued to glare at her sister.

"Oh." Danielle pushed away from the desk and strolled towards the doorway Brenna still stood in. "How boring. Why didn't you just say it was for school? It's pretty interesting though. I always thought coma patients could hear and remember everything said to them. I guess that's only in the movies."

Brenna shook her head. "No, but it's rare. Mainly for people in an induced coma. But they have found talking, music and other sensory input can help."

Danielle brushed past her sister. "Oooh. Don't you

sound all intelligent? I guess at least if I ever end up in a coma you'll know what I need." She grinned.

Brenna pushed Danielle against the wall, her hand on her sister's shoulder, and snapped, "Don't joke about it."

"Don't be so serious. What else is there to do around here other than joke? Join in the fights?" Danielle stepped away, lowering her shoulder as she did.

Brenna's arm fell to her side. "Just don't joke about it. Being in a coma is serious."

"Whatever." Danielle headed to her room.

Brenna watched her go. Maybe she'd been a little overboard, but… her gaze was drawn to her laptop screen, all she could think about was Zach lying there alone. She closed her bedroom door and sat at her desk again. She'd read heaps of comments from family, patients and a few medical articles. They all said talking was the best thing. Joking, reading, music. Anything to give them sensory stimulation. She could do that.

What was she thinking? Was she going back? She didn't even know him. Why would he want a stranger visiting? But who else would? He was alone. No one deserved to be stuck in hospital and have no one care they were there. She reread one of the pages that listed suggestions in point form.

- Talk to the patient like they can hear you.
- Talk to them about your day, their past, hobbies and current events.
- Play their favourite music.
- Tease them and joke with them as if they are awake and participating.
- Keep conversations as normal as possible.
- Don't spill secrets. On rare occasions patients not only hear but also remember.

She could do some of those. Not all of them, but at least some of them. The image of the diary came to mind. Maybe he had written about his friends. People she could contact to let them know how important it was for Zach to hear familiar voices. She printed up the list, folding the page to slip it inside her handbag before she returned to her laptop.

Her gaze dropped to the time in the corner of the screen. She hurriedly started to close down her laptop. Unless she wanted to be grounded tomorrow, she'd better get to sleep. After a quick trip to the bathroom to clean her teeth, she crawled into bed. It took her ages to fall asleep, her mind spinning with the information she'd read.

When the sound of arguing voices woke her, Brenna swore as she peered at the alarm clock on her bedside drawers and saw it was nearly four in the morning. She dragged her pillow over her head to drown out the sounds of her parents. Couldn't they stop? Or at least whisper? Why did everything have to be shouted? She drifted off to sleep again groaning when her alarm went off at eight. She hit snooze and rolled over. What stupid idea had made her think this was a good time to get up? As she started to drift off again she remembered. Zach! Not a stupid idea after all.

She sat up, reaching out to turn her alarm clock off properly. She was going to see Zach. No one deserved to lie alone in hospital without a single visitor. And a stranger had to be better than no one.

It took Brenna longer to reach the hospital than she expected. First breakfast, followed by an argument with her mum, then threatening to fail her classes if she couldn't get to the library for research. It had taken nearly two hours to escape to the bus stop with a handful of schoolbooks in her backpack, her handbag jammed in on top of them. It was better than leaving it around for her sister to snoop in.

When she reached Zach's room, she stood in the doorway, doubts plaguing her. Who did she think she was? A miracle worker? Just because she was going to do everything on that stupid list it didn't mean it was going to make a difference. Her courage failed and she started to turn away. She ran into the nurse who'd seen her yesterday.

"Well, this is nice. Two days in a row. Poor Zach must be feeling overwhelmed by all the attention." The nurse smiled at her. "Come on in. No need to hover. You can't visit him from the doorway."

Brenna slowly entered the room, not certain how to answer.

The nurse lifted the chart from the end of the bed. "I'll only be a minute and then he's all yours." The nurse glanced over to Brenna. "Although I'm surprised to see you here on a Saturday. No dates?"

Brenna shook her head as she watched the nurse fiddle with the machine on the other side of Zach's bed, making some notes in his chart.

"You're probably going to want to learn to talk a little more than that." The nurse grinned. "I've got a feeling you'll be doing most of the talking. Zach here seems to be the strong, silent type." The nurse returned the chart to the foot of the bed and her smile faded. "All joking aside, it's good for him to have company. I bet he'd tell you he appreciates it if he could." The nurse paused, a hand on one hip. "Now, he's all yours. Make sure you let him know you're waiting for him to wake up." She grinned again. "He's not going to want to lie around sleeping when he has a pretty girl waiting for him."

Brenna watched the nurse stride from the room, relieved she hadn't seemed to expect a reply. She sighed. Would it count that Zach didn't know her? Would he want to wake up for a stranger? She returned to the door and closed it. There was no way she wanted other people listening to her talk. She felt like she was pushing herself in where she didn't belong. Once she crossed the room she stared down at Zach, wondering if what she was about to do was right. But she couldn't ignore the fact he was stuck in this hospital alone. There was something so wrong about that. She reached out and opened the drawer in the cabinet beside his bed. Sliding the diary out, her stomach lurched. She'd given up keeping a diary the first time her sister had read it and laughed at her, reading the words out loud as she danced down the hallway out of reach.

Brenna pressed the diary against her chest. She wasn't about to do that. She wanted to help him, not mock him. Well, maybe she was a little curious too. Okay, fine, she was a lot curious. But she hoped she wouldn't have invaded his privacy if it wasn't necessary. She drew a chair up to his bed and sat down, wriggling as she tried to get comfortable. She laid the diary in her lap and cleared her throat.

"I know you probably won't remember a single word I've said, but I've read all this stuff on the net that said I should talk to you like you can hear me." She smiled wryly. "But I still feel like an idiot talking to myself. Anyway one site I was reading summarised what most of the sites kept saying. I need to talk about things you like, your past, current events and put on your favourite music for you. Well, I don't know most of that stuff, or even who would. I don't know where your friends are, but I have an idea of how I can find them as well as how to talk to you about your past and things you like."

Brenna cleared her throat again and shifted in the chair. "I know it's personal and I wouldn't normally do this, but I'm going to read your diary to you. I'm sorry, but I don't know any other way to help you." She stared at the unresponsive boy in the bed trying to ignore her feelings of guilt. She cleared her throat and opened the diary, staring blindly at the words for a moment.

Chapter Three

10th August

Happy Birthday to me. Another crappy day, another crappy year. Who says you have to start a new diary on the first of January? I've turned seventeen, isn't the world meant to revolve around me? Or aren't I meant to at least think that? Yeah right, like we're stupid enough to believe that. So my year will start today, the day I was born. Hope that's self-centred enough for them. It's MY birthday. If I don't want to show enthusiasm for it, why should I have to? That doesn't instantly make me self-centred…

Zach put the bowl, milk, cereal and spoon on the table. He eyed the small pile of brightly wrapped presents in front of him. He could easily guess at what they were by the shapes of the packages. Clothes,

clothes, book, CD. He tried not to sigh. Both his parents watched him as they ate their breakfast. Why couldn't they have given him a gift voucher? How hard was that? Now he'd have to dredge up some enthusiasm for gifts he knew would be so far off the mark he'd be wondering all day who they actually had in mind when they picked them out.

"You going to open your presents?" his father, Greg, asked. His grey hair had receded far enough it was now only a narrow band around the back and sides.

"I was thinking of having breakfast first. You know, drag the anticipation out." Or wait until after breakfast for the usual lecture so he could cut it short. He tipped in cereal and milk at the same time and ignored his mother's frown.

"What about your card? You could open that now." His mother, Deirdre, tucked a lock of grey streaked brown hair behind her ear, her brown eyes hopeful.

"Sure, Mum." He had a mouthful of his breakfast as he sat down and picked up the card. He eyed the purple envelope. Not a promising sight. Another mouthful and then he slowly slid his fingers under the flap of the envelope and pulled it open.

He glanced at his parents. He'd rather go to the

dentist than open birthday gifts in front of them. He shovelled in more cereal before he slid the card out of the envelope. Yep, usual mushy crap, usual picture that was suited to someone a good few years younger. He looked over at his parents and forced a smile. "Thanks." He placed the card carefully on the table so it didn't look like he was dismissing it.

"Happy seventeenth, honey." Deirdre smiled tentatively.

He hurried through his breakfast, ignoring the uncomfortable silence. Think uni next year, he reminded himself. As soon as he finished eating, he eyed the four presents.

Greg checked his watch. "You'll be late for school if you don't hurry up."

Zach opened up the first present. Jeans. You couldn't stuff that up. He shook them out and grinned. Okay, scratch that thought. His parents couldn't even successfully buy jeans. Or more likely his mum. He couldn't picture his father shopping. "Thanks." He opened the next present and eyed the print on the t-shirt. He tried hard not to wince at the picture of the band he'd never even think of listening to. His grin was barely kept in place as he reached for the CD. Yep, great choice if you were in early primary school, not the last year of high school.

"The woman at the music shop said it was very popular with kids," Deirdre said.

Zach only nodded as he reached for the book. It was an effort not to laugh. He guessed a collection of boy's adventure stories was a step up from fairytales. Barely. He gathered the wrapping paper and rose from the table. "Thanks."

"A little more enthusiasm would be nice," Greg said.

Zach shoved the paper in the kitchen bin. "It's in the contract kids sign when they become teenagers. No enthusiasm allowed."

"Zach–" Deirdre began.

"Look, I've got to go. I don't want to miss the bus." Zach checked the kitchen clock. He still had plenty of time even if he walked extra slow.

"And that's it?" Greg pushed away from the table. "Your mother spent hours looking for the right presents and we get a thanks, got to go. We go out of our way and you couldn't care less."

He tried to stay calm. To keep his voice low and not give in to the urge to yell like his father had a habit of doing. "I did say a gift voucher would do since you don't believe in giving money."

"It's the same! What's wrong with them? Not the right brands? Not expensive enough? You expect us to put you through university starting next year. We don't have a fortune. I turned sixty-one this year. Most men my age are setting money away for their retirement, not putting an ungrateful child through university."

"Then maybe you should've thought about that when you had me," Zach said, his voice rising.

"Greg, please." Deirdre grabbed at her husband's arm, but he brushed her away.

"You weren't expected. You think I would've deliberately set out to have a child at forty-four? And your mother was only five years younger. I don't care what anyone says these days, it's not the correct age group to have children."

"Yeah, I know. You've told me often enough." Bitterness filled Zach's voice.

"What did you expect us to do? Of course we've done our duty by you," Greg said.

It was his birthday, supposedly his day. He'd lost count of the number of times they'd replayed this argument. It always ended the same. Well, not today. "Then maybe you should've aborted me when you had the chance." He turned his back on his parents, grabbed his backpack and ignored his mother's shocked gasp when she called his name.

He wrapped his hands around the step rails, vaulted

the handful of steps at the back door and headed along the side of the house to the front gate. It was only a medium sized house, but it made up for its lack of size by being set on a larger parcel of land in one of Brisbane's older and more valuable suburbs. The timber cladding had been recently repainted and a screened verandah ran across the front of the house. He stepped through the waist high mesh gate and allowed it to bang shut behind him. "Happy friggin' birthday," he muttered under his breath. "So great to have you in this world. Yeah, right."

* * *

Brenna closed the diary and stared at Zach. "I can't imagine what it must be like to have parents old enough to be your grandparents. Mine are clueless enough as it is. Oh god… I'm sorry. I guess I'm clueless at times too. I forgot… well, I forgot…" Her voice trailed off. Just because he wasn't really listening didn't mean to say she could bring up his parents' death. "I'm sorry. I wish I could help more." She stared at the diary on her lap. "I wish there was some other way for me to help." She rose, placed the diary on the seat and reached out to take his hand that wasn't connected to a drip. She wondered if that was why he was alone. Maybe his parents had been his only family. "You must have friends who could visit. And I'll find them somehow." She stared at him silently. "It doesn't seem right to walk off and leave you alone. I've got to go though. My parents will ground me if I'm late. And believe me when I say there's enough arguments going on at home without me adding to them." She avoided saying she somehow still added to the arguments

Brenna reluctantly let go of his hand and picked up the diary. She nearly dropped it and a photo fell from the back of the book. She bent and picked it up. "Wow!" She looked between the picture and Zach. She turned it over to read the scrawled words. "Thanks for the great night, Love Tracey." She turned it to stare at the two people in the picture. A tall slim girl with long sleek blond hair laughed at the camera.

"No wonder you were dating her. She looks like she could be a model. If she has brains to go with those looks, I'm going to absolutely hate her. Seriously, how fair would that be? And you! I'm speechless. I thought Travis was gorgeous. Normally I wouldn't be game to say a single word to you." It had taken her months to gather the courage to speak to Travis. It probably would've taken her a year to speak to Zach in normal circumstances. Her gaze was drawn to Zach's dark brown eyes staring up at her out of the photo.

Brenna sighed and pushed the photo into the diary before she returned it to the drawer. "I can't believe she ditched you. But I guess with looks like hers it won't be any great effort to replace you." Brenna shook her head with a groan. "And that didn't come out right. I meant she'd probably have a line of guys wanting her." She stared at Zach and tried to see past the tubes taped under his nose and across his cheeks and his paleness. She brushed his hair away from his forehead. "It was nice meeting you, Zach. I hope you get better soon." She groaned again. "I mean, it's not nice you're here, but well…" her voice trailed off. "I think I need to shut up before I say anything else that's stupid." She wasn't used to carrying the entire conversation. It was unnerving. "I have to go now, but I will come back."

She walked to the door where she stopped and her hand rested on the doorknob. She looked back at him one last time, feeling like the worst kind of person to leave him there alone. What else could she do? She had to get home or she'd be in trouble. Again. It took her a few more minutes before she managed to force her feet to move.

* * *

Brenna glanced nervously along the corridor, relieved no one seemed to pay any attention to her. The nurse she'd met in Zach's room the last two times had seemed okay, but she wasn't taking chances. Who knew if they were all the same? She slipped inside the room and stopped by Zach's bed to look down at him. He looked exactly the same as yesterday. She didn't know what she'd expected. A miracle? Yeah, she guessed she had.

Her mind was full of words she couldn't speak. Not that speaking them would give her any answers. How long had he been in here? Were there any other problems besides his coma? But most of all, where was everyone? No one should be left alone in a hospital. She pushed the questions from her mind and concentrated on the reason she was here.

Brenna pulled the diary from the drawer and turned to Zach. "It's so different talking to someone and not being constantly interrupted. My family does it all the time. So do my friends. And we have a bad habit of talking over each other. But a few words would be nice." She sighed. This was so frustrating. No wonder her parents liked to yell. She wanted to scream at Zach to get up. Now!

She pulled the chair over to the bed and dropped onto it. "It wasn't until I left yesterday that I realised you must've been stuck in here on your birthday. Not the nicest way to spend your eighteenth. I guess you'll have to say even your seventeenth was good compared to it. Anyway, happy birthday for last week."

She slipped her hand in her jacket pocket and pulled out a plastic card and a blue paperclip. "I got you a gift voucher. I thought I'd stick with a major department store so you'd have more to choose from. I'll paperclip it to the first page of your diary. I wanted you to know someone listened to what you wanted for your birthday." She left unspoken the words that came to mind. I really hope you get to use it. She stared at him a moment longer. How did you know if you were making a difference? Was that why he had no visitors? The stress was too much? She barely knew him and yet last night it had taken her ages to fall asleep. All she could think about was Zach lying here alone.

Brenna turned the pages of the diary until she reached where she'd left off. Maybe today she'd find a clue about how to get in contact with his friends. Or maybe she'd come across the right memory to draw him from his coma. She hadn't been able to resist reading more coma patient stories last night, when she was supposed to be doing her homework. Sometimes the strangest things woke them.

There'd been one man whose wife had been in tears while she told him the neighbours had complained about how his dog had howled day and night. It had barely eaten since he'd been in hospital and she was going to have to get him put down. He woke up and told her not to even think about it. It was all he'd remembered from weeks of conversations.

Brenna blinked and cleared her throat as she tried to focus on the words in front of her. "I really hope this helps," she whispered.

* * *

Another crappy Saturday in Crapville

Surprise, surprise, they grounded me. I'm only allowed to go to school or work. Well, Dad was the one who grounded me. And I had to make a major apology to Mum since abortion is completely against her beliefs. Yeah well, I don't hear them ever apologising to me for constantly reminding me of how I screwed up both their lives by being born. Like that was my decision. As if I saw this couple with a perfect life and thought, hey, I'm going to make myself into their unborn child and wreck their world. They're far too happy. Someone has to do something about it. Well, I'm out of here for now. They're at the theatre and that's Jordan and the guys sitting on the horn out the front. Will write all about the great escape later…

Chapter Four

Zach closed his diary and shoved it in the second drawer of his desk. He grabbed his wallet and phone and slid them in the pockets of his jeans as he headed for the back door. The horn sounded again and he grinned. There was nothing like getting out of jail for a few hours.

Zach slid into the back seat of the old Holden to sit next to his best friend, Jordan. "So where are we off to?"

"Kelsey's party. Her parents are away for the weekend," Jordan's cousin, Derrick, answered from the driver's seat. He and his friend Brent, who sat in the front passenger seat, were both twenty.

Derrick and Jordan were uncannily similar in appearance. Derrick's dark brown hair was shorter than Jordan's and he had green eyes while Jordan's were blue. He was also a little stockier than his younger cousin but they were both over six foot. Brent, at five foot ten was the shortest in the car, his blond hair as untidy as the torn jeans he wore.

"Sounds good. You sure you'll be able to get me home by midnight?" Zach asked.

"No drama," Derrick said.

Within twenty minutes, Derrick pulled up behind a line of cars that filled the normally quiet street. It was easy to tell where the party was. They followed the music and stepped inside the open door of the large, rendered brick house straight into a crowd. The beat of the music and the sound of talking and laughter filled the air.

Zach glanced at his watch. "Meet back here at eleven thirty?" Derrick nodded before he disappeared into the crowd, Brent on his heels.

Zach and Jordan pushed their way through the crowd and smiled at people in greeting every now and then. Zach found a spot not far from the sound system that wasn't as crowded.

Jordan leaned close to Zach so he could be heard over the music. "I'll grab us a couple of drinks. How about you grab us a couple of girls?" He grinned.

"Any preference? Blonde? Brunette?"

"At this point I'd take almost anything. I don't know why they have to fall all over you."

"You just need more confidence," Zach said.

"And you've got too much. How about sharing some?"

Zach laughed. "No, my problem is I don't give a shit. You try too hard."

"And here I thought the problem was that no girl's going to look twice at me when I'm hanging around you. I'm going to get those drinks so I can drown my sorrows."

Zach watched Jordan disappear into the crowd and his smile faded. He looked around to see who he knew. Before he had time to take proper notice, his phone, on silent mode, rang. He checked the display and swore. He moved close to one of the speakers before he answered it. This close he could feel the music vibrate through his body.

"What?"

"I've been ringing the home phone for the past ten minutes. Where are you?"

"I probably didn't hear it over my music, Dad."

"We better not get more complaints from the neighbours about the noise level. Is that laughing I can hear in the background? What's going on there?"

"Well gee Dad, I'm in the middle of throwing a party. Think you could give me a call just before you leave the theatre so I've got plenty of time to clean up before you get home?"

"Don't get smart with me, Zachary."

"What the hell do you think I'm doing? Did you ring to check on me? Because you better make it quick. I'm so bored that in another five minutes I might have to put a gun to my head and pull the trigger. At least with how loud my music is the neighbours won't call the cops about the gunshot."

"We don't have a gun in the house."

"Then I guess that option's out."

"This attitude of yours needs working on, Zachary."

"Apparently. If you've finished complaining? I've got to sharpen a knife since there's no gun." Zach smiled at the silence on the other end of the phone. Mission accomplished. Interrogation ended.

"You finished?" The words were sharp and clipped.

"Apparently."

"Your mother wants you to take a chicken out of the freezer and put it in the fridge to thaw for lunch tomorrow. Make sure you put it in a bowl."

"Sure. That all? No more questions?"

"I'm not letting you ruin my night. Your mother and I have been looking forward to this show."

"No, we can't have that. Not after all the effort

I've put into screwing up your entire life." He disconnected and put his phone in his pocket, his mood ruined. He scowled as he moved away from the speaker.

"Zach!"

His gaze was drawn to the crowd, watching as a curvaceous blonde bounced towards him. She threw her arms around him and gave him an enthusiastic kiss on his cheek. Her friend, also blond, a little taller and slimmer than her, stood quietly beside her.

"Hey, Betts. What're you doing?"

Betts chuckled. "If you have to ask that, Zach, then you do have problems." She looked up at him through her lashes. "Well?"

Zach laughed. "Okay. Besides kissing everyone in sight, what are you up to?"

"Oh, you know, the usual. Have you met Haley? She's my latest project."

Zach shook his head, his lips still curved in a smile. "Scrap booking or pottery is a project. People aren't."

"Oh don't be boring. I can have whatever I like as a project."

Zach turned to Haley, still smiling. "Give in. Betts is a steamroller. Trust me when I say your life will be much easier if you do."

Haley hesitantly returned his smile.

"Like you did?" Betts wrapped her hand around his arm and moved closer. She pouted theatrically. "Maybe you should take your own advice."

"Maybe. But then how boring would that be for you? You need at least one challenge." He untangled her from his arm and reached for one of the bottles of beer Jordan brought back with him.

"Jordie!" Betts threw her arms around him and gave him an equally enthusiastic kiss.

Jordan cringed at the name. "Hi, Betts."

Zach grinned at him and raised his brows. "As ordered. Satisfied?"

"You are a sadist."

Zach laughed at Jordan's comment. He ignored Betts' momentary look of confusion. "Jordan, this is Haley. You might want to rescue her before Betts gets her claws in too deep. She's looking for a new project."

Jordan turned to Haley and his smile became more forced. "Hi."

Haley's smile was equally forced. "Hi."

Zach grabbed the beer off Jordan and put both of them on the window ledge behind him. He placed a hand on each of their backs. "Run along children. Sounds like they're playing your song." He grinned at the daggered look Jordan sent him and gave them another gentle shove forward.

"Zach–" Betts started to protest.

"Here." He gave Betts Jordan's beer and took a mouthful of his own. He tugged her back to his side when she would've followed Jordan and Haley. "Besides terrorizing humanity, what else have you been up to, Betts?" Zach tuned her voice out once she got started and made the appropriate 'mmm' and 'ah-huh' each time she paused for breath. When he thought Jordan and Haley had enough of a head start, he interrupted. "I see someone I've been trying to catch up with. See you later, Betts."

He disappeared into the crowd before she could follow. It didn't take long to run into someone else he knew and the rest of the night passed quickly. He arrived at the front of the house a bit before eleven-thirty. He had to look twice at the couple out the front.

Jordan and Haley were entwined closely. The rest of the world stepped around them as they kissed like they'd be separated for months. Seeing Derrick and Brent push their way through the crowds, Zach took pity on his friend.

He crossed the lawn. "Okay, break it up children."

He grinned as they sprung apart. "Time to swap phone numbers. Here comes the chauffer."

Jordan glanced towards the front door in time to see his cousin step out of the crowd, Brent beside him. His cheeks coloured and he turned back to Haley. "Ah…"

Haley looked away, but pulled out her phone. An expression of relief crossed Jordan's face and he took his phone from his pocket. He quickly keyed in her number, saved it then rattled off his.

Derrick clapped Jordan on the back as Haley walked away. "Nice one, little cousin. But seriously, would it have hurt you to kiss the girl goodnight?"

"Like I need tips from you. Isn't your longest relationship a week?" Jordan asked.

"That's not nice, Jordan," Zach protested as they started to walk towards the car. "It was eight days."

"Very funny. You two feel like walking?"

"Sure. And I'll tell my father you kidnapped me and dumped me out here." Zach grinned.

"Harsh. Why don't you just give me to terrorists or something? Your father scares the hell out of me," Derrick said.

"Tell me about it." Jordan shuddered. "I'd rather get yelled at by my father than get one of those looks from yours, Zach. You know the one. The look that makes you think you're an insignificant little bug and he's going to squish you into the ground."

"Give it a decade and it'll start to lose its effectiveness."

*   *   *

Brenna closed the diary and stared at Zach thoughtfully. "You know, I think Jordan's right. I'd rather be yelled at by my parents than have them look at me like that. My parents have never told me they regretted my birth either. And believe me when I say I've been obnoxious enough, at times, I'm surprised they've never said it."

She rose and slipped the diary in the drawer. She noticed a necklace with two rings on it tucked in the back corner. She lifted them out and looked at the simple diamond ring and plain gold band. She wondered who they belonged to. She placed them back in the drawer and closed it. Yet another unanswered question.

"I'll be back tomorrow afternoon. I won't be able to stay as long as I did today. I'll probably have to tell my parents I'm going to the library to research an assignment after school. I don't know how long they'll swallow that for." She moved forward and rested her hand against his cheek momentarily, careful not to disturb the tube. She opened her mouth to speak but words failed her.

How did you tell someone you were glad to meet them, even if it was only through their diary, but sad they were stuck in hospital? Yet if he weren't, she'd never have met him. Instead, she closed her mouth and said nothing. She brushed his hair back from his forehead. Life was so complicated. "See you tomorrow, Zach."

* * *

Brenna stared at the clock on the wall. Only minutes until the bell rang. If she hurried she'd be able to catch Travis alone. Breaking up wasn't something that should be done with an audience. The shrill sound catapulted her from her seat, the sound of chairs scraping across the floor filled the air, accompanied by numerous voices blending into a wave of noise. She grabbed her schoolbag and hurried to where Travis' last class had been. One of the few he didn't share with Adrian. A scream threatened to escape when she saw Adrian stride towards the classroom from the opposite direction. She came to a sudden stop.

"Watch it," a boy growled from behind her as he stepped around her.

She ignored him. Five minutes. That was all she needed. She hoped. Lunch had been a fail too. Was she too old to stamp her feet and throw things? Brenna forced a smile when Travis spotted her.

He reached her side, Adrian with him. "We're all headed into the city. You coming?"

Brenna shook her head. "I have to get home. Mum's still angry with me. I have to go straight home after school this week." The second statement at least was true. Her mum was always angry with her lately.

"What about the weekend? Are we still seeing a movie?"

She hesitated. Surely there'd be a few minutes sometime between then and now when she'd catch Travis on his own. "Ahh, I'll have to see what Mum says. I'll wait till she's not so angry."

Adrian nodded. "Good strategy."

Travis dropped an arm around Brenna's shoulders and started walking with her at his side. "Can we drop you home on our way to the city? It's not far out of our way."

Brenna shook her head. "Better not. You know I'm not allowed to have a boyfriend. She'd ground me for life."

Travis grinned. "I keep telling you I could convince her to drop that rule."

"You don't know my mum." Brenna pulled away from Travis as they stepped outside. "I better run. I don't want to miss my bus."

Travis reached out and took her hand so he could tug her back to him. "That's not much of a goodbye."

Brenna's hand went to his chest as she leaned in to kiss him quickly. It wasn't that it was a chore. It just felt wrong. Like she was cheating somehow. "I'll see you tomorrow." She ran towards the buses, hoping the one headed towards the hospital hadn't left yet. A sigh of relief escaped when she saw something was finally going right. She slid onto a vinyl seat halfway down the aisle and pulled out her homework. It was hard to focus. Her mind swung from thoughts of Zach alone to Travis who never was. Giving up, she returned her homework to her schoolbag and watched for her stop.

With nothing but her thoughts to occupy her, the trip seemed longer than usual. But Brenna finally entered Zach's room and dropped her schoolbag just inside the door.

"You're so lucky you're finished with high school. At least I'm guessing you are. You weren't kept back were you, Zach? You seemed certain you'd be at uni this year." She dragged a chair over to the bed. "I keep forgetting to return the chair when I'm finished. I wonder if it annoys the staff having to put it back."

She took Zach's hand and looked at him for a moment. "Here I am complaining about school and you're-" She broke off, the words 'stuck in a coma and your parents dead' echoed in her mind. "Well, you're… here. I can't believe how thoughtless that was." She sighed heavily. "These one sided conversations are difficult to carry." She recalled the advice to try joking and forced a smile to her lips. "You know you could always wake up and join in. I won't even mind if you want to interrupt."

Her smile faded. How did people cope when it was someone they loved? And how did they drag themselves away each day? She reached out with her free hand and brushed his hair back from his forehead. "Sleeping Beauty with a gender change. We just have to figure out what it'll take to wake you. I'm guessing it's going to be more than a kiss." She smiled slightly. "Sleeping Beauty. Maybe that's just for girls. How about Sleeping Handsome, since you're male. Although that doesn't sound right. Sleeping Gorgeous? Nope. Somehow they all sound wrong. Sleeping Beauty it is. And you're going to wake up, too." She continued to stare down at him.

He was so pale. And still. She dragged her thoughts away from that direction. He wasn't going to always be still. He'd wake up and return to his life. She sighed. And then she guessed she'd never see him again. "So, are you ready for another few pages? I know it's your life and you've lived it, but it's important to talk about your memories and things you enjoy." She paused. "And I guess I should be honest and tell you I'm curious. I mean, I wouldn't read it to you if it wasn't important, but I guess I've got caught up in it." Her voice dropped. "And it's better than focusing on my life."

Brenna lightly squeezed his hand before she released it and turned to the drawers. She lifted out the diary and the rings caught her attention. She put the diary on the top of the drawers, where the magazines still sat, and picked up the rings. "How can anyone know they've met the right person? How can they make a commitment and know they'll want to be with someone until death do us part?" The rings spun on the end of the chain. "And what about when it's over? How do they end things without war breaking out?" She blinked. Questions. Always questions.

Once the rings were back in the drawer, she turned to Zach. "I always seem to have so many questions and no one has the answers." She sat down and opened the diary. Maybe today she'd find a few answers to her many questions about Zach.

Chapter Five

Why won't August end?

Mum cornered me earlier today. She went on and on about how stressful work is for Dad and how I should give him a break. Okay, so she didn't use those exact words, but I'm not about to write three dozen when a handful will say the same thing. What about the stress of year twelve? I know it's been decades for them, but surely they must recall something. About the only good thing to happen this month is Jordan wandering around with a stupid grin on his face because he can't think about anything other than Haley. Okay, so it's not such a good thing for the rest of us who have to see the stupid grin, but at least he's having a good month.

Finally- September decided to arrive

Derrick called in the million favours we owed him for all the chauffeuring. They have a house inspection in about a week and their place is a mess. Too many parties and no one willing to help clean up…

Zach stepped back onto the top step as a paintbrush was shoved at him. "At least let me get in the door." He pushed past Derrick and into the lounge room.

"Don't have time. It's going to take us a year to get this place in the same condition it was when we moved in." Derrick looked around, a troubled expression on his face as his gaze roamed the walls of the old Queenslander.

"Did the other guys round up anyone?"

"Ahh, I think Brent did. Not sure about Mike. He said he would." Derrick rubbed the back of his neck. "Think you can paint over the bogged up holes in here and the hallway? The last party was a smashing success, in more ways than one."

Zach groaned. "Please, no jokes. Or should I say no attempts at jokes?" Zach glanced around the lounge room and noted the couple of places where the fibro walls had been patched. The lounge room had once been an open verandah until it had been enclosed years ago. The carpet was now faded, the lounge chairs could only be politely called well aged, but the flat screen television was large, taking up one corner, and surrounded by a scattering of games and a playstation. "What paint have you got for in here?"

"It's in the kitchen. You be right? I need to start on the yard."

Zach raised the paintbrush. "Yep." He paused. "You do realise that after this weekend you'll be the one owing us."

"No drama. Just don't expect me to give you a lift anywhere until this inspection's over."

Zach headed for the kitchen and found Jordan and Haley in there. Jordan scrubbed out the stove while Haley stood on the sink and took down the curtains. Zach saw the tin of paint on the end of the bench and rested his hand on it while he grinned at Jordan who stepped back from the stove.

Jordan wiped the back of his wrist across his forehead. "I swear this job should be yours. Derrick must have driven you around more than he did me."

"Your cousin." Zach picked up the tin of paint.

"I'm going to walk everywhere if he expects me to clean his stove again for getting in his car. It's not even that great a car. It's got rust and the interior's wrecked."

"I think it's kind of neat they have their own place." Haley sat on the edge of the sink so she could drop to the ground where she'd thrown the curtains.

"Expensive though. He probably eats half of his meals at our place." Jordan eyed the stove again. "Which is why I can't understand the mess the stove's in."

"So, where's your frilly apron, Jordie?" Zach laughed when Jordan threw the steel wool ball at him. He moved out of the way and headed to the lounge room as he ignored Jordan's uncomplimentary reply.

Zach was surprised at how relaxing he found painting the repaired walls. And how quickly the time passed. He looked up as Mike, Derrick and Brent's housemate, came in the front door. Mike was shirtless, sweaty and dotted with lawn clippings. He didn't envy him being stuck outside on such a warm day.

Mike's blond hair was cut short enough to almost be bald and his sandy coloured stubble showed it had been several days since he'd shaved. His face was flushed from the heat and he wiped his hand across his upper lip to remove the beads of sweat. "We should have rented an apartment. Or at least something with a concrete backyard. And probably something modern with solid brick walls that don't let the cold in during winter or that people can't put their fists through."

"I get the feeling you're meant to do a little bit each week and then it's not such an issue."

Mike eyed the lounge room walls. "Hey, not a bad job there. Forget uni and becoming a vet. Get a job as a house painter. You're mad going to uni. And who wants to be covered in blood and gore?"

"They earn good money."

"Is that the only reason you're becoming a vet? No dream of saving animals from cruel humans or something."

"Nah. It's interesting. Besides, animals don't back talk like humans."

"Interesting isn't a good enough reason to choose a lifelong career."

"Then what is? And what do you think I should be doing instead? Following in my father's footsteps? Not happening. A week working at the bank would have them carting me off to a padded cell."

Mike laughed. "Yeah well, there's got to be something more interesting and less gory."

"Blood doesn't bother me."

Derrick stepped inside in time to hear the last

comment. "It will if you're the one shedding it." He turned to Mike. "I thought you were getting a drink and coming right back. Stop distracting the helpers."

"Stop threatening them. I don't have enough chains to put on them so they can't escape." Mike headed for the kitchen.

Derrick glanced around the lounge room. "You look like you've finished in here."

"Yeah. About to start in the hall."

"Thanks for this. We'd never get it done without help."

"Hey, it's the least I can do after all the years you've been running me around. Not to mention teaching me to drive."

"No drama. That's what mates are for."

Zach grinned and held up the paintbrush. "Exactly."

* * *

Brenna leaned back in the chair to stare at Zach. It was impossible to imagine him painting walls. Not with how he looked at the moment. She drew out the photo. Yes. The boy in the photo, with his grin and amused look, would've been capable of anything. She closed the diary.

"I've got to go home. If I'm late my parents will ground me. Besides, the library's shut now. It's not like I can use it as an excuse if it's not even open." She dropped the diary in the drawer and leaned against it. "I hope you realise I'm not reading your diary to invade your privacy. It's the only thing I could think of. I don't know your past, your hobbies, your friends… nothing. I know what it's like to have your privacy invaded. My sister practises on me daily. I don't know what's worse. Sounds like being an only child hasn't been that great for you, but having a fourteen-year-old sister is no joy either. She pretends to be me on the phone and reads my emails if I don't log out of my laptop. Even if I only leave my room long enough to get a drink. And she gets to do everything years earlier than me."

She moved closer to the bed and took Zach's hand. "Like when I turned sixteen in June, I was finally able to wear makeup without having to hide it. A few weeks later she got into my makeup and Mum didn't say anything. Well, she did, she said how well Danielle applied it." Brenna rolled her eyes. "When she caught me wearing makeup just before my fourteenth birthday I was grounded for a week. How fair is that?"

She fell silent a moment. "I wonder how good a

listener you normally are. I haven't had anyone I can really talk to since my best friend moved to Western Australia last year. I was so mad at her parents. So was Bec. And some things I don't want to write in an email or on my messenger, particularly since I risk having it read by my sister. And her internet isn't fast enough for voice calls, which sucks since I'm not allowed to ring her. My parents had a fit over how high the phone bill was the first month Bec left. Now I'm only allowed to ring on her birthday and at Christmas. She got in trouble for the same thing. But we always rang each other every day. Several times a day. It was a hard habit to break."

Bec's parents had said she'd be permanently grounded if their bill was ever higher than usual again. And now they never talked. Not about anything important. It was beginning to feel like she'd lost her best friend forever.

She rested her hand against Zach's cheek for a moment, feeling the ridge of the narrow tube under her palm. "See you later, Sleeping Beauty." A slight smile touched her lips. "You are going to wake. That's the way the story goes. I heard the tale heaps when I was a little kid, and I saw the movie. Sleeping Beauty always wakes up." She moved away to pick up his chart and frowned as she tried to make sense of the doctor's handwriting. She returned the chart. Who cared what it said anyway. He was going to wake. That was all that was important. She stared at him a moment longer. It was past time to leave. Turning, she slowly walked away.

*　*　*

Brenna stomped out of her bedroom and picked up the cordless phone from where it lay on one of the lounge chairs, ringing. "Yeah."

"Answer the phone properly. What if it had been something important?"

"You said you'd ring at four. Who else would it be?" Brenna held the phone away from her ear as her mum's voice rose. A pity she couldn't do that when they were in the same room.

"Are you listening?"

"As if I'd be allowed to do anything else."

"Don't take that tone with me, Brenna. There's no reason you should need to go to the library every day. We pay a fortune for the internet. Use it for something practical instead of playing games."

"We're not allowed to rely completely on the net for our research."

"Do you have to argue everything I say?"

How could she answer that? If she said no, that'd prove the point. If she said yes, she'd be in trouble. She started to pace.

"Well?"

"No," she muttered.

There was a moment of silence. "Take meat out of the freezer to thaw for dinner."

"Okay."

"And if you don't cause any arguments tonight you can go to the library tomorrow."

Brenna bit back the comment she wanted to make. "Okay."

Another moment of silence, this time followed by a sigh. "Just try for once, Brenna."

"I sa–" she broke off the angry words that started to pour out of her as an image of Zach, alone in hospital, filled her mind. "Okay."

"I'll see you this evening. And don't forget to take the meat out of the freezer."

"Okay." Brenna dropped onto the lounge chair, with a groan, as soon as her mum hung up. How was she going to survive the night? But what choice did she have? She needed to visit Zach. He didn't have anyone else.

She rolled off the chair to land on her feet. Meat from the freezer. She better do that before she forgot.

And no arguments. She could manage. Danielle's bedroom door slammed. Hopefully. No, she was going to manage. And nothing her mum or Danielle said or did was going to make her argue.

Brenna opened the freezer and pulled out a parcel of meat to drop it on the sink. Homework. That's what she needed to do. When she sat at her desk and turned on her laptop, she couldn't help doing a little more research on comas. That little bit turned into numerous pages.

She dropped her head into her hands as she tried to work out how long Zach had been in a coma. She tried to recall the information she'd gained from reading his chart. Her head rose. About two and a half weeks. Her gaze was drawn to the page displayed on her screen. The words five weeks seemed to leap out at her. At five weeks his prognosis would start to look grim. That wasn't far away. He had to wake up. Really soon. She wished she'd been able to read the scribbles on Zach's chart that the doctors seemed to think were actual sentences. How bad was he? And what was the risk of brain damage? She closed her eyes. No more. She wasn't going to read another single word. Zach would wake up. It was that simple.

She glanced at the time on her monitor, swearing

under her breath when she realised how much time had passed and she hadn't even started her homework.

"You're not still reading about comas, are you? What are you writing? A book?"

Brenna closed the page and turned to glare at her sister. "Get out."

"Mum sent me to tell you dinner's ready."

Brenna opened her mouth then quickly closed it. At least one thing had to go right today. She'd once again failed at getting Travis alone, but she wasn't going to fail at no arguments.

She pushed away from her desk. "Okay."

Danielle stepped further into the bedroom. "You know your nail polish–"

"What did you do to it?" When she heard how demanding her words were she took a deep breath, trying to remain calm.

"It wasn't my fault. Mum must've been moving stuff around in my room. I knocked it off my duchess and it hit the metal feet of my oil column heater. I had to use up all your nail polish remover to clean it up."

Brenna's jaw clenched. Her hands became fists. She wanted to yell, instead her eyes narrowed and she kept her voice soft. "I hate you."

"I'm gonna tell Mum you said that." Danielle spun away.

Brenna threw herself forward and grabbed her sister's arm to pull her into her room. "Don't you dare." She kicked her door shut behind them. "If you get me into trouble tonight I'll never forgive you and I'll make you pay forever."

Danielle pulled away from Brenna. "What's in it for me?"

"Me not throwing all your nail polish out the window and onto the road."

"You wouldn't."

Brenna held her sister's gaze. "Try me."

"Fine." Danielle spun away and opened the door. She stepped into the hallway then looked over her shoulder. "I'm going to remember this."

"Good." Brenna watched as her sister stalked away. Her hands were still tight fists and anger burned inside her. She tried to focus on Zach, alone in hospital. She couldn't yell at her sister. No arguments. She could do this. One meal then she could escape to her room. How hard could it be?

Brenna was surprised to find it wasn't as hard as she'd expected. Danielle sulked the entire meal, her parents glared at each other silently across the table and Brenna was able to quickly eat without drawing any attention. Not wanting to push her luck, she readied herself for bed in record time and headed to bed early.

Turning her light out didn't make her fall asleep. She lay awake for hours, the words 'five weeks' spinning round in her mind. She wondered if prayer would help then had to drag herself from bed to huddle in the dark at her laptop as she googled how to pray. There were too many religions.

A sound in the hallway made her hastily close the lid of her laptop and slide back into bed. Prayers and the words 'five weeks' tumbled through her mind. She finally fell into a restless sleep to be disturbed late at night by an argument, followed by the slam of the front door, then a car door. Keeping her eyes tightly closed, Brenna pulled her pillow over her face.

Chapter Six

A nurse was in the room when Brenna walked in. She dropped her bag just inside the door and waited while the nurse made notes in Zach's chart. The nurse looked her over once she'd hooked the chart back on the foot of the bed.

"Are you meant to be in here?"

Brenna nodded, words failing her. Again.

"You're about as talkative as my patient." The nurse continued to watch her. When Brenna only answered with a shrug, she spoke again. "How do you know Zach?"

Brenna had spent several restless nights planning her answer to this question in case she was asked. Being confronted with it made her forget her carefully planned sentences. "School. Last year." The nurse continued to look at her. "He was a couple of grades ahead of me." More silence. "I come in and talk to him. I… he… I know I'm talking to myself, but well…" she shrugged.

The nurse smiled slightly. "Maybe not. Some patients have woken up and said they heard everything said to them." Her smile became a grin. "I hope you're not spilling any deep, dark secrets."

Over her initial nervousness, Brenna laughed. "I have a younger sister. She doesn't believe in letting me keep secrets. So no, no deep, dark secrets."

The nurse's grin faded. "You have my sympathy. They don't get any better as they grow older. I have two younger sisters and a younger brother. My brother turned up a month ago and asked if he could stay a week. Longest bloody week I've ever come across. I can't wait until he leaves." She glanced at Zach. "Just make sure you don't touch any of the monitors or anything."

"I only sit beside him and read out loud."

The nurse nodded. "And don't worry. I'd be surprised if he recalls a single word you've spoken to him. But keep reading. The more sensory stimulation, the better. He's a good looking kid. It's sad he hasn't had many visitors."

"I wish I could get in more often. School takes up too much time."

The nurse reached the door and opened it. "I might see you tomorrow."

Brenna shook her head. "I won't be in again until Saturday. I couldn't make it yesterday either." After all her efforts to keep from arguing her mum had only given her a single day for her supposed trip to the library .

The nurse looked sympathetic. "Don't beat yourself up over it. He probably doesn't know he spends most of his time alone." She smiled sadly as she closed the door behind her.

Brenna moved to Zach's side and took his hand. "I wish you could hear me. I want you to wake up. So, can you hear me in there? Hurry and wake up." She stared a moment then smiled wryly. "If you can hear me then I've probably bored you to tears by now. Sorry about that." She frowned. "I'm trying to think what I've told you. Other than how gorgeous you are, that is. But you probably already know that. And I promise not to drool all over you while I'm sitting here keeping you company. Although let me tell you you're not looking your best. Tubes and hospital gowns don't do anything for anyone. But I suppose they don't make you look completely terrible either. Now if I were in the same situation I'd probably scare little kids after they took one look."

Her forced tone of lightness evaporated as the words 'five weeks' echoed in her mind again.

She brushed his hair back from his forehead and her fingers lingered. "I did some research on comas when I couldn't get in to see you yesterday. I even found myself praying last night that you'd wake up. And believe me when I tell you I wouldn't know the first thing about how to pray. I had to google how to go about it. How pathetic is that? And that wasn't a simple thing either. Do you know how many religions have web pages on how to pray? I prayed to four of them and then I worried if that meant they'd cancel each other out."

Brenna shook her head and her lips curved into a self-mocking smile. "So it mightn't have been any help after all. But enough of my sad pathetic little attempts. How about I read more of your diary? Although I don't know how much it's helping. You should have your friends here. Like Jordan and Derrick. Where are they? Did something happen to wreck your friendships? I can't understand why no one's here with you. And I don't count. You wouldn't have a clue who I am. You wouldn't even be able to pick me out of a line up."

As soon as she had the chair by the bed she took the diary out of the drawer. She lifted the necklace again.

"I wish you could tell me who owned these rings." Were they his mother's? But surely she would've had them on her fingers, not a necklace. She sighed. "I always have so many questions." She turned to Zach. "I rarely feel comfortable asking them. Except of my family." She paused. "You know I'm probably going to get into the habit of talking to myself. I'll end up being one of those crazy old ladies who wander around muttering to themselves and carrying on conversations with people who aren't there."

She placed the rings in the drawer before she closed it and sat in the chair near Zach's bed. She opened the diary. The picture taped to the next page caught her attention. She read the names underneath. "That's not how I pictured Haley. She's pretty. I expected a quiet mousy little blonde. And Jordan is gorgeous too. I don't know what he was going on about. Well, maybe I do. He can't compete with you. So who took the pic of the three of you? And where was it taken? How am I meant to talk to you about your past when you haven't written enough information?"

Brenna closed her eyes and took a deep breath as she heard the tone of hysteria in her voice. "I'm sorry. It's just-" she broke off. It's just that I don't want you to die. Instead she whispered. "I need you to wake up. I... worry about you." Her fingers tightened on the diary as she stared down at the words. It was several minutes before she trusted herself to speak calmly.

*   *   *

Hangover Sunday

I hooked up with Betts at a party last night. She's been ringing me all day. I shouldn't have had so much to drink. It makes me forget how annoying she is. It wasn't like I made any promises to her. It was just sex. Anyone would think I'd agreed to love her for life or something. I guess she won't be calling again today after the last call. But what can she expect? I'd had enough. It's not the first time I've slept with her and I had to put up with the same theatrics the next day. Maybe next time I get drunk I'll remember to avoid her like the plague. Who am I kidding? The girl is hot until she opens her mouth to speak. Who can resist when they're drunk and Betts is drunk and on the hunt? My head is killing me. I'd better go and take something for it. I have to work today…

"Hello, bastard."

Zach grinned across the counter at Betts. "Still angry, Betts?"

She sniffed. "I'm only talking to you because I want two pizzas. Otherwise I wouldn't give you the time of day."

"How about the time of night?" He hoped her glare meant she was finally getting the message.

"I really hate you."

"Yep. So you said last time."

"I mean it this time. Now hurry up with those pizzas."

"Usual?" At Betts' nod, he quickly made the pizzas and popped them in to cook. He leaned against the counter. "Odd how you waited for so late in the day to come in and get pizza. Not lunch time anymore and not late enough for dinner. Makes me wonder if you were waiting for me to be all alone."

"I'm not talking to you."

"Betts, I'm not going to change my mind. I didn't last time. You keep ringing me and hassling me and I'm going to keep saying things neither of us wants to hear."

"Then why did you sleep with me?"

Zach grinned. "I've never claimed to be a saint. You were all over me, I'd had too much to drink and I wasn't thinking with my brain. If it were just a matter of looks I'd say hell yeah. But it's not. We both like our own way too much. Look how many arguments we have as friends. We'd probably kill each other within a week if we tried dating."

"Are you going to pull out that stupid old line of, it was great, but how about we just be friends?"

"If you're looking for compliments I'm sure I gave you enough last night." He frowned. "Or was it this morning? Time's a little hazy. Other images are fairly clear though."

"Are those pizzas ready yet?"

Zach chuckled at her change of subject. "Nope."

"You didn't even look."

"I don't need to. You going to keep hassling me about last night? Ringing me every five minutes? Trying to turn it into something it was never meant to be? I'm far too young to die and have a million things I want to do."

"Like breaking every girl's heart you come in contact with?"

"Get over it, Betts. Go and find yourself a new project." He knew if he were the least sympathetic she'd start thinking he wasn't serious.

"That's another thing I'm annoyed with you about. You stole Haley."

Zach shook this head as he turned from her to remove the pizzas from the oven and slice them. "That wasn't me. That was Jordan."

"But you probably put him up to it."

Zach placed the pizzas on the counter and took the money Betts handed him. "I don't spend my days trying to think up ways to annoy you." He grinned. "It comes naturally."

"I still hate you." Betts took the pizzas off the counter.

"I'm heartbroken."

"No you're not." Betts glared at him.

"Would it make you feel better if I asked you in front of your friends if you want to go out next Saturday? But you better turn me down otherwise I'll stand you up."

Betts started to smile. "You'd do that?"

Zach shrugged. "Wouldn't bother me."

"That's your problem, Zach. You couldn't care less about what everyone thinks of you. You'd probably be nicer if you did."

"Now that's where you're wrong, Betts. I do care. But there's only a handful whose opinion means anything to me. Your problem is you want the whole world to love you. Half of them aren't worth the effort."

They both looked up when the door opened and a woman walked in with two children. Zach smiled at Betts. "Enjoy your pizzas." He turned to greet the woman as Betts left with a disgruntled expression on her face.

* * *

Brenna stared at the diary thoughtfully. "I can't help sympathising with Betts. You weren't very nice. Sort of. Maybe it's just too close to Travis and I. Well, not for the same reason. I haven't... actually I'm not going to go any further with that comment. Knowing the way my luck is lately you'd choose a moment I was spilling secrets or saying really personal information to wake up and hear me." Brenna groaned. "That sounded wrong. I do want you to wake up. It's not-" she stopped abruptly.

"Okay. Time to shut up about that before I sound even more idiotic. But what I'm trying to say is Travis is so thoughtless at times. He'll invite me out and the next thing I know he has half a dozen mates with him and they expect me to stand around and watch them ride their motorbikes. Like that's going to be fun for me. And I've been trying to get him alone for days now. Five minutes. That's all I need. But do you think I can get him to give me five minutes? No." Three times she'd tried today. Maybe he realised and was trying to avoid being alone with her. No, that wouldn't be it. He'd dump her first.

She sighed and put the diary back in the drawer. "But I guess you weren't dating Betts. Although it was mean to sleep with her when you were only looking for sex." Brenna frowned. "At least, I think it was. And I guess she was stupid to think this time would be any different than before. Maybe you were both at fault."

Brenna held Zach's hand. "What would I know? I started dating a guy because he looked good and has a friend with a car. How shallow can you get? Well, maybe that's an exaggeration. He's fun to be with. I do like him, I'm just sick of him forgetting about me when his mates are around. Which is most of the time. And it doesn't make it any easier that I'm not allowed to have a boyfriend until I'm seventeen. So I have to come up with other reasons for why I'm going out. It's a stupid rule. Sometimes I think they shove numbers in a hat and pull them out when they need to decide how old I have to be before I can do something. Anyway, I have to go. I've got a million chores to do otherwise I'm grounded for the weekend. I'm sorry I can't visit the next two days. But I'll be here early Saturday if I'm not grounded."

She continued to stare at him, reluctant to let his

hand go. He remained still. "Try and wake up," she whispered as she slowly let go and turned away.

She grabbed her bag and headed for the elevators. A quick glance at her phone showed she'd have to hurry if she didn't want to miss her bus. Then she would be grounded for the weekend. She jabbed the button for the elevator several times, watching the number as she waited, her foot tapping rapidly. She entered the moment the doors slid open and nearly ran into a man who tried to exit.

"Sorry," she mumbled in reply to his glare as she hit the button on the panel. Each stop had her glancing at her phone. Why did so many people need to use it? The moment she reached her floor, she dashed out with another mumbled sorry and headed for the bus shelter. She breathed a sigh of relief when she saw the bus creeping along in traffic, still headed for the stop. A grin erupted at her close call. She started to relax as she watched the bus pull up at the bus stop. The doors opened and she clambered up the steps, automatically drawing out her money as her gaze scanned for seats. She froze.

Travis sat nearly at the back of the bus, his arms wrapped around another girl, the fingers of one hand tangled in her long black hair. Their lips looked permanently fused and they were completely oblivious to their surroundings. Brenna alternated between wanting to run over and demand what was going on and slinking away.

"Are you getting on or not?" The irate voice of the bus driver finally caught Brenna's attention.

She looked from the driver to where Travis was still wrapped around the girl. She couldn't deal with this right now. Not after spending the afternoon with Zach. Shaking her head, she stumbled off the bus, stepping into the shelter to slump onto the seat, leaning her head against the wall. Anger and hurt mingled with the worry she felt for Zach. As she watched the bus pull away in a burst of exhaust, Brenna realised she was going to be late home. Tears welled in her eyes and she wiped at them with the back of her hand.

"Great," she muttered under her breath. "Just great."

By the time Brenna made it home, she was over half an hour late. The sound of arguing in the kitchen met her as she opened the front door. She hurried to her bedroom and closed the door before she dropped onto her bed. The image of Travis and the dark haired girl filled her mind. She swung between hurt he was seeing someone behind her back and anger he dared do that. She didn't know if she should curl up in a ball and cry or plot revenge. Amongst all the images and thoughts that filled her mind were the words 'five weeks'. She groaned as she pressed her hands against her ears. She didn't want to think about her problems and she certainly didn't want to listen to her parents'.

The sleepless night caught up with her and Brenna drifted off to be woken by her mum shaking her. "Why are you tired? What have you been up to?"

"What?" Brenna struggled to sit up.

"What have you been up to?"

"Nothing. What can you expect when you and Dad wake us all the time with your arguing?" Brenna wished she could take back the words the moment she said them. She held her breath waiting for her mum to ground her.

"Dinner's ready." Sandra spun on her heel and marched from the room, leaving the door open behind her.

Brenna stared after her, wondering if she'd been dreaming. She swung her legs over the edge of the bed and her feet touched the carpet. Did that mean she still had a chance to go out on the weekend? And obviously no one had noticed she was late. Brenna started to smile in relief until the image of Travis and the girl filled her mind. That tiny bit of luck still didn't make it any less of a crappy day.

Chapter Seven

Brenna strode down the corridor towards Zach's room. The past two days had seemed to take forever. Even worse, Travis hadn't been at school. How could she break up with him when she couldn't speak to him? And she wanted to tell him to his face, regardless of who was with him. She came to a stop at Zach's bed and looked down at him. He lay unmoving. "I'd hoped… it's just that… well you've been here nearly three weeks." Brenna's gaze fell to her hands that were clasped together and she dropped them to her sides, taking a deep, unsteady breath.

"I'm sorry I couldn't come and see you the last two days." She sighed. "I really wish you could talk. You're the only person I have to talk to right now. Although if you were awake, I'd probably lose my nerve and not be able to say anything." Brenna groaned. "And that sounded terrible. I don't mean I

want you to wake up just to talk to me. I mean…
okay, forget my babbling."

She reached out and brushed his hair back from his
forehead. "Sometimes I think I'm a hopeless judge of
character. I really liked Travis. I know I kept saying I
was going to break up with him, but I still liked him.
He just wasn't… I don't know." She shrugged. "He
made me feel insignificant a lot. And that isn't good."
She stared at Zach a moment, wanting to shake him
awake. But that wouldn't help. Her gaze was drawn
to the monitor and quickly away again. She took a
deep breath.

"Travis can be fun to be with, but only when we're
doing his things. Self-centred. That's the word I was
looking for. He can be very self-centred. Anyway,
the slimy bastard's been two timing me. At least I
guess he has. I saw him when I was going home last
time I visited you. He had his tongue so far down a
girl's throat I'm surprised she didn't gag. It makes me
angry every time I think about it. But I guess being
angry is better than crying because someone who'd
do that isn't worth tears. Or at least any more tears.
And the worst part is I still haven't broken up with
him. He hasn't been at school. And the longer it takes
the angrier I get. And I know it's probably shallow

and won't make me feel any better in the long run, but I want to hurt him as much as he hurt me."

She took his hand and lightly squeezed it. "Come on, Sleeping Beauty. Will a kiss help?" She reached out with her free hand and lightly touched two fingers to the middle of his lips. "Please wake up," she whispered. He remained silent and she moved back closing her eyes momentarily. "I guess," she cleared her throat and started again. "I guess I should read to you."

Once the chair was in place she sat down with the diary and turned the pages. She stopped at the photo of Zach with Haley and Jordan. They all looked happy. Haley was in the middle with her arms around their waists while they had their arms around her shoulders. She looked small sandwiched between them. And like someone cared about her. Brenna stared at them a moment longer before she turned to the page she was up to.

* * *

First Saturday of the September school holidays

I really don't know how I managed it, but I'm spending the first week of the holidays at Derrick's place. Jordan's parents agreed to let him stay too. That isn't much of a miracle since his parents regularly let him, but I nearly died of shock when Mum agreed. She did say a break might help Dad and I get over our problems, but I have a suspicion she just doesn't want me at home all the time. I guess I can't blame her. Dad and I have been at each other's throats more than usual. When he starts on me I lose it. There's no way I'm going to stand there and listen to his lectures on how ungrateful and self-centred I am. When he gets started I always want to give him a few more reasons to complain. Sometimes I think I should stop while my mouth is busy getting me in trouble, but most times I'm just thinking of more ways to piss him off. It might be petty to say he started it, so what. Might as well add that to the list. And how about vindictive, vengeful, vile, hey got a theme starting here. Maybe I better get out a dictionary and see what other words start with 'v'. Guess I can completely forget about virtuous.

Enough of that crap. At least the holidays have started out on a high note. Friday night was a party. I managed not to get drunk enough to have sex with Betts. Don't know which poor bastard did. But she was drunk enough someone would've got lucky. Or unlucky, depending on how you look at it. And

Jordan kicked me out of the bedroom we normally share and I had to take the spare mattress into Derrick's room. He said he was coming down with a cold and didn't want to share it around. With the way he was making out with Haley last night it wasn't too much of an issue then…

Zach opened the door and stepped into the room Jordan slept in. He paused in the doorway as both Jordan and Haley blinked sleepily up at him from the double bed pushed against one wall of the small spare room. Haley grabbed at the sheet and pulled it up to her chin as she slid further down the bed. Jordan sat up and angled his body so he blocked Haley from Zach's view.

Zach grinned. "Coming down with something, hey? No wonder you made me share Derrick's room last night. Did you honestly think you could sneak Haley in and out again before any of us noticed?" He chuckled. "Morning, Haley." He laughed at what he guessed was her mumbled greeting.

"Did you want something? Or are you going to stand there and hassle us?"

"A few of us are going out to the forestry with motorbikes. You coming?" Zach leaned against the doorframe.

Jordan turned towards Haley, still blocking Zach's view. After a whispered conversation, he turned back. "Not today."

Zach nodded once. "I'll catch you both later. See ya, Haley."

"And tell Derrick he needs locks since no one can knock on a closed door."

"Hang a sign in future." Zach laughed as he blocked the pillow that soared towards him and shut the door. He strode to the kitchen where Derrick and Brent ate cereal standing at the bench, as there was no table. "Jordan won't be coming. He's got other plans for the day."

"Like what?" Derrick asked around a mouthful.

"Haley." Zach couldn't stop the grin that erupted.

"What? She in there with him now?" Brent asked.

"Don't go hassling them." Zach put a hand on each side of the doorframe.

"You did," Derrick said.

"Yeah, but Haley's likely to sink through the mattress if anyone else goes in there."

Derrick laughed. "Okay. You can get out of the doorway. She's safe for now."

Zach picked up the cereal box and shook it. "What am I meant to have for breakfast?" He tossed the empty carton in the bin at the end of the bench.

Derrick shrugged. "It's not a bed and breakfast."

Zach picked up the half empty bottle of milk. "Haven't you heard of guests?" He rummaged in the cupboard until he found a tin of Milo, which he had to scrape out because it had gone hard.

Brent shook his head. "Nope. Don't have them around here."

Zach put the lid back on the milk bottle and shook it until the Milo was mixed in. "You might get some if you gave them breakfast."

"Thanks for the warning. Breakfast not allowed here anymore." Brent grinned.

"Hope you're going to buy more milk later," Derrick said as Zach drank from the bottle. "If Mike doesn't have enough coffee we'll have to drag him out the back and shoot him. Either that or shoot ourselves so we don't have to put up with him."

Zach pulled out his wallet and tipped the coins onto the bench. A couple of gold coins and some silver fell out. He grabbed the notebook they kept on the fridge and tore a page out. He scribbled the word milk on it and shoved it under the coins. "Done. He can get it himself. Are we going? The day will be over before we get there. And I have to work tomorrow."

"You can crash here again tomorrow night if you

bring pizza with you." Derrick rinsed his bowl under the tap and put it in the draining rack.

"You already agreed you'd put up with me for a week. The pizza depends on which assistant manager is working. I'll see what I can do. I finish at ten, can you pick me up?" He drank the last of his Milo.

Derrick grinned. "Depends which assistant manager is working."

Zach put the lid back on the plastic milk bottle and threw it at Derrick.

Derrick caught it and tossed it in the bin. "Didn't you say something about getting out of here? Who's mucking around and holding us up now?" Derrick headed out of the kitchen.

"Leave Jordan alone," Zach called out to him.

Derrick's answer was a laugh.

*   *   *

Brenna closed the diary and looked over at Zach. "Seriously, what is it with guys and motorbikes? I've never understood the fascination. Not that I've been on one for long." Sliding the diary back in the drawer her gaze fell on the rings. She stared at them thoughtfully. Taking them from the drawer, she slipped the diamond ring off the necklace and slid it on her finger. A plan started to form and she turned towards Zach.

She really wished he could answer her, but then again he probably wouldn't be talking to her if he was awake. "I hope you don't mind, but I'm going to borrow the rings in your drawer. I'd buy one but I'm just about out of pocket money because…" her voice trailed off. She couldn't tell him it was because of the gift voucher she'd bought him and bus fare even if he wouldn't remember her saying it. "Well, because. Anyway, I'll put my name, address and phone number in the back of your diary. I'll take good care of the rings and return them as soon as I've finished. But if you wake up before then, you can call me and tell me to return them immediately. When I end things with Travis on Monday I don't want to be the one pitied. It's bad enough-" she broke off. Some things shouldn't be said aloud. "I just don't want to be pitied. He's so popular no one could imagine anyone willingly breaking up with him. It was different when I didn't know about the other girl. I don't want him saying he planned to break up with me for her."

Brenna opened to the last page of the diary and grabbed a pen out of the small backpack she used as a handbag. She wrote her details down on the last page, that she was borrowing the rings and for him to call and she'd return them. "I shouldn't need them until Monday, but in case I run into him tomorrow, I want to be prepared." She took the ring off, put it on the necklace and hung it at her neck. The chain was long enough she was able to tuck the rings into her shirt. "I won't be able to wear them at home or my parents will have a million questions." Guilt nagged at her as she stared at Zach, pale and unmoving. "I really hope you don't mind. But I don't-" she swallowed. "I won't let him make me feel insignificant again."

She closed the drawer once she'd placed the diary inside and went to stand at Zach's side. She rested her hand against his cheek. "I'll be back tomorrow, Sleeping Beauty. Maybe you could work on waking up before then." She brushed her lips across his cheek, avoiding the tube, then returned the chair before she left.

*   *   *

Brenna entered Zach's room with a smile. "You can't imagine how good it is to get away from home for the day. Mum and Dad spent half the night screaming at each other and then picked up this morning where they left off when they went to bed.

Dad even slept on the couch in the study and you can imagine how cheerful that made him this morning since the couch is about half a metre too short for him. Some days I can't imagine why they bothered to get married."

She took hold of Zach's hand. "So how are you today? Any plans to wake up?" She tried to maintain her cheerful voice, but failed. "Please." He'd been in a coma for three weeks. She momentarily closed her eyes as she tried to ignore the words 'five weeks'. They had started to sound like a ticking clock.

A wry smile curved her lips. "I can't believe I come here and talk to someone who isn't even listening. How pathetic does that make me? And even worse, you're the only person I have to talk to. Travis has never been anyone who listens and all my friends seem to be his friends. I didn't realise that until I was thinking last night about what breaking up with him would mean. I sort of wandered away from all the people I used to hang out with when he became my boyfriend. We only ever seemed to do his stuff so I didn't have time for anyone else."

She brushed her knuckles across his cheek. "Enough of my sad, pathetic life. I didn't come here to bore you." She moved to the drawer and opened it. Once she had the chair in place and the diary on the correct page, she pulled out the photo of Zach and Tracey. She stared at the picture for a few moments before her gaze was drawn to Zach. It was hard to believe the energetic, smiling young man in the photo was the same, pale unresponsive person in the bed. She tucked the photo into the back of the diary, wishing she'd known him before. Before he'd lost his parents and before he'd ended up in hospital, all alone.

* * *

Sadly started the second week of the school holidays

I could've easily moved in with Derrick and the guys. A pity I can't work fulltime and go to school. I also couldn't afford uni. Dad was firm about that. If I leave home before completing uni I'm not his responsibility and he doesn't have to pay for it. I sometimes wonder if that's why he's got harder on me the closer we get to him having to pay for it. Wouldn't surprise me.

I went for my provisional licence today and passed. Dad had to ruin it. The moment he heard all he could go on about is how he's not wasting money on a car for me. He couldn't stop complaining that the stricter testing to get your license was hype and he couldn't understand how I'd managed to pass with how badly I drove the few times he took me out. He was constantly grabbing the wheel when he gave me duty driving lessons. Good thing Derrick didn't mind helping me rack up the hours I needed.

Wednesday, busy waiting for Friday.

How sad is it when you're wishing school holidays would go quicker? About the only excuse they find acceptable for going out, is work. I even rang my boss and told him to roster me on for every shift he could, no matter how short the notice. Dad said I should be focusing on assignments and helping out around the house. I can go out Friday and Saturday night. The highlight of my week has been visiting Grandma. At least she's easier to deal with than my parents. She's only in her mid seventies and was about twenty when she had Mum. She said they were mad having me so late in life. Grandma always said it was hard enough keeping up with a kid when she had one when she was young. Anyway, we don't see her much. She can't drive anymore, public transport is too much for her and she lives a few hours away…

Chapter Eight

Zach came to a stop in front of the shrub planted in front of the last apartment. He barely gave it a glance before he turned to Marian. "Okay, Grandma. I know you didn't really drag me out here to look at the neighbour's plants. I know nothing about gardening and I plan to keep it that way. What's the real reason you wanted to see me alone?"

Marian chuckled, laughter lines deepening around her green eyes, her hair a frosty white. "If I'd said I wanted to talk to you, your mother would have been full of questions. And it's not like you visit me on your own."

"Just because I've finally got my license doesn't mean I can miraculously afford a car."

"Does that mean you'd visit me more if you had a vehicle?"

"Truthfully?"

Marian nodded, still smiling. "Go ahead, break my heart, love."

"With how busy life gets I'd be lucky to visit once a month. Possibly only every second month."

"That'd be more than I see you now. So, you just humouring an old lady or you really mean it?"

Zach grinned. "I really mean to humour the old lady?"

Marian held out her closed hand. "I want you to have something. I considered giving it to your mother, but she isn't in the least sentimental."

Zach held his hand under hers and watched as a chain slithered into his palm, two rings threaded on it. "Grandma?"

"Don't go giving them to some girl. Keep them for one of your children if you ever have them."

"But-"

"I want you to have them. I'm not going to wait until I'm dead for your parents to come along and turf them out with the rest of my stuff. I can imagine your father having a secondhand shop come in and take whatever they offer to get it all off his hands. Just don't let him get rid of my pictures. I've written it in my will that I want you to have them."

"You've always worn your rings."

"I can't even get them on my little finger now. It's time to put them aside. Getting old is a killer."

Zach smiled like she expected him to. "Thanks, Grandma. I'll take care of them." He put the necklace on and slipped the rings under his shirt.

"You don't have to wear them."

"I know." He grinned. "I still remember Grandad telling me about the day he gave you the engagement ring. He said his hand shook so hard he dropped the ring when he tried to put it on you and it took nearly an hour for you both to find it in the grass."

Marian smiled, her eyes becoming distant. "You remind me of him sometimes. Oh, not in looks, more in personality. There were people who said he had a smart mouth on him. I never thought so. He just had a good sense of humour. I always wished a man with a sense of humour for your mother, but she values different qualities to me."

"Yeah, well I'm still trying to figure out what they are," Zach muttered.

Marian reached up to pat his shoulder. "Sometimes it takes becoming an adult before you can get along with your parents."

"And sometimes you never do."

"True. Now, I have a birthday card for you. But you're not to open it until you leave and not around your parents." She pulled a card from the deep pockets of her dress. She eyed him. "Not sure where you're going to hide it though."

Zach grinned. "Nothing is impossible." He bent, pulled up the leg of his jeans, and tucked it down the side of his well-worn motorbike boot.

"And that's why I never worry about you, love. You have an answer for everything, regardless of if it's the right one."

"Ask Dad. It never is."

"Give it time, Zach. Now, let's rejoin your mother before she comes looking for us. Tell me, did we figure out the name of the plant?"

"Not likely."

Marian grinned. "Just wanting to get our stories straight."

When they stepped inside the apartment, Deirdre was washing the dishes. "Go and sit down. I can do them later." Marian took the dishcloth from her. "I didn't invite you here to do my housework. I have a lovely young lady from Blue Care who comes in once a week to take care of things. The rest I can manage."

The conversation turned to more general topics until it was time to leave. Zach watched Marian wave to them as they drove down the street. She was still standing there when they turned a corner and then she was lost from sight. When they were partway home Zach, who couldn't wait any longer to find out what was in the card, spotted a service station.

"Think we can pull over at the servo. I need to use the toilet."

"Can't you wait? It's only an hour until we're home." Deirdre glanced at the steady flow of traffic.

"Do you think I can wait if I've gone to the trouble of asking?"

Deirdre pulled up at the service station, her lips pressed tight together. "You could have gone before we left your grandmother's place."

Zach didn't bother answering. He grabbed his backpack from the floor at his feet, climbed out of the car and shut the door hard behind him. Within minutes he entered one of the toilet cubicles, shut the door and pulled out the card. He grinned when he noticed the picture on the card was far more appropriate than the one his parents had chosen. He opened it up and his jaw dropped when he saw the fifty-dollar note, cheque and letter held in place with a paperclip.

The letter was short. 'Get yourself a car and visit more often. Tell your parents I gave you the fifty for your birthday.'

Zach looked at the cheque again and then put it and the money in his wallet. The card he slipped into his backpack. He tore up the letter and threw it in the rubbish bin that overflowed with paper handtowels and returned to the car in a daze.

His first thought, when he was finally able to think, was to text Jordan. Within minutes Jordan's message came through. Ten exclamation marks. Zach grinned as he returned his phone to his pocket.

Last time his grandma gave him more than fifty dollars for a birthday his father had made him return it. There'd been a fight that had lasted six months and even his mother hadn't talked to his grandma. And all over seventy dollars for his thirteenth birthday. His father would tear up the cheque. And his grandma would be offended. It would have taken her ages to save the money on her pension, but as she often said, he was her only grandchild and it was her duty to spoil him occasionally.

As soon as they arrived home, Zach was out of the car and hurrying to his room. He turned on his laptop and drummed his fingers on the desk as he waited to start looking online for a car.

* * *

Brenna used the photo of Zach and Tracey to mark her place then closed the diary. "Your grandma sounds nice. I wish I could meet her." She hesitated. Now she knew they were his grandma's rings, she wished she could've come up with another plan. "I know you don't know me, but I will take care of her rings for you. I just… I can't figure out what else to do. I won't let anything happen to them. I promise." After a moment, Brenna rose to her feet. "I hate to leave, but I've really got to go. I'm not sure I'll be able to visit tomorrow. But I'll be back as soon as I can."

Once the diary and chair had been returned, she bent over Zach and dropped a kiss on his cheek beside the tube. "Wake up soon, Sleeping Beauty." She stared at him a moment longer, almost hearing the clock ticking away the five weeks. Her steps were slow as she walked to the door.

* * *

Brenna headed for the area of the school Travis usually hung out at. She twisted the ring around on her finger, trying to ignore the lurching of her stomach. She forced a smile at the couple of greetings some of Travis' mates gave her and watched as he turned towards her.

"Can I talk to you for a minute?" Brenna asked when she stopped in front of him.

"Sounds like you're in trouble."

Brenna didn't turn to see who spoke. She kept her gaze on Travis. "It'll only take a minute."

"Sure. What's up?"

Brenna hesitated. Should she tell him in front of his mates? Maybe that was too harsh. And how would she find the right words with them all listening?

"Come on, Brenna. Don't make me wait all day. The bell for next class will ring at the rate you're going."

Brenna's anger returned and she found the words. "I wanted to tell you we're over. I've met someone else."

"What?" Travis looked surprised.

"I didn't want to go behind your back so I'm letting you know we're over. You'd have to be pretty low to two time someone." She ignored the snigger behind her.

Travis' look of surprise changed to one of arrogance. "You made him up because you heard about the girl I met."

"What girl?" Brenna shook her head. "Forget that.

It's unimportant. He is real. He even gave me a ring."
She held out her hand. "I told him I had to let you know we're over first."

"What's his name?"

"Zach."

Travis' eyes narrowed. "I don't believe you."

Brenna shrugged. "It doesn't matter." She turned to walk away.

"Brenna."

She glanced back. "What?"

"Where is he then?"

"He doesn't go to this school." She walked away, ignoring the hushed comments from Travis' mates. She bit back a grin when Travis told one of them to shut up. A twinge of guilt rose when she thought of how she'd used Zach's name. And part of what she'd said was true. She had sort of met Zach, he just wasn't her new boyfriend. The bell rang and Brenna picked up her pace. At least now she could forget about Travis.

Forgetting had been her plan, but she soon found no one was willing to let her. She was asked numerous times throughout the rest of the school day if she really had broken up with Travis and there was even a couple of rumours he'd made up a girlfriend to hide how heartbroken he was.

Brenna was glad to escape the attention and head home, until her parents arrived home arguing. Sitting at her desk, doing her homework, she closed her eyes and rested her forehead on the desk. Couldn't they shut up for ten minutes? She was nearly finished her homework. A tap on her door brought her head up. "Yeah?"

The door swung open and her mum stood there. "Out to the kitchen. I need to talk to you."

Brenna watched her mum stalk away and she tried to rack her brain as to what she could have done wrong. She came up empty. Her hand went to her throat to make sure the necklace was hidden. All safe. With a sigh she pushed away from her desk and headed for the kitchen. She froze in the doorway. Both her parents and her sister were seated at the table. And everything was quiet.

Adam sat with his arms crossed, leaning back in his seat. His hair was a shade lighter than Brenna's, his eyes the same blue as both of his daughters. Danielle shifted in her seat, glancing between her parents.

When Brenna continued to stand in the doorway, Sandra gestured towards her seat. Brenna eyed it and her mum warily. She cautiously crossed the room and sat down with a quick look at her sister, who also seemed confused.

"Your father and I need to discuss something with you."

"Will it take long? I'm missing my TV show," Danielle complained.

"You know we both love you," Sandra said and glanced towards Adam who nodded.

Brenna's stomach dropped. This wasn't going to be good. Why weren't they yelling at each other? They were not only in the same room, but also within arm's distance.

"Even though we both love you, that doesn't mean we still love each other," Sandra continued.

"What your mother is slowly trying to say, is we're getting a divorce," Adam said.

Sandra glared at him. "Didn't we agree I'd tell them?"

Adam stared at her a moment before he made a go ahead gesture.

"As I was saying," Sandra bit the words out. "There will be some changes. We're going to try and keep things as easy as possible for you, but it's time for your father and I to go our separate ways. Your father's going to move closer to his work and you girls can visit him."

"Now wait a–" Adam started to say.

"Did we or did we not agree I was going to explain this?" Sandra's tone was cold.

"What about all my things I do on the weekend?" Danielle wailed. "I can't stay miles away from everything. I thought you said you weren't making a heap of changes."

Brenna stared at her family, the sudden rush of noise as they all started to shout at once washed over her. How was she going to see Zach on the weekend? And when would her dad move? Their life might not be perfect, but she knew what to expect. Maybe it was past time, but they could've waited another few years. Why'd they have to change everything now?

The arguments continued. Adam and Sandra rose to their feet and Danielle shouted that no one cared how she felt and stormed from the room. Brenna sat frozen, trying to figure out how she felt.

Sandra turned towards Brenna. "And what about you? No arguments like usual?"

Brenna leapt to her feet. "You've always got to pick on me. And why should I bother arguing? It's not like you're going to listen. You should just suck it up. Another few years and I'll have finished school and be out of here. Then you can do what you want." She spun away, knocking her chair over as she ran towards her room, her vision blurring. She scrubbed her eyes with the back of her hand and slammed her bedroom door.

Great. Just what she needed to completely ruin her day. She threw herself onto her bed, and tossed her pillow on the floor. It didn't make her feel one bit better.

Chapter Nine

Brenna could barely wait for school to end the next day. She tried to ignore most of the rumours floating around, but it was impossible when people wanted to make sure she heard them. The moment school ended, she caught a bus to the hospital and hurried to Zach's room. She ditched her schoolbag at the door and reached out for Zach's hand before she even came to a stop.

"I can relate to your diary entry about a crappy day in Crapville. And I had thought Monday was going really well. You should have seen Travis when I told him we were finished. He was stunned. And all the rumours are out of control, but at least most of them are about him and his rebound girlfriend. I'm glad I'm not the one they're talking about." She paused. "I hope you don't mind, but when he asked who I dumped him for, I could only think of your name.

He'll never get to meet you, so it doesn't matter. I mean, I wasn't-" she broke off. "Anyway, you don't have to worry. There won't be any problems for you because of it."

She reached out and touched his cheek. "When are you going to wake up?" She hesitated, words burning inside her. "I really don't know how to say this. How to tell anyone, really. Maybe there's some way of leading up to it. I don't know. But, my parents are splitting up. I wasn't very nice when they told us. Actually, I was really nasty if you want the truth."

She smiled wryly. "They were so civilised for a change. And it was like being at a funeral." She recounted the evening for Zach, sighing when the words finally stopped flowing. "I know it's not that bad really, I mean, not like being in a coma, but it's the worst moment of my life. I'm worried about what changes they're going to make. Dad's moving to a suburb so far from the city centre it might as well be on the Gold Coast and we're expected to spend every second weekend with him. All the people I know live in suburbs nearby. So maybe I haven't had much to do with most of them lately, but I'm changing that."

She sighed heavily. "I guess I should stop whining. I'm here to read to you, not spend all my time moaning about my life." She left unsaid the words, not when I'm worried about yours. Less than two weeks. She closed her eyes and tried to calm her racing thoughts and jumbled emotions. Letting go of Zach's hand, Brenna pulled out the diary and instead of getting the chair she sat on the edge of the bed. She reached out and tangled her fingers in his. Once again her gaze dwelled on his picture, ignoring Tracey completely, before she started to read.

* * *

October started with usual arguments

Dad tried to ruin what should've been a milestone. My first car. Nope, can't feel any excitement about it. Even writing about it is flat. Makes me want to shove a nail in each of his tyres and ruin how he feels about his car. I bought a commodore that's a decade old and has a towbar. Need to make sure there's always someone who can tow the trailer to get the motorbikes to wherever we're planning on riding them. Derrick can't always take us. Work gets in the way sometimes.

Still stuck in October

I've nearly been grounded for the whole of October. Well, what we've had of the month so far. And it's been for the flimsiest of reasons. Ever since I bought my car. Surprise, surprise. Some things are just too much of a coincidence. Nearly two weeks and no end in sight. Been asking for extra shifts at work so I can at least get out of the house.

Halloween

Life just plain sucks sometimes. Either he's upping his efforts to make me move out or he misses me when I'm gone. Yeah, and that's a likely story. The whole month! Grounded! And they haven't gone out of an evening so I've had no chance to do anything except go to work and do schoolwork. Which probably isn't a bad thing anyway, since school's been trying to overwork us.

Finally reached November

Not that the situation has changed as far as being grounded. But school's taking up my every moment so it hasn't been too big a loss. Well, not much. And I'm not even allowed to lend my car to Jordan. Apparently when I'm living under Dad's roof I have to follow his rules…

Jordan stood in the doorway of Zach's room, not speaking, just standing there.

"Come in and shut the door. Mum will check on us soon and if that door's open she'll take it as an invite."

Jordan stepped in far enough to be able to close the door. He looked everywhere but at Zach.

"Need help burying a body?"

"I only wish."

Zach moved over to press play on his stereo. He sat on the edge of his desk. "I can't help you if you don't tell me the problem."

"You know how you told your parents they should've aborted you? Did you mean that?"

"What's this about?"

"Did you?"

Zach shook his head. "I just wanted to strike out at them." He shrugged. "It probably makes me a complete bastard, but it felt good at the time."

Jordan pulled a book from the bookshelf that sat against the wall to the left of the door. He flicked through the pages then put it back on the shelf.

Zach frowned. "You aren't thinking of killing yourself, are you?"

"No!"

"Then hurry up and tell me. The suspense is killing me. And I'm probably thinking of problems that are a million times worse than yours actually is."

"Haley's pregnant."

Zach stared at Jordan in open-mouthed silence. "Okay. Didn't think of that one." He paused. "It's yours?"

"Of course it is!"

Zach held up his hand. "If you end up keeping it, that's the first thing most of the people we know are going to ask. So what are you going to do? You thinking of aborting it?"

Jordan ran his hand through his hair. "I've made such a mess of things."

"Haven't you heard of safe sex?"

"Of course I have. And of course we were. It's just not one hundred percent reliable. Obviously." Jordan fell silent. Then he met Zach's gaze. "What am I going to do?"

"How does Haley feel?"

"Confused. Terrified. Like the world is about to end. And I don't blame her. I feel exactly the same."

"I guess the bottom line is, do you want the kid?"

Jordan's expression changed to one of amazement. "The whole time she was telling me I went from, 'what the hell are we going to do', to 'I'm going to be a dad.' I don't know what to think. I can't sleep. I can't eat. I feel like I'm going to throw up every time I think about it and then I have an urge to go out and buy booties or whatever it is you buy for babies. See? I wouldn't even have a clue what they need. How the hell can I be a dad? I'm meant to be going to uni next year. So's Haley. There's no way we can do this."

"There's always adoption if you can't go through with an abortion."

"What if they don't look after the kid? How do you know they've picked the right person?"

"Jordan. You know I'm here for you, man. Just tell me what you want help with."

Jordan laughed sharply. "As if I know." He shook his head. "I can't believe I screwed up so badly.

Zach laughed. "Appropriate choice of words."

Jordan smiled weakly. "What am I going to do?"

"I can't make that decision for you. You're going to have to make that one yourself."

"We've only been together a couple of months."

"You bored with her already?"

"No!"

"Well that's something anyway." Zach pulled the

chair out from under his desk and spun it around. "Sit down before you pass out. Have you eaten yet today?"

Jordan shook his head as he dropped onto the chair. "I couldn't. I think I'd throw it straight back up."

"It's the mother that's meant to have morning sickness, not the father."

"Very funny."

"Where's Haley?"

"She had some family thing to go to."

"Have you talked to her about this?"

Jordan shook his head. "We sat there and freaked out together. Quietly."

"You're going to have to talk to her. She'll think you don't want her or the baby or something."

Jordan leapt to his feet. "Of course I want her."

"Then go and tell her."

"Now?"

Zach shrugged. "Depends what she's doing."

"Some family barbeque at the Parklands."

"Then catch a bus or get Derrick to give you a lift. I wish I could lend you my car, but you know how Dad went on about that. It's not a toy, responsibility and whatever other crap I tuned out. And I don't think they're going to give me time away from this grounding to drive you there."

Jordan shuddered. "Don't remind me about the lecture your father gave me about never asking to borrow your car."

Zach smiled. "I keep telling you a look isn't too bad if you watch him with your eyes out of focus and the lecture is bearable when you tune him out. So, you going to see Haley now?"

"I don't know what to say to her."

"Does it matter? If she's taking it anything like you are, she's probably wishing she were a million miles away from her family. Think about exactly what you want to do before you get there. You've got three options. Keep the baby, adopt it out or abort it. Forget strategies and planning. That can be sorted later. You only have one decision to make now."

"What will I tell my parents if we keep it?"

"Congratulations, you're going to be grandparents?"

"And that will go down real well."

"Better than if I was the one having to tell my parents."

Jordan shuddered. "Thanks for that image. I think I can tell everyone now. Just not your father."

Zach laughed. "You can't imagine the amount of times I'd have loved to tell him something like that just to see his reaction. Can I tell him it's mine? And that you don't know and I'm letting you take the blame."

Jordan chuckled. "You're evil, you do know that."

Zach nodded. "Yep. My father regularly tells me."

Jordan became serious again. "Thanks for listening."

Zach clapped him on the back. "We're mates. Of course I listen."

"I might give Derrick a call and see if he can give me a lift."

"A bit of advice. Don't tell your cousin until you've told your parents. He couldn't keep a secret like that if his life depended on it. Well, not from relatives who know when he's hiding something. And who'll bug him until he tells."

Jordan smiled. "Tell me about it. I can't count the number of times he got us into trouble when we were kids by caving during interrogations." He walked to the door.

"Ring me later. Let me know what happens. Or text me and I'll go online."

"Will do. And Zach…"

"Yeah?"

"Thanks, man."

"Anytime."

* * *

"Wow!" Brenna turned back to look at the picture of Zach, Haley and Jordan. "I certainly didn't expect that either." Her gaze focused on Jordan. "But where is he? You sound like you're best mates. So why isn't he here?" Brenna sighed as she used the picture of Zach and Tracey to mark her place and returned the diary to the drawer. "I have to go." She kissed him on the cheek. "I'll try to come back tomorrow and I'll find a way to get Jordan here for you." She brushed her hand across his cheek above the tube. "Please, Zach. Wake up." She reluctantly dragged herself from him, gathered her schoolbag and headed for the bus stop.

She shivered in the cold air wishing spring would hurry up. Then she instantly took that wish back. Time was already passing too quickly. She didn't need spring. She needed Zach to wake up. When the bus arrived she found a seat by the window and leaned her face against the cold glass. She couldn't even bring herself to do her homework. Her mind was too cluttered to focus.

* * *

The next afternoon Brenna dropped onto the edge of Zach's bed. "Life's back to open warfare at home. They're arguing over everything. Even the linen. Who cares who gets the extra tea towel? I felt like tearing it from their hands, ripping it in two and say, done. All split evenly now."

She took hold of Zach's hand. "When are you going to wake up?" She lifted his hand and rested her cheek against it. "Most people would say I don't know you. But I feel like I do and I'm worried. I know you won't want me hanging around when you wake up, but I just want you to get better."

She silently watched him, trying to see any improvement. There was none. He looked exactly the same as the first day she'd seen him. After another moment she took out the diary and had a long look at his picture before she began to read.

Chapter Ten

**Grounding finished before November did, what
a surprise**

The news is everywhere. It's the only thing everyone
can talk about. And the rumours are a laugh. Even
I've been linked to Haley as the father, and in one
story she doesn't know which one of us fathered the
kid. Some people have nothing to do but gossip. Poor
Jordan won't come around. He's terrified of what my
parents will say now they know. I swear, for such
a large city too many people know each other in
Brisbane.

At least now I'm not grounded I can spend time
with them. I told Jordan he shouldn't feel privileged,
Dad treats most people like insignificant bugs in need
of exterminating.

I'd be going crazy now school's finished if I was
grounded. It's probably Mum not wanting me

underfoot all day. We'll be staying at Derrick's. Hoping to go for a week if I can convince my parents. Won't be holding my breath though.

Glad to be finished school. I've got all my applications in and I'm waiting to see which uni I get into. I've got a suspicion my parent's are only willing to pay if I get into a local one.

Schoolies week without me

Not a surprise I was suddenly grounded again. I guess I should be happy I managed to escape to Derrick's for a couple of days. Jordan and Haley aren't going. Haley feels too queasy. She told Jordan to go without her. He said it wouldn't be the same without the two of us. Betts rang to see if I was going and had heaps of wild plans to help me escape.

I've played with a few ideas myself. Even going to the Gold Coast for a few hours one night would be good. Maybe let my parents think I'm working. At least my parents don't class pizza as a food. That used to annoy me, now it's great. Work's the one place I know they aren't going to bother me.

The great escape

Still grinning. Had the best time at the Gold Coast. Betts, as usual, was on the hunt. I was late home, but the assistant manager from work covered for me. He's only a few years older than me so he can relate to how frustrating it is.

I also managed to visit Grandma today. She's certain this constant grounding is because Dad doesn't want me to visit her. I mentioned my theory that he doesn't want to pay uni fees. She agreed it's another possibility. Grandma and Dad have never liked each other.

A week into December and not grounded once since schoolies

As soon as schoolies was ended I was no longer grounded. An amazing coincidence. And I'm back at Derrick's. Such a relief…

Zach plumped the large pillow so he could see the television better from where he lay on Derrick's lounge room floor. Another pillow hit him in the face. He turned towards the couch where Jordan grinned at him.

Jordan's expression of innocence failed. "You looked like you needed it."

Haley, who was stretched out on the couch with her head in Jordan's lap, giggled.

"You wouldn't have been game to do that if you weren't hiding behind Haley."

"I'd come over there and prove you wrong if Haley wasn't so comfortable." Jordan ran his fingers through her hair.

"Liar, liar." Zach stared at them wistfully. They might have a lot to face, but he'd never seen his friend so happy. Well, he did seem a bit preoccupied tonight.

"Sticks and stones."

"Now you don't seem so taken with the movie and not trying to shut me up every time I talk…" Zach let his words trail off and smiled at the guilty expression that crossed Jordan's face.

Haley sat up. "I'm going to get a drink."

"Hales-" Jordan began but stopped when Haley shook her head. She rested her hand on his shoulder and they shared a look before she wandered off to the kitchen.

Zach rose to his feet and dropped into the armchair behind him. "What's wrong?"

"We've figured out how we can have the baby and still go to uni." Jordan, forearms resting along his legs, leaned forward and stared at the floor.

"Spit it out. Obviously I'm not going to like it, so just tell me."

Jordan met Zach's gaze. "I don't like it either. But Haley and I can't think about giving this kid to some stranger. It's ours. We might make terrible parents, but that kid's ours and we're not giving it away."

Zach nodded, his expression serious for a second before he grinned. "You never were good at sharing your toys either."

Jordan smiled fleetingly. "Mum said she'd take care of the kid while we're at uni. The rest of the time we're going to have to work it out between us so we can study and still manage to look after it."

"That sounds reasonable. Be tough since I hear babies are time consuming, but I'm willing to help. You only have to ask."

"Well, that's where the problem is. Work's transferring Dad. To Rockhampton."

"What?" Zach leapt to his feet.

Jordan hastily rose too. "I don't have much choice. Without Mum's help one of us won't be able to go to uni. Actually, neither of us would probably be able to afford to. Kids cost money."

"You don't have to remind me. My father does a good enough job of that."

"Zach–"

Guilt hit him hard when he saw the expression on Jordan's face. "Don't worry, Jordan. Of course you have to go." Zach forced a grin. "But since I'm making such a sacrifice letting my best friend move so far away you're going to have to name me the kid's godfather."

"Done." Jordan held out his hand.

Zach took it and shook solemnly, before he pulled Jordan forward, grabbed the pillow off the ground, grinned and hit him in the face with it. They wrestled for several minutes over the pillow until a sound in the hallway had them both turning in that direction.

Haley rolled her eyes. "Children."

"Yep." Zach grinned.

Haley grinned back at him. "All's well?"

Zach draped an arm around Jordan's shoulders. "Yeah."

* * *

Brenna placed the photo on the page she was up to

and closed the diary. "I guess that answers why Jordan isn't around. But you'd think he'd come the moment he heard. Unless he doesn't know. It's really annoying you never mention people's last names. I want to find him for you, but I don't know how with only a first name."

She slipped the diary into the drawer and sat on the bed beside him. Her fingers threaded between his. Her other hand smoothed his hair back from his forehead. "I need you to wake up, Zach. Wherever it is you are, you need to come back to this world. Please." She stared silently at him. "I have to go. I don't want to. There's nothing to look forward to at home." Brenna dropped a kiss on his cheek. "I'll be back tomorrow." She smiled wryly. "And I guess you need something more than a kiss to wake you, Sleeping Beauty." Her expression was filled with worry again as she whispered, "Please wake up."

* * *

Brenna opened the door and stepped inside Zach's room. She came to an abrupt halt when she saw the elderly woman sitting beside his bed. The woman turned her way the moment the door opened and Brenna saw tears stained her cheeks.

"I'm sorry. I didn't mean-" She opened the door and stepped into the corridor.

"Wait!"

Brenna turned to face the woman, putting her hand out to stop the door from closing.

"Are you the girl who visits my grandson nearly every day?" The woman struggled to her feet.

Brenna nodded.

The woman crossed the room, stepped into the corridor and put her arms around Brenna. The door swung shut behind her. "Thank you. You can't imagine how hard it's been knowing he's alone."

Brenna awkwardly returned the hug. "I... yeah... um well..." The rings at her neck felt ten times their weight. Why had she ever come up with that crazy plan? She could have handled the teasing. Well, maybe not.

"Come back into Zach's room and sit with me. You can call me Marian. What's your name, love?"

"Brenna Reardon."

Marian opened the door and stepped into the room. "Sit down and tell me about yourself. I'm afraid our boy here is being a little uncommunicative." She smiled fleetingly and pointed to the other chair. "Bring it closer. Come on now, no need to be shy."

"How did he end up here?" Brenna blurted out

the question that had been burning in her mind ever since she'd met Zach. She blushed and dropped into the chair she'd dragged close. "I'm sorry. I shouldn't have asked. I mean…" She felt her cheeks grow hotter.

Marian reached out and patted her hand. "Don't fret. You deserve to know with how much time you've spent with him. He came to spend the night with me. A friend of mine turned eighty and he took me to her party." Marian fell silent as her eyes became unfocused. "When he went to leave the next morning, his car wouldn't start. Tom, a gentleman who lives two apartments over had his son visiting. He's a mechanic. Nice young man too. He had a look at the car and said Zach needed a part he wouldn't be able to get until Monday. I insisted Zach ring his parents and tell them what the problem was."

Brenna automatically made a sound of dismay.

Marian grinned. "Exactly. I should've called that bastard and told him Zach was staying to help me. He insisted on collecting Zach with the excuse he had work. I knew it was so he'd be without his car. We both knew it. Anyway, they turned up, Greg was going on about Zach's choice in cars, and Deirdre barely said hello and goodbye. She had a sour, puckered up expression on her face. Probably from listening to Greg." Marian fell silent.

When she continued to remain quiet, Brenna spoke. "You don't have to tell me. I shouldn't have asked."

Marian shook her head. "There was a group of young boys, between fourteen and sixteen. Five of them. They were drunk and stole the car of one of their parents. It was late afternoon. The driver died. Two of the boys were in intensive care for about a week. The rest had barely a bruise. Deirdre and Greg were killed instantly. At least that's what they tell me. And Zach…" Her voice trailed off. A tear slowly made its way down her cheek. "My Zach has to make it."

Brenna reached out to take Marian's hand. "He will. We won't let him give up."

Marian's hand tightened around Brenna's. "He's a fighter, my Zach. Just like his grandfather. The two of them were always stubborn." Marian looked at Zach. "He's all I've got now. Just me and him."

Brenna's throat tightened at Marian's words. Her problems seemed insignificant. "Do you know how to get in touch with his friends? Jordan? Haley? Derrick?"

Marian shook her head. "I can't help you there, love. I know their names, but that's it."

"Their last names?"

Marian shook her head again. "No. When he spoke of them it was always by their first name. I worried about it too. He was sad when Jordan moved to Rockhampton. They've known each other since primary school. There's probably a heap of school photos at the house with his full name on them. Probably even address books. But I can't get around much. Getting old is a killer."

Brenna smiled at the familiar words. "Can't someone take you there so you can have a look?"

Marian shook her head. "A friend of mine has to come in every few weeks for specialist appointments. Her daughter brings her. Rather unwillingly. Kids always seem too busy to help these days. Anyway, this is the second time she's brought me in. She'll get me when it's time to leave. It doesn't give me time to catch a taxi to the house, search for address books and get back. That prune-faced woman would leave me behind if I wasn't here waiting for her. I'm not even game to go to the loo."

"If you need to go, I'll be here to tell her not to leave you behind."

Marian laughed. "You're a love. No, I'm fine.

Now, tell me about yourself. I know little more than your name and you care about my grandson."

Brenna shrugged. Shyness rushed in on her. "I'm not very interesting."

"Let me be the judge of that. Do you have any siblings?"

The next hour passed quickly as Brenna started off telling Marian about her sister, her parents and all the dramas their break up was causing. She was surprised how easy it was to talk to Marian after the first few sentences. Marian didn't judge her words with either expressions or comments. When the woman who was to give Marian a lift arrived, Brenna was disappointed.

"You'll keep visiting him?" Marian asked once the woman stepped back into the corridor.

"Of course."

Marian pulled out a notebook and scribbled her phone number on it. Next she wrote down an address in Brisbane. She tore out the page and pressed it into Brenna's hand. "There's a birdbath in the backyard. It has a little stone bird sitting on the side. The key's under the birdbath directly below the bird. Find his friends for him."

"But–"

"I've always been a good judge of character."

Tucking the notebook away, she reached out to clasp Brenna's empty hand between both of hers. "Maybe it'll help him to have his friends around."

"I won't be able to go until Saturday." Brenna watched as Marian nodded, walked to the door and grabbed hold of the frame. "Are you okay?"

"Just a little dizzy. Part of why I don't do well on public transport. Happens all the time. You'll call me and tell me how he does? The nurses are nice enough, but they don't spend as much time with him as you do."

"If he even twitches I'll call you."

Marian gestured towards the phone on the drawers beside Zach. "You can use that. I had hoped he'd use it to call me."

"He will."

Marian smiled sadly. "Of course he will, love."

Chapter Eleven

Brenna moved back to Zach's side once Marian had left. She took his hand in hers. "I'm sorry I couldn't read to you, but I'm sure you were glad to have your grandma visit. That was probably a lot better than putting up with some random person." She tried to swallow past the lump that formed in her throat. Once she found his friends he wouldn't need her. "I'll be back tomorrow. But Saturday I'll track down your friends." She brushed her lips across his cheek, a single tear falling onto his face. She reached out and wiped it away then ran the back of her hand across her own cheek. "You've got to wake up. We're worried about you."

She hurried away, barely making it to the bus stop in time. She was going to have to try and leave a little earlier in future. She couldn't afford to miss the bus. On the ride home, she kept pulling the piece of paper from her jacket pocket to stare at the address. Not long and she'd be able to find Jordan for him. Maybe that's what he needed to wake up. His best friend talking to him. Seeing her stop ahead, Brenna tucked the paper in her pocket. Not that it mattered if she lost it. She'd read it enough times she knew it by heart.

Once inside, Brenna managed to spread her homework out on her desk, just before she heard a knock on her door. "Yeah."

"In the kitchen. Now." Sandra walked away without waiting for a reply.

Either she was in trouble or there was more bad news. Brenna sighed. She couldn't think of a single thing she'd be in trouble for. Well, nothing her mum knew about. She rose from her seat and slowly walked to the kitchen, finding her sister already at the table. Her dad was nowhere in sight. That wasn't a good sign. She wondered what bad news would be dumped on them now. The wait was far too long. They were expected to eat dinner first, even though it was earlier than usual. As soon as the table was cleared Sandra told them her latest news.

Brenna stared at her mum, certain she'd misheard. "What?"

"You'll move with your father. Danielle will stay with me."

"No!'

"This is not negotiable," Sandra said.

"I'm old enough to decide where I live."

Sandra leaned forward, her arms resting on the table. "That has nothing to do with it."

"Does that mean I can have her bedroom to turn into a study?" Danielle asked. "Or a lounge room?"

"No. I'm not moving." Brenna glared at her sister.

"Don't be difficult, Brenna."

"Difficult! Why should I be the one to change schools? Year eleven's meant to be an important year. You're shifting me part way through it!"

"I can't change schools. I'm in too many groups," Danielle protested. "You don't participate in anything."

"I do so," Brenna argued.

"Name one."

"Girls!" Sandra slammed her hands against the table. "Enough! Your father and I have decided."

"I noticed he wasn't here to tell us." Brenna said.

"He's looking at a house to rent."

"Where?" Brenna demanded.

Sandra sighed. "We've already been through this."

Brenna shook her head. "No! I'm not moving that far."

"Stop carrying on, Brenna. You'll be back here every second weekend."

Danielle crossed her arms between herself and the table. "Does that mean I can't have her room?"

"You'll be visiting your father every second weekend."

"You're kidding!" Brenna leapt from her seat. "On the same weekend?"

"It'll be the easiest."

"She might be a pain in the a–"

"Watch your mouth, Brenna." Sandra jabbed a finger in her direction. "I won't tolerate swearing."

"Well, she is. But she's my sister. Now you're telling me we'll never see each other." Brenna tried to make sense of it. But nothing made sense. It wasn't enough they had to split up, now they wanted to split up her and Danielle.

"That's no loss," Danielle muttered, disbelief written all over her face.

"You don't like each other and rarely get along, why should it be a problem?"

"I've never said I don't like her," Brenna argued.

"I believe the exact words were you hate her," Sandra said.

"So? That doesn't mean I don't like her. She's my sister."

"I'm not in the mood for these theatrics, Brenna." Sandra closed her eyes for a second.

"Then stop trying to ruin my life. I'm not moving."

"You'll do as you're told. Now get ready for bed. This conversation's over."

"No it's not."

"Don't start with me, Brenna or I'll finish it. If you don't want to be grounded this weekend you'll get ready for bed. Now!"

Brenna's hands tightened into fists. Anger and frustration washed through her. Why did they have to go to bed early? She glanced at Danielle who poked her tongue out. Brenna glared at her before she turned to her mum. "I guess I'll have to get a job and find my own place to live."

"Bed. Now!"

Brenna spun on her heel, strode from the room and slammed her bedroom door. It didn't help. She dropped onto her bed to stare at the ceiling. Her head filled with the words her mum had used to tell her the world was falling apart.

Her door swung open and Danielle stepped in, shutting the door behind her. "Can I come too?"

"What?" Brenna sat up.

"When you leave home."

"No!"

"I can get part time work and help pay for everything."

"If I move out you might get my bedroom."

Danielle looked at her feet. "I didn't really mean that."

"Then why say it?"

"Because."

Brenna rose to her feet. "Then you can't move in with me... because."

Danielle glanced up at Brenna before she looked at her feet again. Her voice was barely above a whisper. "Because I don't like to cry."

Brenna stared at her sister, speechless. "I–" she still had no idea what to say.

"Forget it," Danielle muttered as she turned to open the door.

"Dani."

Danielle kept her back to Brenna. "What?"

"If I had a house you could live with me."

Danielle turned to face her. "Really?"

Brenna nodded.

"What are we going to do?"

Brenna shrugged. "I'm not sure. But I can't move. I just can't." She thought of Zach alone in the hospital.

She couldn't leave him. Not until she found his friends and not until he woke up.

* * *

After a restless night and an equally long day at school, Brenna finally entered Zach's room. She dropped her schoolbag inside the door and went immediately to his side. She wordlessly took his hand and stared at him. "They're splitting us up, my sister and me. Just like the dishes. Mum's getting the good dishes and Dad the everyday ones. I wonder what that says about me since I'm the one who has to go with Dad?" Brenna's voice faltered.

Her hand tightened on Zach's. "I wouldn't have a clue what to do. About anything. I wish you'd wake up. You can't stay like this. You have to wake up. I couldn't-" she broke off before she could speak the words, stand to lose you. She wiped away the tears that stained her cheeks and rested her head on the bed beside Zach. Her eyes closed.

"I couldn't sleep last night. All these stupid plans kept going through my mind. I can't think of anything realistic. I'm so tired." She lay there quietly, her head near his hand. She sat up abruptly. "Did you move your fingers?" He remained as still and quiet as ever. She sighed. "Now I'm imagining things." Another heavy sigh. "How about I read to you?" She thought back to the moment she'd printed the list from the internet. She'd been certain she could help. What if he didn't wake? There wasn't much more than a week left. Brenna reached over and withdrew the diary from the drawers. Something had to wake him.

* * *

Another year, hopefully not as crappy as the last one

I've barely had time to write. Jordan leaves next week. I've been helping him sort through all his stuff. His parents don't want to cart a heap of junk around the countryside. There's six cardboard fruit boxes filled with things he can't part with stacked in my room. Said his kid might want them when she's older. Yeah, it's going to be a girl according to the ultrasound. There goes my plan to hassle him to name the baby after me. Not that I'd let him.

I'm not sure what I'm going to do with the boxes. Mum goes lemon faced every time she sees them. Said he should leave them at Derrick's place. With the parties they have, that's not a good idea. But

I didn't explain that to her. At least they're being half reasonable and letting me spend more time with Jordan. Well, Mum is. Dad seems to be doing a lot of overtime so he hasn't had much say in what goes on around the place.

Jordan and Haley even dragged me into a baby shop. I couldn't believe how small everything was. When they said they expect me to hold her at the christening, I nearly panicked. Babies are so little. And breakable. What if I dropped her? I didn't tell them though, just asked if I could attend via web cam. That got Haley's eyes rolling. Jordan thought it sounded like a good idea, but he lives and breathes computers, at least he did. Now they come in second to Haley and the kid. It amazes me how wrapped up in them he is. I hope he still feels the same way once the kid's born. Everyone goes on about sleepless nights, how loud they scream and changing nappies. No thanks. Not for me.

Moving Day

I can't believe how quickly it arrived. One minute there were days left, then time evaporated…

They stood around in Derrick's kitchen. Jordan

and Haley had stayed the night, while his parents had booked into a motel. Zach had been amazed his parents let him stay too. Derrick and Brent were also in the kitchen.

"You'd swear they were going to a different country," Derrick said. "He's only going to be about six hundred and thirty kilometres away."

"What did you do? Google it?" Jordan asked.

Derrick grinned. "Pretty much. I need to know how far away it is for when I come and see my new cousin." He glanced at Haley's stomach. You couldn't even tell she was pregnant. If it hadn't been for the morning sickness, hardly anyone would've known.

Haley's hand went to her stomach. "I hope you all visit when she's born."

"As long as no one expects me to pick her up," Brent said.

A horn sounded out the front. Jordan glanced towards the front of the house. "I guess that's my parents."

"I'll take your bag to the car and let them know you won't be long," Derrick said.

"Uhm… I'll head out the front too." Brent followed Derrick.

Haley wiped her eyes. "I hate how emotional being pregnant makes me."

Zach wrapped his arms around her. "You take care of my goddaughter."

Haley smiled, eyes still damp. "Absolutely."

Zach drew Jordan into the hug. "And take care of each other." He stepped back. "Hey, we'll only be six or seven hours apart."

"Try again." Haley grinned. "Derrick isn't the only one who can google things. It's closer to nine hours with fuel stops."

"Maybe with you driving," Zach said.

"With you driving too." Haley frowned at him.

"Yes, Mum. I was just teasing."

"I hope so."

Jordan dropped his arm around Haley's shoulders. "He was." He turned to Zach. "I never know what to say at times like this."

"How about goodbye? And catch you online."

"Of course," Jordan said.

The horn sounded again and they looked towards the hallway.

Jordan sighed. "I guess this is it."

"You only have to ring and I'll drop everything and be there," Zach said.

"Thanks."

"No thanks needed. Isn't it part of the pact?"

Jordan laughed. "I sometimes forget about that."

Haley looked from one to the other. "About what?"

"First grade. We'd known each other a couple of weeks and were moaning about the fact neither of us had a brother. Zach came up with the idea that being blood brothers would be just as good. We swore some oath that involved always being there for each other. I can't remember the exact words."

Zach grinned. "I vaguely recall them sounding like a cross between wedding vows and the Boy Scout oath." He shrugged. "What can I say? Dad had forced me to join Scouts and we'd recently attended a wedding."

Hailey sniffed. "How sweet."

The horn sounded twice. Zach stepped between them and put an arm around their shoulders. "Best get you out there before someone comes looking." He guided them to the start of the hall where he let them go ahead. When they reached the front door, Zach stopped. "I'm not coming out to watch you drive away."

Jordan nodded. "I'll text you when we arrive."

With a quick smile Zach turned away. He wandered into Derrick's room where his things were scattered around his bag. He focused on repacking.

It was going to be different not having Jordan around. They'd been friends since the first day of school and in each other's company every minute possible. Zach dropped onto the mattress and stared at his closed bag.

* * *

Brenna shut the diary. "I'm going to find him for you. I promise. But right now I have to go home." She placed the diary in the drawer and turned to Zach. She cupped one cheek with her hand and dropped a kiss on the other. "Please wake up, Zach," she said softly. She stood and stared at him. "Please." She closed her eyes for a moment and then opened them to watch him for a few seconds longer before she turned and left.

Chapter Twelve

Brenna put a note under a magnet on the fridge. She carefully unlocked the back door, slipped outside and quietly closed it. A backpack was slung over one shoulder and she slid an arm into the other strap.

When no one called out, Brenna hurried to the front of the house and ran to the bus stop. There was about a ten-minute wait until the bus arrived, but she didn't want to risk being spotted.

There'd been no choice other than to sneak out. When she'd arrived home yesterday it was to find her dad had signed a lease on a house and they'd move over the weekend. She wasn't moving. And her note had said that. She'd also written she was going away for a couple of days and wasn't staying with anyone they knew.

Brenna was relieved when the bus arrived. Now to find Zach's house. She looked at the notes she'd made with the help of an online trip planner. There'd be two bus changes and approximately a five-minute walk from the bus stop. She was used to walking. It was ages before she could go for her provisional license and at the rate she was logging driving hours, it'd be more like never. If she could have waited for a later bus there would've been no bus changes. But she didn't have time to wait around and be caught sneaking out.

The bus changes were made without incident, but lost in thought Brenna nearly missed her destination. She quickly hopped off the bus and looked at her printed pages before she started down the street. She'd brought her laptop with her in case clearing the online history wasn't enough to wipe out where she'd searched. She was determined to stay away for a couple of days and had even packed her school uniform.

She looked at the address again. Yep, this was the correct house. It was several steps up from the ground, with a screened verandah across the front. The mailbox was full so she took the mail with her and left it on the back step while she fetched the key. It was exactly where Marian had said. Under the birdbath, below the little stone bird.

Brenna stared at the back door, key in hand,

butterflies in her stomach. It felt odd. Even though Marian had given her permission, it felt a little like breaking into someone's home. Thinking of Zach lying alone in the hospital, she unlocked the door and swung it open.

The house smelled stale so Brenna dumped her backpack and the mail on the kitchen table and opened some windows. There was a sudden sound and she gasped. A nervous giggle followed as she realised it had been made by the fridge. She opened it.

"Eww." There was a bottle of sour milk, vegetables that dripped slime and several unidentifiable objects. She quickly closed the fridge. She sorted and stacked the mail neatly on the bench and kept back the two letters addressed to Z. Reed. She flipped the oldest one over and saw the sender was J. Burns. Surely it couldn't be that simple.

She stared at it, unable to open someone else's mail. But if it led to finding Zach's friends shouldn't she? Calling herself an idiot, Brenna ripped open the letter.

'Where are you? You haven't been online, not answering phone calls. Ring, text, email. Something. Let me know what's going on. Jordan.' She frowned as her hopes evaporated. That hadn't helped. She looked at the envelope. It had a post office box address. Not much help. And Burns was a common name. How many were likely to live in the Rockhampton area?

Brenna dropped the letter on the bench and looked at the next. Same address, same sender. She hesitated. It didn't feel right. And what if it was similar to the last and very little help? What else could she do? Her fingers shook and she nearly dropped the letter. She closed her eyes and took a deep, calming breath before she unfolded the piece of white A4.

'I'm getting worried. RING ME!' Brenna smiled in relief. There was a mobile phone number written large enough it went from one side of the page to the other. "Thank you, Jordan." She searched through the house until she found a phone in the lounge room. Her earlier butterflies were back and they bounced around her stomach as she lifted the cordless phone from its base.

The phone answered on the first ring. "Zach! Where've you been?"

Brenna didn't know what to say.

"Zach?"

"No. Sorry. Ah… you don't know me… I–" she faltered. How did you tell someone their best friend was in a coma?

"Who's this? Where's Zach? And why are you ringing from his home phone?"

"Brenna."

"You better explain before I ring the police to tell them you're there."

Panicked, words tumbled out. "Zach's in hospital and his parents are dead." Brenna cringed. *How pathetic could you get?*

There was a long silence before Jordan spoke, his voice uncertain. "Is this a joke?"

"I'm sorry," Brenna whispered.

"Zach… is he… will-"

"Who's this?"

Brenna nearly dropped the phone when a female spoke. "Brenna. Umm… Jordan… is he okay?"

"What did you tell him? And we don't know any Brenna."

She cringed at the accusation in the words. "Zach's in hospital."

There was more silence. "Where? I want all the details. And don't go anywhere. As soon as I check for myself I'll ring you back."

Brenna gave the hospital and room details and hung up the phone when she was disconnected. Her legs gave out and she sat on the floor, unable to make it the few steps to the couch. She closed her eyes and dropped the phone beside her. She'd made a real mess of that. With a groan she lay back on the carpeted floor. What an idiot!

She jumped when the phone rang, quickly picked it up and pressed the talk button. "Yes?" Her voice was hesitant.

"This is Haley. I'm sorry I snapped at you. We'll be there as soon as we can. The hospital won't tell us anything. How is he?"

"Not good. He's been in a coma nearly four weeks. I'm sorry."

Haley swore. Then fell silent. "What number can I reach you on?"

Brenna gave Haley her mobile number. "But I might not have it on this weekend." Not when her parents got her note. "There's a phone in Zach's room."

"Okay. If we need to get hold of you I'll ring your mobile first. And Brenna, thanks for ringing."

"I opened the letters Jordan sent. I'm sorry. I didn't know how to find you."

"That doesn't matter. I'll call when I know our arrival time. We'll have to talk to uni about time off, and Jordan works part time. There's so much to organise. Can you ring Derrick? You know more about what's going on than we do and he's sure to have questions."

"I don't have his number. I only have this one because Jordan wrote it in his letter."

Haley chuckled. "And to think I teased him about that." She rattled off a number and Brenna had to ask her to repeat it after she stumbled to the end table, the phone base was on, to pick up a pen.

As soon as Haley hung up Brenna stared at the notepad with Derrick's number. She sighed. Now she had to go through the same conversation all over again. She dialled the number and waited for him to answer.

"Zach! Where've you been? I thought you'd dropped off the face of the earth. I've even come over a million times but no one's ever home. You didn't leave town, did you?"

Brenna sighed. Did everyone have caller ID? "It's not Zach. Haley asked me to call."

"Then who the hell are you?"

"Brenna."

"Nope. Don't know you."

"I know. Ah… I sort of made a mess of this conversation last time. Maybe I should have asked Jordan where he was first."

"Make sense, girl."

"Is it okay to… what I mean is… where are you?"

"At home. Problem with that?"

"Zach's in hospital."

"What's wrong with him? And how come no one rang me earlier. I know his parents are complete bastards, but they should have rung."

"They're… well, they're not… they've… passed away."

"What!"

"They're–"

"Yeah, I heard you. They're dead. I just don't believe you. You're at Zach's place? Right?"

"Yeah."

"Stay there."

Once again someone hung up on her. Brenna sighed. The day wasn't looking good. She gathered both phone numbers and slipped them into the front pocket of her jeans. Putting the phone in its base, she gazed at the immaculate lounge room. The couch and armchairs were evenly spaced, a coffee table in the middle of the room. A television cabinet was in the centre of the wall opposite, with a television placed dead centre. There were two paintings hung on the wall on either side of the television. No clutter and everything in its place. Brenna frowned. The room was more a showcase than somewhere to relax.

She wandered from the lounge room and glanced in doorways. Bathroom, study, main bedroom with an ensuite, spare bedroom and finally, the only room that looked like someone lived in it. Zach's room.

Posters on the wall, books jammed into a bookcase, a desk with a laptop in the middle surrounded by scattered paper, a cricket ball, pens, and two empty coffee cups that now had an unhealthy growth. The built-in wardrobe was half open and clothes were scattered on the floor. The bed was unmade and another cup sat on the bedside table along with a lamp and a clock radio. There were even six fruit boxes pushed into one corner.

Brenna smiled slightly. This was more what she was used to. She gathered the three cups and took them to the kitchen where she put them in the sink to soak. A knock on the back door made her heart leap. She'd locked it when she'd come in. She cautiously eyed it.

"Brenna, you better still be in there."

She recognised Derrick's voice and opened the door. Her mouth dropped open at the sight of him and she blurted out, "You look like Jordan." She closed her eyes and stepped back. Why did the floor never open up and swallow you when needed?

Derrick laughed. "Our fathers are twins. Don't

worry, I get that all the time. Now why hasn't Jordan ever mentioned you?"

Brenna opened her eyes to have a proper look at him. There were some differences. Derrick's dark brown hair was shorter and his eyes were green while Jordan's were blue. Derrick was a little stockier than his cousin. She didn't know how tall Jordan was, but Derrick had to be more than six foot. She realised she was staring.

She glanced away. "He's never met me. I've only seen a photo of him."

"Tell me what's going on."

Brenna told Derrick the bare bones of what Marian had said. She watched as he strode into the room and dropped onto a kitchen chair.

He shook his head, opened his mouth and then closed it only to shake his head again. He swore, rose and started to pace. "Jordan knows?"

Brenna nodded.

"He's coming?"

Brenna nodded again.

Derrick pulled out his phone. He stopped pacing as he waited for his call to be answered, his foot tapping instead. "You're staying at my place... of course you are... let me know when you do... and don't speed, maybe you better let Haley drive." He laughed abruptly. "Take care and ring me along the way." He put his phone away and looked towards Brenna, who still stood by the door.

"You going back to the hospital?"

She nodded again.

"Not very talkative, are you? Want a lift?"

"Yeah."

"Yeah you're not very talkative or yeah you need a lift?"

Brenna couldn't help momentarily smiling. "Yeah I need a lift." She gestured towards the fridge. "Should we do something about the mess in there first?"

Derrick took one look inside the fridge and quickly closed it. "Nope. Not today. Come on, grab your gear and let's get out of here. I want to see how Zach's doing."

Brenna nodded, swung her backpack onto one shoulder, shut the windows and locked the door. When she was about to take the key to the birdbath, she looked towards Derrick.

He grinned. "I know where it's kept. But don't worry about returning it. I'll get another one cut for when I come back and clean up the mess. There's probably other things that need dealing with. A good thing Greg didn't believe in owning pets." Derrick took the key and pocketed it.

"Eww!" Brenna screwed up her face at the thought of an animal left in the house four weeks without food. She quickly pushed it from her mind.

Derrick laughed at her as he unlocked his car. Brenna eyed the rubbish on the floor as she climbed into the front seat. She kept her backpack on her lap and pulled on the seatbelt. The drive to the hospital was made in relative silence. She always found it difficult talking to people she didn't know well.

Brenna led the way to Zach's room once they were inside the hospital and watched as Derrick hovered in the doorway. "You want me to leave?"

"No!" Derrick reached out and placed his hand at her back to guide her further into the room. "Do you know… have you heard… is he going to make it?"

"I don't know," Brenna said softly. "I can give you his grandma's phone number."

Derrick shook his head as he slowly walked over to Zach. He stood silent and every now and then shook his head. He turned around. "You right to stay? I've got to get out of here."

Brenna nodded.

Derrick paused at the door. "Call me if… just let me know… whatever happens… I can't stay."

Brenna watched Derrick as he nearly ran from the room. She worried at her bottom lip with her teeth.

She picked up the phone beside Zach's bed and pulled the letter from Jordan out of her pocket.

"Yeah?"

"Ahh… Jordan?"

"Yeah. Who's this? Is this Brenna?"

"Yeah."

"Zach-"

"No, he's still the same. Sorry. It's your cousin."

"What happened?"

"He came up to see Zach. I don't know. He didn't look too good and he just about ran from the room."

Jordan was silent for a moment. "Thanks. I'll call him."

"Will he be okay?"

"His mum was in hospital on and off for ages with cancer. She's been clear for five years, but I guess… well, it probably brought it back. And Zach?"

"Still hasn't woken. Do you know when you'll get here?"

"Early tomorrow morning at a guess. Tell him I'm coming?"

"Yeah. I will."

"And thanks for ringing me. Sorry I freaked."

"Sorry I didn't break the news better."

Jordan laughed wryly. "Not an easy thing to tell anyone. I'd probably have made a worse mess." A baby screamed in the background. "I've got to get Lily. See you tomorrow."

Brenna hung up the phone. Jordan had disconnected before she had a chance to say goodbye. She turned to Zach and took his hand. "Jordan and Haley will be here tomorrow." He remained silent and Brenna sighed.

She turned back to the phone and rang Marian to let her know what was happening. Once she'd hung up, after actually managing to say goodbye to someone, she took the diary out of the drawer. She ignored the chair in the corner and sat on the bed.

Chapter Thirteen

Uni started and I couldn't give a shit

I'd expected to be attending with Jordan. I know I've got other friends, but it's not the same. We didn't even need words half the time. I hate having to explain myself. Derrick isn't too bad and I've known him as long as Jordan. But he still doesn't get everything I say.

I'm stuck with this idiot called Nic, who also plans to be a vet. It's enough to make you want to skip lectures just to have a break from him. If you listen to him, he's been everywhere and done everything. I always get the urge to want to show him up. Usually I manage to control it. Most people are easy to ignore, but some are just so in your face you want to push them out of your view.

There has been the usual parties on the weekend.

Some of the crowd has changed. Some hasn't. I still see Betts around. She has a new project. I'd say this one is going to be long term. Dad tried to ground me the other week. I locked the door, turned up the music and jumped out the window. Derrick met me down the road. I had the music plugged in to a timer to turn off at ten. I don't know if they banged on the door or yelled, since I wasn't there to hear, but the next day he glared at me all through breakfast. I was glad I had work. I half expected him to break down the door so he could turn off the music. Guess he wasn't willing to go that far. But I'd had enough. I had put in hours studying and needed time off.

April already

I can't believe how much time has passed. I've been really slack about writing anything this year. Between uni and work I barely have a spare moment to myself. Not that I've got any news to write. Same shit, different day. Or maybe that should be different month. Dad's still doing his best to drive me out of the house. Work's a relief from home. Uni's great. Fascinating. And I've been going out every weekend. I made a deal with Mum. I don't play my music loud at home and I can pick one night a week to go out. Doesn't have to be the same each week. She even stood up to Dad when he wanted to ground me on the night I chose to go out. The grounding was moved forward a day, but it certainly was a sweet victory.

How the hell did we get to May?

I'd planned to write more and here May is nearly over. I stuck a heap of photos in the diary to make up for the lack of writing. I'll get around to labelling who's in each of them later. When I find more time. But nothing's changed. I could scan most of the last entry, cut a few parts out and paste it straight in.

* * *

Brenna looked at the photos. She smiled slightly. "I guess you never found the time to label them. Although I can recognise a couple of faces now. Derrick and Tracey anyway." She closed the diary and put it back in the drawer. "I've got to have lunch. I'll be back soon." She leaned forward and kissed his cheek, her hand cupping his other cheek for a moment. "Think you can surprise me while I'm gone and wake up?" It wasn't as difficult to sound cheerful for him today. Jordan was on the way and he was sure to wake up for his friend. He had to. She stared at him a moment longer before she left.

It didn't take Brenna long to find somewhere outside the hospital to buy food. While she waited for her burger, she turned on her phone and rang home. She held the phone away from her ear when her mum began to yell. She tried to speak, but it was impossible. She disconnected.

Brenna grinned when the phone rang and she saw it was her mum. "I'll turn my phone off if you're just going to yell."

"Where are you?"

"That doesn't matter. No one's listening to what I want. I'm not moving. I'm not changing schools. You and Dad can't live together. Fine! But don't wreck my life too." Brenna sighed when her mum started to yell again. She turned her phone off and put it back in her pocket. Nothing had changed.

As soon as she finished eating, Brenna returned to Zach's room. On the drawers beside the bed was a folded piece of paper torn from a magazine. Brenna saw her name written along the edge where the print didn't reach. She opened it and a blue key fell out. There was more writing inside, around the edge of the page.

'I returned the original key. Give me a yell if you need a lift anywhere. A hand to clean the fridge would be good. Derrick.'

Brenna grinned. She wondered if the offer of a lift was a bribe to clean the fridge. She pushed the paper into her backpack, which she carefully dropped on the floor near the drawers. Next she pulled out her key ring and put Zach's key on it. She stared at the two keys. The blue one she'd added and the worn silver one. There was probably some metaphor or deep meaning, but she didn't want to know. She was emotionally drained from dealing with her family. She shoved the keys in her pocket and turned to Zach.

Sitting on the bed next to him, she took his hand. "You're probably getting sick of the sound of my voice. Not long and you'll have your friends here." She sighed heavily. "You probably won't need me around then." Not knowing what else to do, she pulled the diary out and continued to read to him.

* * *

June has begun just like all the other months

I'm seriously sick of Nic. Everything's a

competition with him. And I don't know why he has to choose me to compete against. I've never felt the need to prove myself. I guess I never gave a shit what people thought. Jordan has always accepted me the way I am and if others couldn't, that was no loss. I still had my best friend. I wish to hell he didn't have to move so far away. I'll be going to see him end of this month. That's when the baby's due. They did say it might be early July because sometimes babies are late.

June is creeping by

I know it's because I'll catch up with Jordan and Haley at the end of it. That's probably part of the reason I finally let Nic goad me into a bet with him on Wednesday…

Zach strode towards Tracey where she stood talking with friends. Anger burned in him. He wasn't about to let Nic get away with cheating. "Tracey."

"Zach." She barely looked at him.

"Can I talk to you for a minute?" He glanced at the two friends with her.

Tracey checked her watch. "If you're quick."

Zach grinned. "I can be." He placed his hand at the small of her back and guided her away from her friends. "I was wondering if you wanted to go out Saturday night."

"It's Thursday, Zach. It's short notice and I'm already going out with someone."

"I know. With Nic." The bastard had asked her Tuesday. He'd already known he was going to win when he started the bet.

"Then why are you asking me?"

Because this will either sabotage Nic's chances of winning or improve mine. He hid his thoughts with a fleeting grin. "Because I'll split the hundred dollars with you. He won't."

"Hundred dollars? You've lost me."

"How do you feel about back handed compliments?"

"I think you've taken up more than a minute." Tracey looked at her watch.

"Nic and I have a bet. Now keep in mind we see you as a challenge. You're popular, gorgeous and not lacking in guys who want to date you. So you were the obvious choice. Whichever one of us takes you somewhere Saturday night is paid one hundred dollars by the loser."

Tracey tossed her head, her hair falling neatly into place. "And what if I decide I don't want to go with either of you?"

"Then neither of us wins." Zach grinned. "But I'm hoping you'll ditch Nic and go out with me. I was upfront about the bet."

"That kind of seems like cheating."

Zach laughed. "There was nothing said about you being kept ignorant." And he didn't want Nic to find out he knew Nic had cheated. Let him think he'd got away with cheating, as long as he also lost.

"Wouldn't that be implied?"

"If it's not spelled out, it's not part of the rules."

"I've already agreed to go out with Nic."

"Tell him you've had a better offer."

Tracey stared haughtily at him for a moment. "The whole hundred dollars."

Zach shook his head. "Fifty-fifty. And I'll foot the bill for Saturday night. Don't worry, I'm sure we'll more than exceed the other fifty."

"I'll think about it." She turned away and started to walk back to her friends.

He watched her go, his gaze drawn to her long legs. When she slowed, he looked up again.

Turning her head, she met his gaze. "Pick me up at seven. If you're late I won't answer the door." With a quick smile, she continued towards her friends.

* * *

Brenna looked up from the diary. "I don't know if I'd have gone out with either of you. I think I would've been offended. And I certainly wouldn't have gone out with Nic." She grinned. "I guess he wasn't happy about her cancelling at the last minute." She looked at the diary. There was so little of it left to read. But she needed a break. She wasn't used to talking non-stop for so long. Returning the diary to the drawer, she said goodbye, promising to be back soon.

As soon as she was outside the hospital, she turned her phone on. She listened to the demanding messages left by her mum and then dialled her home number.

"Don't you dare hang up on me."

"Then stop yelling at me."

"You're a kid. It's up to us to tell you where you'll live and what you can do. You can't expect to run your own life."

"You moved out of home at seventeen. That's one year older than me."

"And look how well that turned out. You'll come home immediately. Your father will pick you up tomorrow and I'll hear no more of this."

"I'm not living with him."

"Why?"

"Because I'm not changing schools. I'm not leaving my friends behind or completely changing my life."

"You can catch up with friends every second weekend."

"Not good enough. And what about school holidays? And Danielle. Am I supposed to forget I have a sister?"

"We've talked about that. We'll split the school holidays. You girls can be together then."

"You and Dad were the ones who screwed up your lives. Why should we be the ones to pay? It's not fair."

"You're old enough to realise life isn't fair."

"Then maybe you should consider that statement too. We're not linen. You can't share us out between you like we're one of your possessions."

"It's not your decision to make."

Brenna laughed abruptly. "That's where you're wrong. I am making the decision. And I'm saying no. I'll ring you tomorrow."

"I want you home tonight."

"This conversation was a waste of time."

"Where are you staying?"

"Nowhere. I've got nowhere to stay. Just hanging out wherever is open late." Brenna held the phone from her ear when her mum started to yell at her for being stupid and pigheaded. She turned the phone off. She wasn't the only pigheaded one in the family. Putting her phone away, she returned to Zach's room. She opened the door as his phone stopped ringing.

There were only a handful of people who'd ring. She tried Jordan first.

"Yeah?"

"Did you ring?"

"Brenna?"

"Oh, yeah, sorry."

"Yeah, I rang. We should be in Brisbane about six tomorrow morning. We'll go to Derrick's first. Get all our gear unpacked and have something to eat. We should be up there before nine."

"Thanks."

"You'll be there?"

"Yes."

"I'll see you then."

Brenna didn't have a chance to say goodbye. She hung up the phone and turned to Zach. "What's with your mate, Jordan? Doesn't he believe in saying goodbye on the phone? Or at least letting other people say goodbye."

She took out the diary and sat on the bed to read to

him. This might be the last time she got to spend with Zach. There was a good chance she'd be grounded for life after this weekend. But at least Zach would have his friends with him.

Chapter Fourteen

The Sunday after winning the bet

Tracey is actually fun to be with, in a vindictive sort of way. I was surprised. She has a unique way with words that even when she's tearing someone to shreds, her disturbing sense of humour makes you want to smile. At least she's not boring. She told me as long as it stays fun, she's willing to go out with me again.

One of the best parts of the whole date was seeing Nic towards the end of the night and having him pay up. I know, petty, vindictive and all the rest of it. But I couldn't resist accepting the money with a smile. And he still doesn't know I found out he cheated.

Nearly the end of June

The days seem to have gone back to a normal pace. The kid should be born soon. It'll be good to catch up with Jordan. It's been different without him. Tracey isn't too bad to hang out with and she keeps me entertained. So does her no strings attitude towards sex. Big difference to Betts who thinks every encounter's going to lead somewhere.

Start of July and I'm back home again

I forgot to take my diary with me. Not that I'd probably have had time to write. I was only gone a couple of days. They had a little girl and called her Lily. She's so tiny. They wanted me to pick her up, but I managed to get out of it each time. Probably wouldn't have if I'd stayed around much longer. I'll wait until she isn't so tiny and fragile looking. She seems fairly quiet, unless they're trying to hand her over to me and then she goes off like a siren. I'll have to thank the kid for that when she's older. Told them I make it a policy not to pick up any kid that's screaming.

Tracey was annoyed I took off on short notice. She went to a party with Nic while I was away. I told her if she does that again, I'll be the one walking due to lack of fun. I'm not going to let her set Nic and me against each other. If she wants to play games like that, she can play them alone.

August already

Life has been completely busy. I barely have enough time for sleep let alone writing. I'm at Grandma's. I gave her a lift to a party tonight. It didn't last as long as the ones I normally go to so I'm still wide-awake.

Dad hasn't been as bad lately. I think he might be resigned to the fact I'll out stubborn him over the 'if you leave home I'm not paying for uni' issue. He never calls it uni, it's always university and there's emphasis on the word as if to remind me how to say it. Like abbreviating things is a crime.

He lost it when he heard I was going to stay at Grandma's to take her to a party. I half expected him to have a heart attack he got so worked up. I can't understand why he has to act like she's the enemy. She's in her seventies. How threatening an enemy is that?

* * *

Brenna turned the page to find the next one blank. "I guess that was the night before the accident." She put the diary in the drawer and sat quietly beside Zach for several minutes while she figured out what to do. "I'll go and get a magazine to read to you. I won't be long."

As soon as she'd bought the magazine, Brenna returned to Zach's room. She pulled the chair close to the bed and curled up in it, reading only the articles she thought might interest Zach. When she finished the magazine, she stood and stretched. Her stomach rumbled.

"I need something to eat." She stepped close to him and took his hand. "I wish there was something I could do. I feel so useless." She brushed her lips across his cheek. "Wake up, Sleeping Beauty." She closed her eyes as Zach blurred. One week left. He had to wake.

After she'd eaten, Brenna reluctantly turned on her phone. There were more messages from her mum. She dialled her home number, let it ring once, then hung up. If they wanted to talk, let them foot the bill. Her phone was still low on credit. The phone rang almost immediately.

"Yeah."

"Come home and we'll discuss it."

"Does that mean I don't have to move?"

"It means we'll discuss it."

"I'm not an idiot. You always say that when the answer's no and you're humouring me."

"Brenna, I'm fast losing patience with you."

"Well you're lucky. I'm way past that stage."

"Don't be smart, Brenna."

"I should've known this was a waste of time. I'll ring you tomorrow."

"Don't hang up."

Brenna hesitated. Giving in wasn't going to make them listen to her. "Bye, Mum." She turned the phone off and slipped it in her pocket. She looked around. Night had fallen while she'd been in Zach's room, but the amount of traffic on the move hadn't slowed. People hurried in and out of the hospital focused on their own lives. Brenna envied them knowing where they were going. She forced herself to stop thinking about her life. Compared to Zach's her problems were insignificant.

When she arrived in Zach's room, the chair was back in its usual place and the bed sheets had been smoothed. She hesitated and then sat beside him. She yawned. "You can't believe how tired not doing anything makes you feel. I'm going to sit near the power point and use my laptop. I have an assignment due Wednesday. I've got the research done, I just have to write it." She cupped his cheek with her hand. "Come on, Zach. Please wake up." When he didn't respond, she sighed and rose to her feet.

She moved the chair near the power point and took out her laptop. Several hours later, Brenna stretched, put her gear away and dimmed the lights. She eyed the chair but then, with a half smile, she sat on the edge of the bed.

* * *

A hand shook Brenna's shoulder and dragged her from sleep. She sat up and blinked as she tried to focus. Her cheeks were damp and the last images of her dream hung on. She reached out to touch Zach's warm hand. He was alive. She turned to see who'd woken her.

It was the same nurse who'd previously asked her how she knew Zach. "What are you doing here?" The words were quiet.

"Do you think he'll make it?" Brenna's voice was barely a whisper.

The nurse's expression softened. Her smile was

tinged with sorrow. "I never saw you." She patted Brenna's shoulder before she left the room.

The nurse's actions hadn't been promising. "Please. Please wake up." Her hand curved across his cheek. "Zachary…" her throat tightened and she put her head down on the bed again. At least if she went back to sleep she wouldn't have to keep thinking about everything. Providing her dreams cooperated.

*   *   *

Next time Brenna was jarred awake, it was from a hand on her head. She sat up and gaped. "Zach?"

"What's your name?" His voice was a raspy whisper.

Brenna couldn't stop a grin forming. "Brenna."

"Pretty." He smiled slightly and his eyes closed.

She reached out to hesitantly touch his cheek. "Zach?" There was no response. Had she dreamt it? She felt awake. She slid off the bed and moved around. Did people hallucinate when they hadn't had enough sleep? Was this still a dream? That was possible. She could be dreaming she was awake. Her gaze fell on the phone. She took Marian's number from her pocket.

"Yes?" There was fear in Marian's voice.

"Please tell me I'm awake."

"Who is this?"

"Brenna."

"What's going on?"

"I think he spoke. And moved his hand. But maybe I was dreaming."

"You're not at the hospital, are you?"

"Ah… yeah." Becoming more awake she wondered how late it was.

"Where do your parents think you are?"

"Not here. But that's unimportant. I think Zach spoke. He opened his eyes and asked my name. But he went straight back to sleep. I'm almost certain. But maybe this is all a dream."

Marian chuckled. "Then how about we both agree not to wake up, love."

Brenna grinned. "Deal."

"I was worried when you rang. It's four twenty-one."

"I'm sorry. I was so excited. And then I didn't know if I was awake and I didn't think. I just-"

Marian interrupted her babbling. "I'm glad you rang."

"Maybe I should ring Jordan."

"Yes. A wonderful idea. Those two are thick as

thieves. He'll be worried to distraction. I wish I could be there."

"He's asleep."

Marian sighed. "Call me the moment he opens his eyes again. I'm going to ring the hospital and ask how this changes his prognosis. Thanks for calling, love."

"Okay. Bye."

Brenna stared at Zach, the grin still plastered on her face. She tore her gaze away long enough to call Jordan.

He answered hesitantly. "Yeah?"

"He spoke. Zach spoke!"

"What did he say?"

Brenna laughed self-consciously. "He asked my name."

"And that was it?"

"Well…"

"Come on, don't keep me in suspense."

"When I answered, he said pretty."

Jordan laughed. "Yep, that sounds like Zach. I always told him he'd be chatting up girls even if he was on his death bed."

"Oh no, it wasn't like that. He meant my name," Brenna protested.

Jordan chuckled. "We'll be there later this morning. I bet I'm right."

Brenna didn't know how to answer so she remained silent.

There was more laughter from Jordan. "I'll see you later." He hung up.

Brenna put the phone back and her head came up quickly as the door opened. Two nurses and a doctor entered. Within minutes, she'd been sent from the room, her backpack in place. She didn't know where to go. There was no one to ask. Although if she did ask, she guessed they'd show her the exit. At that thought, she hunted around for somewhere to hide. Seeing a sign for the restrooms, she slipped inside. She crossed to the far wall and perched on the basin dotted bench after first checking it was dry. Leaning against the wall, she closed her eyes for a moment.

It seemed like it was only seconds later when she nearly slipped off the bench. She came fully awake and realised she must have drifted off. Pulling out her phone, she turned it on to check the time. She stared. It was nearly six. She smiled wryly as she realised she must have slept propped against the wall.

As soon as her phone was off, she slipped it in her pocket and slid off the bench. Her knees buckled and she grabbed the wall for support, holding on until she was able to stand straight. After using the toilet she peeked outside. The corridor was empty. She hurried to Zach's room and was relieved to find him alone. The backpack was carefully dumped inside the door on her way to the bed.

She stared down at him. He looked the same. The tubes were under his nose and across his cheeks, he had a drip in one hand and he was hooked up to the monitors. She'd hoped that something would have changed.

"I'm glad you woke earlier. Do you think you can do it again? Please, Zach?" She sighed when he remained unresponsive. Her hand reached out and rested against his cheek. When his eyes slowly opened she smiled so wide her cheeks ached. "Zach."

"Ren?" His voice was a whisper. He turned his head so her palm rested against his lips. His eyes drifted closed again.

She wanted to shout in excitement. Instead she sat on the bed beside him, uncertain if she should move her hand. She wasn't disturbing the thin tubes taped across his cheeks and under his nose, but she couldn't stay at this angle forever. Finally she laid her head down, her legs hanging over the edge of the bed.

Chapter Fifteen

It seemed like no sooner had her eyes closed than a sound caused them to open. She felt the comforting warmth of Zach's hand resting on her head. Her gaze was drawn to the doorway where Haley and Jordan, with Lily in his arms, stood. She struggled to sit up.

"Don't move on our account." Jordan grinned. He glanced at Haley when she hit him lightly on the arm.

Brenna brushed her hair back from her face and gazed at Zach. His eyes were closed. She looked towards Haley and Jordan, who'd come into the room to stand within arm's reach, and slid out of the bed.

After giving her a good look over, Jordan laughed. "I told you I'd be right."

Brenna felt her cheeks heat and couldn't meet their gazes for a few seconds.

"Stop teasing her." Haley gave Jordan a speaking

glance before she stepped close to Brenna. "You must be exhausted. You didn't need to stay all night." She dropped an arm around Brenna's shoulders.

"I would have missed him waking up." She stood there awkwardly and wondered if she could move away without seeming to reject Haley's friendly action. "Ah… I was thinking I might have something to eat while you're here. I hate leaving him alone."

"Of course." Haley squeezed her shoulder. "You want company?"

Brenna shook her head. "I… ah… well… I'm not much of a morning person."

Haley chuckled, nodding towards Jordan. "Don't worry, I know all about people who think mornings should be banned. Have something to eat and take some time for yourself. Being here for Zach is our only purpose."

"Thanks," Brenna mumbled before she pulled away, grabbed her backpack and hurried from the room. She was halfway down the corridor when she realised she hadn't said goodbye to Zach. She came to an abrupt stop and looked back the way she'd come. She forced herself to turn away. There was no way she could bring herself to go back and say goodbye to him in front of his friends. How crazy would that make her look?

Outside the hospital, Brenna turned on her phone and listened to the messages from her parents. She groaned and reluctantly dialled her home number. She hung up as soon as it had rung once. It took a couple of minutes for them to call and she wondered if it was part of a new plan. Make her think they couldn't care less.

"Yeah."

"We're willing to let you finish year eleven at your current school and you can move in with your father next year."

"Not good enough, Mum."

"You can't expect everything to go your way. Life doesn't work like that."

Brenna was silent while she thought it over. "And weekends?"

"This year it'd be every second one with your father, both you and your sister together and half the school holidays."

"Not half. What about if I want to sleep at a friend's place?"

"You haven't asked to sleep at someone's place since Bec left."

"Then maybe it's time I did."

"Okay, that's negotiable."

"And I want to be able to have a boyfriend before my seventeenth birthday."

"That's not open for negotiation."

Brenna closed her eyes for a second. It only took a moment to come to a decision. "Too late. I've had one for months but I dumped him recently. I don't want to have to hide the fact next time. And at least you'd have a chance to meet and interrogate him." The silence stretched out so long that Brenna began to think she'd lost phone coverage. She checked the display screen and saw the time was still moving as it counted up the seconds of the call.

"Why are you telling me this?"

"Because I want things to change. It's not like I'm going to run out and have sex because I have a boyfriend, if that's what you're worried about."

"It's an issue."

"Although there are girls that have it without having a boyfriend."

"I'm aware of that." There was a moment of silence. "Where are you, Brenna? Your father will pick you up."

"I don't want to be grounded either."

"You've got to be joking. You run away, have us mindless with worry and expect not to be in trouble?"

"You weren't listening to me. How can you blame

me for something you were responsible for?" Brenna sighed as her mum started yelling. She turned the phone off. She should've known it was too good to last.

She looked around and wondered what she could do while she gave Jordan and Haley time alone with Zach. People walked briskly past and cars flashed by on the road until they came to a stop when the lights not far from her changed to red. There was nothing to do around here. She pulled Derrick's number from her pocket and turned her phone on. She quickly dialled in case her mum tried to ring.

"I was sleeping."

"Sorry."

"Who's this?"

"Brenna."

"How's Zach?"

"He woke up twice and spoke."

"Really?" Derrick sounded more awake.

"Yeah. Sorry I woke you. I thought you'd be awake since Jordan went there first."

"Nah, he has a spare key. Why'd you ring? To tell me about Zach?"

"I was wondering if you wanted help cleaning out Zach's fridge. I'm at the hospital."

"Probably can be there in about half an hour. That do?"

"Thank you."

"No drama."

After sorting out where to meet Derrick, Brenna rang Zach's room to let them know she wouldn't be back for a bit then got something to eat while she waited. Derrick double-parked in front of the hospital and she quickly got in. Other than a grunted 'morning' and a couple of yawns, Derrick was silent. He drove with the heel of his hand on the gearstick and the other at the base of the steering wheel, looking half asleep. She hoped he was more alert than he appeared.

When they pulled up in front of Zach's house, Brenna reached out to open the door and realised there was no handle. No wonder Derrick had walked around and opened the door for her last time while she'd been struggling to unbuckle her seatbelt.

Derrick grabbed a grocery bag from the back seat. "I'll let you out. I've been meaning to fix it for a while."

Brenna nodded and waited for Derrick to open the door. She grinned at his theatrical bow.

"My lady."

"Thank you, kind sir." Brenna walked towards the back door, dazed she'd answered Derrick so easily.

He fell into step beside her and glanced at her hands. "I got gloves to use when we clean out the fridge. Hope small fits."

Brenna unlocked the backdoor. "If they don't, you're on your own."

"We'll make them fit." He handed her a pair of gloves and pulled out a pair for himself.

It took over an hour to clean the fridge. Derrick took the garbage bag to the wheelie bin and swore he'd return when the rubbish was due to be collected and put it out. Brenna stared at the pile of mail and wondered what to do about the phone and electricity bill she could see. She pointed them out to Derrick when he came inside.

He opened them. "No need to worry yet. They're barely overdue. And they'll send reminder notices before they disconnect." He grinned. "At least they do for me. I'll have a wander through and see if there's anything else that needs doing."

Before Brenna could answer, her phone rang and reminded her she'd forgotten to turn it off. She checked her caller ID and was relieved it wasn't her mum. She didn't recognise the number. "Yes?"

"Brenna, it's Jordan."

"How's Zach?"

"Missing you." When Brenna laughed disbelievingly, Jordan replied, "No, really. He opened his eyes earlier and said Ren. It took us a few minutes to realise he meant you. He wanted to know where you were and when you'd return."

"He said all that?"

"All he said was Ren, where and when. But I've known him long enough to know what he meant. So, where are you and when will you be back?"

"I'm helping Derrick clean out the food that was masquerading as slime in Zach's fridge."

"Urrr. Rather you than me. When do you think you'll be finished?"

She hesitated. She wanted to see Zach, but didn't want to interrupt his time with Jordan and Haley. "I'll be back this afternoon."

"Okay. And Brenna… I wanted to thank you for being there for him when no one else was. And for tracking me down." Before Brenna could answer, Jordan was gone.

Derrick returned to the kitchen. "All done. Ready to go?"

"Well… I guess." She felt torn. Zach had asked for her, but Jordan was his best friend and he hadn't seen him in ages. Jordan had also driven a lot of kilometres to see him.

"You need a lift to the hospital?" When Brenna hesitated, he asked, "Or somewhere else? Do you need to go home?"

Brenna shook her head. "No, not yet."

Derrick laughed at her quick reply. "What did you do? Run away from home?"

"Ahh…" She couldn't meet his gaze.

Derrick laughed harder. "You plan on going back?"

"Hopefully."

"Want to talk about it?"

Brenna shrugged. "I don't know. It's pretty boring." Before Derrick could say anything, her phone rang again. She checked the display and saw it was her home number. Some weeks she was lucky to get a single call. This weekend she'd had far too many.

"Aren't you going to answer that?"

"I'm thinking about it."

"Your parents?"

Brenna nodded. "Probably Mum. Dad doesn't really talk to us."

"Come on, let's get out of here."

When they pulled up in front of an old highset

Queenslander with a yard that looked like it might hide wild animals, Brenna sent a questioning look to Derrick.

"My place. Come on." He walked around the car and opened the door for her.

"I–"

"Zach's not going anywhere."

"But–"

Derrick leaned against the door. "Have you been at the hospital since I dropped you there yesterday?"

"Yes, but–"

"Time for a break. Out you get."

Brenna hesitated a moment longer before she climbed out. When they were in the lounge room, she looked at the walls to see if she could figure out where Zach had painted them. Before she could look closer, Derrick ushered her into the kitchen. There was still no table.

"Coffee?" He filled the kettle.

"No thanks."

"There's soft drinks in the fridge. Help yourself."

Brenna took a can from the fridge and popped it open.

Derrick leaned against the bench while he waited for the kettle. "If you want to tell me the problem, I might be able to help."

Brenna worried at her bottom lip with her teeth. "It'll probably bore you."

"My sleep was interrupted this morning. I wouldn't mind a bit of a nap."

Brenna returned his smile. "Okay, but don't say I didn't warn you."

Derrick finished making his coffee and they sat in the lounge room. Brenna started hesitatingly at first. Derrick asked her questions and nodded at other times.

"Not wanting to head to bed yet?" Brenna asked when she was finished.

He shook his head. "Have you had a look online to see what the UN has to say about the rights of kids and the Family Law Act?"

"No."

"It might help to approach the issue from where you stand legally."

"I don't know."

Derrick shrugged. "Up to you. I can turn on my computer and you can have a look."

"I have my laptop with me. Can I use it instead?"

"Sure. You can plug it into the modem."

Within an hour, Brenna was sending an email to her mum with links to relevant articles. She sat back with a satisfied smile and stretched.

"You want to go to the hospital now?" Derrick shared the desk with her while he used his computer.

Brenna closed down and unplugged her laptop. "Yeah. I didn't plan to be gone this long."

"Okay. Give me a sec to save this document."

Brenna nodded as she rose to her feet. She'd barely put her laptop in her backpack when her phone rang. When she saw it was from home, she wondered if this meant her mum had read the email.

"Yeah." Brenna quickly held the phone from her ear.

"If you think I give a shit what the UN has to say, then think again. You're not their kid. I make the decision where you live. You keep this up and you'll be grounded for life."

Brenna started to protest when Derrick took the phone from her hands and walked away. He held a hand up when she started to follow and closed his door. Brenna's hand hovered over the doorknob. It was her phone. Not to mention her mum. It wasn't up to him to interfere. She'd just finished convincing herself when the door opened and Derrick handed her phone back. It was turned off.

"What did you tell her?"

"That you have friends who aren't willing to stand back and let them ignore your rights. If they get too difficult, we'll set Betts loose on them. She loves a good project."

"Betts?" Brenna couldn't understand what Betts had to do with her situation.

"Yeah. A friend of Zach's who's studying law. She's terrifying to watch when she gets started."

"Oh." Brenna guessed for someone who saw people as projects law was a good choice. Although she wouldn't have been surprised to hear Betts was doing psychology.

"You ready to go back to the hospital now?"

"You didn't tell my mum where I've been hanging out, did you?"

"No. I didn't even tell her my name."

Brenna breathed a sigh of relief and picked up her backpack. "Thanks."

"Come on, let's get you back to the hospital."

The drive was made in silence until Derrick pulled up in front of the hospital. "Ring if you need a lift."

"Thanks. It's much quicker than taking a bus."

Derrick grinned. "No drama."

Brenna wound down the window so she could open the car door from the outside. "I'll probably be stuck using buses forever at the rate I'm learning to drive."

"Can you drive at all?"

"Yeah. Kinda." Brenna shrugged. "I'm not good in heavy traffic."

"You can drive next time."

"Really?"

"Sure. Why not?" He grinned. "A few more dints won't be noticed."

Brenna returned his grin. "Thanks." A car horn sounded. "Whoops. Better let you get out of here." She waved as he drove off and then hurried to Zach's room.

Chapter Sixteen

Haley sat on a chair breastfeeding Lily and Brenna looked away. Jordan sat by the bed and read a magazine out loud. Brenna smiled fleetingly when she saw it was a motorbike magazine. Typical. He looked up as she came further into the room and stopped.

"How is he?" Brenna asked softly.

"He woke twice."

"Oh." She wished she'd been there.

"He asked for you each time."

Guilt hit her. "I'm sorry."

"Hey, you can't spend every second here. I'm sure you have a life to live."

Brenna shrugged, not sure how to answer.

"Do you want the chair?" Jordan started to rise but stopped when Brenna shook her head.

She moved to the bed, sat beside Zach and took his hand. "Thanks, but I like to sit here."

"Fair enough. So how'd you and Zach meet?"

Brenna felt heat rush through her cheeks and wished she'd waited until Jordan and Haley were ready to leave before she returned.

Jordan chuckled. "Looks like it'll be an interesting story."

Brenna shook her head. "Random chance," she mumbled.

"Now you have me more interested."

"Jordan, leave her alone and stop teasing." Haley shifted Lily to her shoulder.

"Now would I tease?" Jordan's innocent expression failed.

Haley rose to her feet, patting Lily as she spoke to Brenna. "Do you mind if we take a break? We'll be back in a few hours. I can bring you something for dinner."

"Thank you." Brenna watched as they gathered their things and with cheerful goodbyes, left silence behind.

Brenna reached out and brushed her knuckles across Zach's cheek, above the tube. She pulled her hand back when his eyes opened.

"Talk... please."

"I don't know what to say."

"Want to hear your voice." His eyes slowly closed.

Brenna glanced around to see what there was to read. Her gaze fell on the motorbike magazines. She tried to convince herself they wouldn't be completely boring.

Time passed quickly as Brenna read to Zach. Before she knew it, Jordan had returned. This time he was alone.

Without being asked, Jordan answered her question. "Lily was cranky. Haley thought it best not to bring her back." He held out a blue lidded glass Pyrex bowl. "Dinner."

"Thanks." Brenna opened the lid and breathed in the strong smell of stew. "It smells good."

Jordan handed her a spoon and shortly she was finished and handing the sealed bowl back. Jordan sat in one of the two chairs and Brenna worried at her lip as her gaze darted between the magazines, Zach and Jordan.

"What's wrong?" Jordan asked.

"Do you mind if I read out loud? Zach asked me to."

"Of course you can. Look, if you feel uncomfortable I can leave." He rose to his feet.

"No! I'm sorry. He's your best friend. You have to be here."

Jordan smiled slightly. "Yeah, but he keeps asking for you. I don't care who he wants around. I'm just happy he's recovering."

"I want you to stay. I didn't want to bore you." Brenna shrugged. "Or something like that."

Jordan moved to the drawers and took one of the magazines off the top, handing it to her. "I haven't read this one. I'll sit back and pretend I'm old, decrepit, half blind and need someone to read my favourite magazine to me." He grinned.

Brenna couldn't resist returning his smile. She opened the magazine to the first article and began to read. She read for the next couple of hours and was relieved and disappointed when a nurse came and said it was time for visitors to go home. Brenna reluctantly returned the magazine to the top of the drawers. She guessed she'd been lucky last night and couldn't expect to stay two nights in a row.

She watched as Jordan rested his hand on Zach's shoulder, bent forward, said something too quiet for her to hear and then stepped away. He looked at her and gestured towards Zach, a slight smile on his lips. Brenna hesitantly stepped forward. She reached out and rested her hand against Zach's cheek, leaning closer.

"I'll be back tomorrow after school."

Zach's eyes slowly opened. "Visit in the morning first?"

"I don't know. I can't be late to school."

"Call Jordan."

Brenna started to turn and began to pull her hand away as she did. Zach covered her hand with his and lightly pressed it against his cheek. Even though she could've easily pulled free, she left her hand there. She met his gaze. As soon as she did, he turned his head slightly so his lips were against her palm. Heat spiralled through her as Zach continued to watch her. Then he blinked slowly, his eyelids appearing to grow heavy. His head moved so her hand was on his cheek again.

"Jordan," Zach whispered.

Brenna nodded. "Jordan?"

Jordan was instantly beside her. "What's wrong?"

"Bring Ren in the morning. Then to school." Zach's eyes closed. This time they didn't open.

"Sure, Zach."

Zach's hand fell back to the bed and Brenna automatically bent forward and brushed a kiss against his cheek. She reluctantly moved away, grabbed her backpack and followed Jordan who stepped into the corridor.

"Can I give you a lift home?" When Brenna looked like she struggled with a reply, Jordan grinned. "Or do you want to crash at Derrick's tonight?"

Brenna's gaze narrowed. "What did he say?"

"Nothing. Just that you might prefer to sleep at his place tonight. Told me to let you know you're welcome."

Brenna nodded. "Yeah. That'd be good."

When they were in the car, Brenna turned her phone on. She decided to listen to the messages from her mum, but after two she quit. There were a couple of text messages. More demands and threats. She stared at the phone for a minute before she decided to ring. She hung up after one ring and waited. It was a short wait.

"Yeah."

"We can't talk over the phone. Come home so we can talk."

"I'll be home before dark tomorrow."

"What about school?"

"I'll be there. I just have something to do after."

"What?"

"I'm too tired to argue. I'll talk tomorrow."

"You'll talk right now."

Brenna sighed. "Goodnight, Mum."

"Don't you dare hang up on me, Brenna."

Brenna closed her eyes. "I wanted to let you know I'm safe. I'll be home tomorrow."

"Where are you? You can't run off when things get difficult."

Brenna managed not to snort in answer. "How many times have you or Dad stormed out of the house when a fight wasn't going your way? Guess you taught me well."

"Don't carry on again. I–"

"No more arguments. I'll be home tomorrow." When Brenna heard her mum continue to argue, she turned the phone off and closed her eyes.

"You want me to pick you up after school tomorrow too?"

Brenna's eyes flew open and she turned towards Jordan. "If it isn't too much trouble."

"Nah, no problem." Jordan glanced at her. "If you need another ear, I'll listen. And Haley. She's good at solutions."

"Thanks."

"So? Need an ear or two?"

"I'll think about it.

"Okay."

By the time they arrived at Derrick's, Brenna had

made the decision to tell Jordan and Haley everything she'd told Derrick. Maybe they'd be able to think of more suggestions to add to the one Derrick had already made. She needed all the help she could get.

When Brent joined them in the lounge room she almost changed her mind. Instead she forced herself to stick with her decision and after she stumbled through the first few sentences the rest flowed easily. When she reached the end, she stared at the four people that watched her with various expressions on their faces. The silence stretched out and Brenna began to think no one could help.

Haley smiled. "When you don't want a boat to drift away, you drop the anchor."

"Yes." Brenna drew the word out, uncertain what it had to do with anything.

"You have nothing to anchor you to this area, but you should slowly add anchors so your parents don't guess what you're doing," Haley said.

"Look for part time work. Join a club that only meets in this area," Jordan said.

"Have you done any work before?" Derrick asked.

Brenna shook her head. "I never needed more than my pocket money so I didn't bother."

"I've got an uncle who owns a fruit and vegie shop. He'll give you a go," Derrick said.

"But I don't know anything about fruit and vegies."

Brent laughed. "Neither did Derrick the year he worked there. I don't think he knew much more by the end of the year. All Derrick will have to do is threaten to come back and his uncle will beg to let you work instead."

"I wasn't that bad," Derrick protested.

"Really?" Jordan asked. "I believe you threatened to shove an avocado down one woman's throat if she didn't stop mauling them and wrecking your display.

"I was polite." Derrick grinned. "I used the word please."

"I seriously don't think that's what Uncle Matt meant when he said to always be polite to the customers." Jordan grinned at Derrick before he turned to Brenna. "I'll have a chat to Uncle Matt too. We can go by there before the hospital tomorrow afternoon."

"Well, I guess," Brenna said hesitantly.

"You'll like him," Haley assured her. A scream from the bedroom brought Haley and Jordan to their feet. "Sounds like Lily might be hungry. I'll say goodnight." She smiled at Brenna before she turned to Jordan.

"I'll come too. Probably best to get some sleep

while I can. Might be a busy night with her by the sounds of things." Jordan looked around the room. "Night all."

Brenna watched them leave the room, arm in arm. Lily quietened a few minutes later. She turned to Derrick. "If you think your uncle won't mind, I'd like to give it a go."

"He always employs family when he can. He thinks of Zach as family. We'll tell him you're Zach's girl," Derrick said.

"Oh no, that's–"

Derrick laughed. "Don't worry about it."

"Yeah, if you're even slightly better than Derrick, he'll have you. And that won't take much," Brent said.

"I'll tell her some of the stories about your first job," Derrick threatened with a grin.

"He was brilliant. His uncle was devastated when he quit," Brent said with false sincerity.

Brenna couldn't help smiling. "What do you do now?"

"We're both in construction. Need a house built, give us a call," Derrick said.

"Only the house." Brent sent a pointed look towards Derrick. "We don't do the landscaping."

Derrick rubbed the back of his neck. "Okay, so

I didn't get around to mowing this weekend." He shrugged. "I'll do it next weekend."

"We should give in and pay someone to take care of the yard," Brent said.

"Between the three of us, we should be able to deal with it," Derrick protested.

"Might as well say two since Mike's at his girlfriend's place more than here."

Brenna tried to hold back a yawn as she watched the conversation jump back and forth.

Derrick noticed instantly. "You should've said you were tired." He rose to his feet. "You can have my room. I'll throw a mattress on Brent's floor if I can find a clear spot."

"I can sleep on the couch. You don't need to give up your bed," Brenna protested.

"Nah, bad idea. If Mike decides to come home instead of crashing at his girlfriend's place, he always turns on the light. But only after he's managed to trip over his own feet and make a tonne of noise. You'll still hear him in the bedroom, but at least you won't have your eyes fried." Derrick threw an arm around Brenna's shoulders, guiding her from the room.

"Night Brenna," Brent called after her.

Brenna glanced over her shoulder. "Night."

"Bathroom, my room." Derrick pointed at a closed

door then swung open his bedroom door and switched on the light. "Give me a yell if you need anything. I'll be up at four a.m. and out of here by five. Night."

Brenna hovered in the doorway. "Thanks for everything."

"No drama." A quick grin and Derrick headed towards the lounge room.

Brenna closed the door and looked around. A large bed dominated the middle of the room, a bedside table with matching lamps on either side. A tall chest of drawers stood on one wall and was covered in oddments, loose change and a couple of photos in wooden frames.

Brenna dropped her backpack by the bed and turned down the black doona to reveal matching sheets. She pulled her phone from her pocket and turned it on for an alarm. With a glance at the door she wished she'd thought to ask for a towel. But she wasn't going to disturb anyone now. She rummaged in her backpack for her toothbrush, used the bathroom and returned to the bedroom. As soon as she turned off the light she shed her jeans and climbed into bed.

Chapter Seventeen

Sleep was a long time coming and she was woken a couple of times by Lily. Her phone rang when early morning light struggled in the half open curtains and made her groan. She groaned again when she saw it was a call from the home phone.

"Yeah?"

"Where are you?"

"Mum, I'm trying to sleep."

"I'm glad you can. How am I meant to sleep when I don't know where you are?"

"I told you I was safe."

"You'll come straight home after school today."

"I already told you I have something to do first."

"What?"

Brenna was silent for a moment and then smiled. "A job interview."

"What!"

Brenna held the phone away from her ear. She put it back when her mum stopped at one shriek. "I'm looking for part-time work."

"What for?"

"I'm saving for a car."

"You've barely gone for your learners."

"I know, but it'll take ages to save enough money."

"You're not-" she stopped in mid sentence. "Stop trying to distract me. You'll come straight home after school. That's the last I'm going to say."

"After my interview."

"Don't keep pushing, Brenna. You're on thin ice."

Brenna opened her mouth to answer back, but the sound of Lily screaming halted her. It gave her the few seconds she needed to rein in her anger. "I'll see you later." She strived for calmness. She achieved gritted teeth instead.

"Was that a baby?"

"Yeah."

"Where are you?"

"It doesn't matter. See ya, Mum."

"Don't you hang up, Brenna."

She hesitated at her mum's tone. Letting out the breath she held, she hung up, turned the phone off and dropped it on the bedside table. She fell back against the pillow, letting her arm cover her eyes.

Sleep was impossible now. Brenna hopped out of bed and pulled on her jeans.

Jordan was in the kitchen, organising breakfast, when she entered. "You hungry?"

Brenna nodded. "Ah… I was wondering… a towel…"

"Linen cupboard in the bathroom. Help yourself."

"Thanks." Brenna hurried to the bathroom and quickly showered.

When she returned to the kitchen, dressed in her school uniform, Haley stood at the kitchen bench eating egg on toast with Lily in a cloth pouch hanging at her front. She took the plate Jordan handed her and had some of the egg and toast.

"I hope it wasn't Lily who woke you," Haley said.

Brenna shook her head, swallowing her mouthful. "My mum. She's adamant I come straight home after school and I can't get a job."

"What do you say?" Jordan asked.

"Can you pick me up after school?"

Jordan grinned. "No problem. Tell me where and when."

Brenna returned his grin. "Thanks."

* * *

That afternoon, Brenna dropped her backpack inside the door and crossed the room to stand beside Zach's bed. She smiled and was surprised when Zach's eyes opened.

"Ren."

She reached out and grasped the hand he held out to her. "They removed your tubes. When will they take out the drip?"

"Don't know."

"Well, it must have been a good day getting rid of the tubes. And hopefully it was more interesting than my day."

"I slept most of it."

"I think I could have slept through most of mine without missing anything of importance."

"Tell me."

Brenna hesitated. "You'll be bored."

"More than I already am?"

Brenna laughed nervously. "Maybe."

"Tell me."

Brenna met his gaze a moment longer before she made herself comfortable on the bed. "My sister warned me Mum would be waiting for me outside my classroom when school ended so I cut out early and Jordan picked me up a couple of blocks away. Then he took me to his uncle to see if he had any work. I start tomorrow after school. He said depending on how fast I learn, he'd have two to three days a week for me. I'm saving for a car."

"Does that mean you won't be interested in a boyfriend with a car?"

"You heard me?" Brenna groaned, covering her face with her hands. "Did you hear everything I said?"

"Possibly. Although I guess it's unlikely."

"Oh no." Brenna groaned again and leaned forward so her head could press into the mattress.

Zach chuckled. "It wasn't that bad."

"I wouldn't have said half what I did if I'd known." Brenna felt Zach's hand stroke her hair. "Couldn't you have let me know you were listening?" She bit back a groan as she realised how stupid her comment was.

"Where would the fun have been in that?"

Brenna raised her head to meet Zach's gaze. "I'm glad you woke up."

"Me too. I kept hearing your voice and I wanted to wake up and see you."

"Ahh… okay." Brenna started to rise from the bed.

Zach's hand tightened on hers. "Don't run off."

"I brought a book to read to you." She tried to suppress her smile.

"What?" he asked cautiously.

Brenna's smile became a grin. "The book I have to read for English."

Zach chuckled. "Go ahead. I like listening to your voice."

Brenna was only a few chapters in when Jordan arrived to give her a lift. She moved forward and leaned over Zach to kiss his cheek in farewell. She'd done it so many times it was automatic. At the last second, Zach turned his head and their lips met. Startled, Brenna pulled back.

Zach slowly smiled. "Come back tomorrow?"

Brenna could only nod before she turned, grabbed her backpack and fled. Jordan called for her to wait. Brenna didn't get far before she remembered that without Jordan to give her a lift home she wouldn't be able to make it before dark. Her feet slowed until she stopped moving.

Jordan dropped an arm around her shoulders as he reached her side. "No need to run off. I promise not to tease you… much." Jordan grinned.

Brenna felt her cheeks warm and guessed they must be traffic light red. She closed her eyes for a second and then opened them. Nope, the floor in front of her hadn't opened up while her eyes had been closed. Jordan started to walk, his arm still around her shoulders so she had to move with him.

"I'll pick you up in the morning so you can see Zach before school. I guess you won't have time after school since you work till five. I can give you a lift home in the afternoon too."

"Are you sure? I can catch the bus. I mean, look at all the driving you did today. You and Haley. I forgot to ask Zach about seeing his grandma. I bet she was glad to see him. And did you get his car back here like you planned?"

"No problem, yes and yes."

Brenna frowned. "You've lost me."

Jordan laughed. "You were the one who fired questions at me."

"Oh. Sorry."

"We're staying for a couple of weeks. You need a lift during that time, give us a yell. We owe you for being there for Zach."

"There's no-"

"Don't argue. We owe you. Simple. Now, the other questions. Marian cried buckets and couldn't stop smiling. Haley tells me that's good. I'll have to trust her on that since I thought Marian had seriously lost the plot. And Zach's car is parked in their...

ahh… his garage." As they reached Jordan's car, he dropped his arm and pulled out his keys to activate the central locking.

Brenna quietly got in the car, dropping her backpack on the floor at her feet. She glanced at Jordan when he slid into the driver's seat and started the car. She worried at her lip with her teeth, trying to think how to word the questions she wanted to ask. She glanced at Jordan again.

"What's wrong?" Jordan checked for traffic before he pulled onto the road, then took a quick look at Brenna.

"How will he manage?"

"What?"

"Zach. He has no parents. Will he still be able to go to uni? Or will he have to get a job?"

"I don't know. Marian said that when he was feeling up to it he'd have to talk to his parents' solicitor. But whatever the situation, Zach will manage. He always does."

"You sure?"

"Yeah. He's got me into and out of enough trouble over the years I know he can manage anything."

Brenna smiled weakly. "I hope so."

Chapter Eighteen

Brenna dropped onto Zach's bed. She smiled as his eyes opened. "Hey. How are you feeling?" He looked so much healthier now. No monitors, no drip and he no longer looked ghostly pale.

"Bored. I've been waiting all day for you to finish work."

Brenna smiled. "It's barely one. You should be glad it's not a school day and you have to wait longer. Or a school afternoon when I'm working and can't visit."

"Okay. I'll quit complaining if you tell me what you've been doing. You've barely talked to me this week. Mainly read your school book."

Brenna shrugged. "There isn't much to tell. All I do is go to school and work. And here, of course."

"You're not very talkative anymore."

Brenna felt her cheeks grow warm and glared at

Zach when he laughed softly. "Maybe it's because life's boring."

"Would it help if I closed my eyes? You can pretend I'm not listening."

"I'd know you were."

"I've always been listening."

"I never believed that."

Zach patted the bed beside him. "Come closer."

Brenna moved along the bed. She let him take her hand and bring it up to cup his cheek like she'd done many times.

Zach smiled. "I have heard your voice so often that even if I'd never laid eyes on you I could pick you out of a line up if you said one word. Any word."

She opened her mouth to speak, but could think of no coherent sentence.

"Speechless, Ren?"

Brenna recalled the line up comment she'd made to him. "When I asked you if you'd heard everything you said it was unlikely. Tell me you don't recall everything."

"Truthfully?"

She nodded, shook her head and then nodded again. She closed her eyes as she felt her cheeks grow warm. "I don't know," she whispered.

"Sleeping Beauty."

Brenna's eyes flew open to see Zach smiling at her. She pulled away from him and headed for the door.

"Ren. Come back. I wasn't teasing. Well, I was, but I wasn't being mean. Or I wasn't trying to be."

Brenna hesitated in the doorway.

"Please. I can't chase after you."

"No more teasing?"

"I'll try, but I didn't mean to hurt you. I didn't like being called Sleeping Beauty, but I was glad to hear your voice, no matter what you said. Sit beside me." When she didn't move, he added, "Please?"

Brenna walked hesitantly towards the bed. "Did you hear everything I said?"

"I think so. I re-read my diary. I recall hearing every word of it from you."

Brenna closed her eyes and tried to think of everything she'd said. Her mind was blank. When she heard Zach softly say her name, her eyes flew open.

"Come back here. Please."

She took another couple of steps until she was next to the bed. Zach held out his hand. She stared at it warily before she placed hers in it. She allowed him to tug her forward and sat on the bed again. Her gaze dropped to watch his thumb make lazy movements on her hand. She swallowed hard and met his gaze, surprised by the intensity. Her mouth went dry and her pulse sped up. Her lips parted but words didn't follow, instead her mind remained blank.

The door opened and dragged their attention to it. Brenna tried to tug her hand from Zach, but he tightened his grip. She knew she could pull away, but a glance at him changed her mind. She turned towards the door, leaving her hand in his.

Jordan entered. "I was wondering how long you were planning on being here."

"I can catch a bus home," Brenna said.

"I'm going with Derrick and a few others to the forestry. We're taking the motorbikes. Haley said she can give you a lift home any time after the next couple of hours. Her and Lily are out with friends."

"There's no need. I normally catch the bus."

"Were you planning on leaving in the next couple of hours?" Jordan asked.

Before Brenna could answer, Zach did. "No."

Brenna turned to him, about to argue.

"Please," Zach said softly.

Brenna hesitated then nodded. She turned to Jordan. "I'll be here for another couple of hours."

"Haley will pick you up at four-thirty, give her a call if you want to leave before then. I'll have her text you her number. Catch you both later." Jordan grinned before he disappeared through the door.

"Think you can tell me what you've been doing lately?" Zach asked as soon as they were alone.

"No."

"You know all my secrets."

"Only for the past year."

"That's more than most people. Don't censor your thoughts. You had the complete uncut version of mine."

"I'm sorry."

"I don't want you to apologise. I understand why you read it to me. I want you to stop hiding your every thought from me. I liked listening to what you had to say."

"Yeah, but I didn't think you were listening. I can't tell you stuff like that when you are."

Zach moved over in the bed. "Hop up here beside me." He patted the pillow.

Brenna stared at the white linen for a moment before she rose from the bed and then sat with her back to the pillow. She leaned against it, but was unable to relax. She could feel the warmth of Zach's body beside hers, but remained looking straight ahead.

"Not an interesting view, is it?"

Brenna turned to look at him, then back at the blank wall. "I guess not." She met his gaze and wondered what he thought. She missed being able to read his diary. She didn't even know if he was writing in it. A few times she'd considered asking.

"What are you thinking?" Zach reached out and captured a lock of her hair, twisting and untwisting it around his fingers.

"That's exactly what I was wondering. What you were thinking."

"You. I was thinking about you. I was wishing we were going with Jordan."

"No way. I'm not going to stand around and watch you ride a motorbike while I'm bored senseless."

"You wouldn't be sitting around. You'd be on the back of the bike with me."

"Travis tried that. Once. He said I was a rag doll and I'd cause an accident."

"All you'd have to do is hold on tight and plaster yourself to me. If I lean to one side, you lean too."

"I don't know," Brenna said softly.

"I do. As soon as I'm out of here we'll go."

Brenna shook her head. "Not likely. I'm not letting you push yourself the moment they let you out of here."

"Think you can stop me?"

Brenna looked at him thoughtfully for a moment.

"I'll hop on the back of a motorbike with you if you take things easy for a while."

"Deal." Zach grinned.

Brenna stared at him. "Was that deliberate?"

Zach laughed. "What makes you ask?"

"You knew I wouldn't let you overdo things."

"Are you trying to get out of going already?"

Brenna sighed. "You're not going to tell me, are you?"

"You have your secrets. I guess I'm entitled to mine."

"I don't have any secrets. If you want to be bored by my week, then fine." Brenna told him about her classes, teachers, work, but none of it was anything other than superficial. She couldn't bring herself to be as open as she'd been when she'd thought no one was listening.

Zach eventually interrupted her. "Are you going to tell me about the weather next?"

"Fine!" She glared at him. Her words hadn't been that bad. "My parents are adamant I'm moving in with my dad next year. I'm meant to be going to his place next weekend. My sister is treating me like I've died, Travis is telling people my boyfriend I claimed to have when we broke up is a figment of my imagination, it's two weeks to the September school holidays which I'm meant to spend at my dad's place and technically I'm grounded."

"Then how did you manage to come here?"

"Matt thinks my parents are unreasonable and is covering for me. But only as long as I'm visiting you and not gallivanting around the countryside as he puts it."

"And what about visiting me before school? How do you manage that?"

"My sister covers for me. We leave a bit early and Jordan picks me up from the bus stop. With how long it takes for the bus to reach school with all the stops it has to make, I still manage half an hour here."

"Sounds like it takes some effort to spend time with me. Does that mean you enjoy visiting?"

"I guess." Brenna looked away.

Zach laughed softly. "Are we back to not sharing again?"

"It was so much easier when you didn't answer." Brenna momentarily closed her eyes and groaned. "That sounded terrible." She met Zach's gaze. "I'm glad you're awake."

"I know." He paused. "You can ask me questions. About anything."

Brenna looked down at his hand that still played

with her hair. "Have you continued to write in your diary?"

"Jordan bought me a new one earlier in the week. You won't be reading this one. If you want to know what's going on in my head, you're going to have to ask. And share what's in yours."

Brenna remained silent.

Zach smiled. He reached out and tilted her head up with a finger under her chin. "Tell me about the rumour Travis is spreading."

"Mainly about how convenient it is no one has met the guy I dumped him for."

"Okay. We'll see what we can do about solving that problem."

"How?"

Zach smiled with a shake of his head. "Don't worry about it for now. Have I told you they're moving me to a different room tomorrow? Now they don't need me hooked up to all those machines and I'm eating solid food I can go to a normal room."

"Where?"

"I don't know. I'll ring you the moment they shift me."

"On my mobile, not the home phone. My parents would interrogate you and still not let me talk to you."

"Why not?"

"Ahh… well…"

"Come on Brenna."

Brenna closed her eyes and her words came out quickly enough there was no gaps between them. "Because I asked if I could have a boyfriend before I was seventeen." When Zach remained quiet, she opened her eyes. She closed them again when she saw he was smiling. Her eyes popped open when she felt his lips brush against hers.

"What was their answer?"

"I think the third time I talked to them about it… or was it the fourth? I guess it doesn't matter since the answer was when hell freezes over."

"Think they'll change their mind?"

"My mum's stubborn."

"And your father?"

"I don't know."

"What do you mean?"

"We always knew it was Mum who had the final word so we stopped asking him years ago."

"When do you turn seventeen?" He frowned. "You told me that, didn't you? June, right?"

She nodded. "Yeah, June next year."

"That's too far away."

Brenna couldn't resist smiling. She opened her

mouth to ask him a question, but chickened out. Her smile faded. What was she meant to do? Ask him his intentions like some father from centuries ago? Not likely. The door to the room opened and saved Brenna from having to think of a reply.

Chapter Nineteen

Haley stepped into the room with Lily in her pouch she wore like a backpack on her front. "Sorry I'm a little early." She grinned. "Not interrupting anything am I?"

Zach shook his head. "Nah. But I do need you to take some photos." He turned to Brenna. "Pass me the button up shirt in the second last drawer."

"Photos?" Brenna asked.

"Yeah. Give your phone to Haley. She can take photos so Travis can see you didn't imagine me."

Brenna stared at him a moment, his words playing over in her mind. She had to ask him. But she couldn't. Not with Haley in the room. Who was she kidding? Probably not even if they were alone. Slipping off the bed, she chickened out again. "Okay." She handed Zach his shirt and gave Haley her phone. Brenna watched as he slipped the shirt on over his hospital gown.

He grinned at Haley. "Make sure you only get from the waist up. We wouldn't want to ruin the pictures with the wonderful hospital fashions." He rose, paused for a moment then slowly walked to the wall opposite his bed.

As soon as Brenna reached his side, he dropped his arm around her shoulders. "Thanks for this. Are you sure you don't mind? I mean, the photos should stop the rumours he's spreading, but-" She wasn't certain how to finish.

Zach grinned momentarily. "Why would I mind?" He ran his thumb across her cheek, then her lips, stepping closer. He lowered his voice. "I didn't mind that. Did you?

"You want me to take these photos or are you going to talk all day?" Haley asked.

Zach held Brenna's gaze. "Take the pictures, Haley."

Zach smiled and Brenna automatically smiled back. He pulled her even closer and his lips met hers. Brenna forgot about Haley until she eventually spoke.

"Hello? I'm not into voyeurism."

Zach pulled back slightly and stared down at

Brenna with a smile on his lips. "Think those photos will help?"

Brenna could only nod. Conversation was momentarily beyond her.

Zach took the phone when Haley tried to hand it to Brenna.

She finally found her voice. "What are you doing?"

"Choosing the best one for your background. And I've found it." He tilted the phone so Brenna could see it.

She blushed. "I can't-"

"Yep. You can." Zach looked up from the phone to meet her gaze. "Don't change it." He paused. "Please?"

"Okay," she said softly. When he turned back to the phone, she asked, "What are you doing now?"

"Adding my phone numbers. You have everyone's but mine. Here you go." He handed the phone back before he took her hand and walked to his bed. He sat on the edge and tugged her hand so she sat beside him.

"I'll wait in the corridor." Neither of them said anything as Haley left the room.

He threaded his fingers through hers. "Will you be back tomorrow?"

"I'll try. I don't have any excuse and I'm meant to be grounded."

"Just say the word and I'll send someone to bust you out."

"I wish. But I don't want them to completely ground me."

"I miss you when you're not here."

Brenna shook her head. "That's only because you're bored. If you weren't stuck in hospital you wouldn't feel that way."

"Yes I would."

Brenna rose to her feet and tried to tug her hand out of his. "I have to go. I'll never hear the end of it if I'm late."

"What about a kiss goodbye?"

"I think you already had one."

Zach grinned. "That wasn't a goodbye kiss."

"Then what was it?" Brenna wanted to sink through the floor when Zach laughed. She turned away and tried to tug her hand from his.

"Brenna, I wasn't laughing at you. Well, not exactly. There's only one answer I can give and it would embarrass you." He stared at her a moment. "What? No question?"

Brenna shook her head. "I have to go."

"Are you going to forgive me for teasing? It's a

habit. Probably a bad one. I don't usually apologise for it either."

"Are you apologising now?"

Zach stared at her thoughtfully. "Yeah, I guess I am."

"Why?"

"Because you don't like it and I care how you feel." Zach grinned suddenly, all seriousness fleeing. "So, do I get my goodbye kiss?"

Brenna couldn't resist smiling. "I suppose."

She'd barely spoken when he took his goodbye kiss, then rested his forehead against hers. "It's frustrating being stuck in the hospital right this second." His words were barely a whisper.

"Why?" Brenna's words were equally quiet.

Zach pulled back slightly. "You better go. Try and visit tomorrow."

Half dazed, Brenna nodded and walked to the door, letting herself out of the room.

"I was beginning to think I'd have to come and get you," Haley said.

"Sorry."

"No problem. We better move quickly or you won't be home before dark."

When they were in Haley's car and on the way to Brenna's place, Haley asked, "What's with you and

Zach?" The silence stretched out. "Zach usually goes for girls who won't take things seriously. You seem like the type to take things very seriously."

"I don't know."

"You don't know what? About you and Zach or if you take things seriously?"

"Anything. I don't know anything."

"Are you trying to tell me to stay out of your business? You're welcome to say that. I won't be offended. I think Betts cured me of not speaking up. It was either that or be walked all over by her in the end."

"No. I wasn't meaning that. I guess... I... I'm a little confused."

Haley slowed for a red light. "I'm here if you want someone to help you figure things out."

"Thanks. I'll keep that in mind."

Haley laughed. "Yeah, but you won't take me up on it."

"I–" Brenna couldn't think what to say without sounding rude.

"It doesn't matter. It's your choice."

"I've never been very good at sharing my thoughts with other people."

"Neither was I for ages. But I learned sometimes you need to so people don't take you for granted."

Haley grinned. "But even if you don't want to share your deep dark secrets, give me a yell if you want to talk about anything. I don't mind if all you want to do is complain about boys and how annoying they can be."

Brenna laughed. "Okay. I-"

"Yeah, I know. You'll keep it in mind."

* * *

Brenna hurried towards Zach's room. She'd barely have any time with him before she had to go to school. They'd been held up by traffic. She froze in his doorway. A television was in the corner, a playstation hooked up to it with movies and games scattered nearby. A wheeled table was on the left of Zach's bed and another one was pushed over the bed from the right, with a laptop on it. The first held paper, books, pens and a calculator. Zach was on the phone.

The moment he noticed Brenna, he smiled and beckoned her forward. "I'll ring you back." He disconnected and put the phone on the table before he pushed it out of the way.

"What-"

"Later." Zach tugged on her hand to bring her closer. "How about a hello kiss?"

Brenna's eyes closed as their lips met. Her hand reached out to curl around Zach's neck as his hand splayed against her back. After several minutes she reluctantly pulled away.

"I missed you yesterday," Zach said softly.

"I warned you I mightn't be able to visit. And how much of a chance did you have to miss me when you must have rung a dozen times. Your phone bill is going to be ridiculous. And what's all this?" She gestured towards the tables and television. "Should you be working on whatever that is?" Another gesture towards the table.

"I was bored. You can only watch so many movies. Same with games."

"That doesn't tell me what you're doing."

"I got in touch with some of the guys from my classes and they lent me their notes. I'll ring uni later and my parents' solicitor and get my life back on track. The doctors said I should be able to go home in about a week."

"That soon? Really?"

Zach nodded. "Yep."

"Have you told Marian?" When Zach nodded, Brenna asked, "What does she think?"

"That they're kicking me out because they don't have enough beds."

"Are they?"

"Of course not. I feel great. I could probably go home today."

"Why don't I believe you?"

Zach laughed. "What time does your school have lunch?"

"Why?"

"You're highly suspicious today."

Jordan popped his head in the door. "Time to move."

Brenna nodded and turned back to Zach. She gave him the time for lunch and then hesitated a moment before she kissed him goodbye. When she would have pulled away, Zach's arms went around her.

"Will you visit this arve?"

She desperately wanted to say yes. "I have to work."

"Tomorrow morning?"

"Yeah." This time when Brenna pulled away, Zach dropped his arms.

Chapter Twenty

By lunch, Brenna had shown the photos to what felt like a million people. Her reply early that morning when someone had asked about her weekend had been to pull out her phone and show the pictures. People had been asking to see them ever since.

She sat under a tree to eat a sandwich with Ellen and Jessica, who'd cautiously welcomed her back when she'd broken up with Travis. Both girls were blue eyed, with dark blond hair, Ellen's several shades darker than Jessica's. Ellen was also several centimetres taller than Jessica and had a lot more curves. Only minutes after Brenna had finished her sandwich a shadow fell over the three of them and they all looked up.

"What do you want?" Ellen demanded of Travis.

He ignored Ellen, his gaze on Brenna. "I hear you've got pics of your imaginary boyfriend."

Brenna rose to her feet. "Don't tell me you want to look too."

"Why not? Apparently everyone else has. Is there a reason why you wouldn't want me to see them?"

Brenna handed over her phone and watched as Travis scrolled through the photos.

"Whoops. I think I deleted one." Travis smiled as he returned the phone.

Ellen rose to her feet. "Now we know the real reason. He wants to sabotage your phone."

Jessica continued to sit with her back against the tree. "Are you jealous she found someone better than you, Travis?"

"It wasn't deliberate," Travis said. "I'm just not used to that phone."

Brenna shrugged. "It doesn't matter. I backed them up on my laptop."

"Aren't you lucky."

Brenna nodded when she'd much rather say something insulting. Or at least tell him she didn't believe a word he'd said.

"Where did you meet him?"

Brenna didn't know how to answer and was relieved when her phone rang. She checked and saw Zach's name displayed. She smiled as she answered. "Why are you ringing? And seriously, how many more texts are you going to send me today? I can't answer them in class or I'll lose my phone."

"I miss you. Are you sure you can't pop in for even ten minutes after work?"

"I'll catch you tomorrow before school. And I don't work tomorrow arve."

"Is that him?" Travis demanded.

"Who was that?" Zach asked.

Brenna turned her back on Travis. "No one."

"It's Travis, isn't it? So what did he think of the photos?"

"Zach." Brenna drew his name out.

"Aren't you willing to tell me while he's listening?"

"No. And you knew when you asked."

"What's he saying?" Travis demanded as he moved to face her.

Zach laughed. "Doesn't he like me ringing?"

She tried to ignore the insults that Ellen and Travis started to trade, the occasional one thrown in by Jessica. "Doesn't seem that way."

"Looks like I picked a good time."

"You're terrible," Brenna said with a laugh.

"Yep. But you know exactly where I'm coming from. Otherwise you wouldn't have borrowed the rings."

"I keep forgetting to give them–"

"Shh. Remember your audience. Besides, they're probably safer with you then in a hospital room drawer."

"When you're home then."

"I'll call you later."

She would much rather see him. "Okay."

"Miss you."

"Me too."

Zach laughed. "Not going to say it with an audience? You know that's a common response when someone says 'love you' on the phone."

"Thanks! Just what I needed to hear." Brenna could feel her cheeks grow warm and turned her back on Travis who'd finished insulting Ellen.

"Bye." Zach hung up.

Brenna was still smiling when she put her phone away.

"What did he want?" Travis demanded. "And what was he saying?"

"I'm not about to discuss our private conversation."

Ellen smiled at Travis, not a single bit of mirth in it. "Are you worried she was talking about you, Travis?"

Travis glared at Ellen. "Stay out of it. This has nothing to do with you."

Brenna tried to suppress her smile. Ellen and Travis

had hated each other for years. Ellen had been the only one to congratulate her on dumping him.

"It's none of your business either," Ellen said.

"Don't worry about it, Ellen. Let's go," Brenna said.

With one last glare, Ellen turned away from Travis. "You're right, we've got better things to do."

"Brenna."

She turned back to Travis.

"There's a party at my place this weekend. Saturday night. My parents are away. You and… what's his name? Never mind. It's unimportant. Come along. Unless there's a reason no one has met him."

Brenna forced herself to laugh. "Nice try, Travis. We'll come if there's nothing more interesting happening."

"More interesting than one of Travis' parties?" Ellen rolled her eyes. "Please! A dental appointment would be more fun."

Brenna didn't need to force her laughter this time. "Well, I guess if my dentist can't fit me in, I'll be there."

Ellen linked arms with Brenna on one side of her, Jessica on the other. "Why are we still standing here? I seriously have better things to do."

Brenna didn't argue that statement, but she was

left thinking that Travis wasn't taking their break-up very well. She knew it wouldn't be because he still wanted her. No, it would be because she'd been the one to dump him.

*   *   *

"Will you all stop hovering?" Zach glared at them.

Brenna, Jordan, Haley and Marian were seated around Zach's kitchen table. It was Friday, his first day home, and they had just finished eating the celebration meal Haley had cooked.

Haley went to speak, but Lily screamed from the lounge room where they'd set up her port-a-cot.

"You want me to get her?" Jordan asked.

Haley shook her head. "No, she'll be hungry. You see if you can sort your mate out."

Jordan laughed. "Ignore him and go ahead as planned."

Haley shook her head again before she left the room.

"Grandma-" Zach began.

"You're not giving me a lift home. It's been a long day for you," Marian said.

"I'm fine. I feel great," Zach protested.

"Why don't you stay here, Marian?" Brenna asked.

"Because Greg would probably come back and haunt me. I was never welcome here when he was alive. It wouldn't feel right to stay now he isn't." Marian rose to her feet and began to gather dishes. "Discussion over. Jordan will give me a lift home. We'll leave as soon as the kitchen's in order."

"I'll take care of it. Derrick isn't due to pick me up for another half an hour." Brenna looked at Zach when he opened his mouth again. "And you're not giving me a lift home either. You're not overdoing things. Besides, Derrick said I could drive."

Zach pushed away from the table, glared at each of them and strode from the room.

Brenna stared worriedly after him. She took a step in his direction.

Jordan came to stand beside her. "Give him a few minutes before you talk to him. He calms down quickly. Are you right to clean up the kitchen so Marian and I can leave?"

"Yes. Of course. There's not that much mess."

Jordan smiled. "That should give him enough time to cool off." He turned to Marian. "Ready?"

Marian faced Brenna. "Normally I wouldn't leave without helping clean up." She turned to Jordan. "But you have a lot of driving ahead of you." She reached out to Brenna and wrapped her arms around her. "Don't be too hard on him," she said softly.

"I won't."

Brenna cleaned the kitchen and then wandered through the house. She stopped in front of Zach's closed bedroom door. She raised her hand to knock and hesitated. What if he told her to go away? She rested her hand on the doorknob and worried at her lip with her teeth. The door was pulled from her light grip and Zach stood in the doorway.

"Are you planning on standing there all night?"

"Maybe."

Zach smiled, reaching for her. He pressed her head against his shoulder. "I'm sorry." He pulled away slightly so he could meet her gaze. "Not quite what I imagined when I thought about the first time we were alone in my room." He stared at her a moment. "What? No blushes?"

"Maybe I'm getting used to your teasing."

"That'll be sad." Zach ran his fingers along her cheek.

A car horn sounded twice outside. "I have to go," Brenna said softly.

"Stay. Please."

"You know I can't. It's only a week until the school holidays. If I manage to follow their rules my grounding ends. It was hard enough to get them to let me out tonight. I'll see you after work tomorrow. And Matt said tomorrow's the last day he's covering for us since you're out of hospital. I had to promise we'd be on our best behaviour."

Zach laughed. "I bet that conversation made you blush."

The car horn saved Brenna from answering. "I'll see you tomorrow. Oh, and you'll have to give me a lift to the shop because Dad's picking me up from there. I was meant to go to his place Friday after school but he agreed to pick me up after work. Danielle's getting out of going because she has a rehearsal Sunday." She kissed him before she hurried from the room.

She refused to look back since she knew she'd be tempted to tell Derrick not to bother giving her a lift home. Saturday was always a busy day at work so tomorrow morning would go quickly and then she'd be able to spend the entire afternoon with Zach. That was the only thought that kept her feet moving as she collected her bag from the kitchen and went outside to get in the driver's seat of Derrick's car.

Chapter Twenty-One

Brenna's eyes opened and she wondered what had woken her. She checked the time and saw it was nearly four a.m. A light was lit up on her mobile phone and she picked it up to read her message. It was from Zach.

Are you awake?

She smiled wryly. Well she was now. She sent back the word yes. Seconds later her phone rang.

"Why aren't you asleep?" Brenna asked.

"I could say the same to you."

She got comfortable. "What's wrong?"

"Nothing."

"Are you sure? I mean…" her voice trailed off. What could she say? You sound strange?

"I woke you sending that message, didn't I?"

"I like hearing from you."

"Just not in the middle of the night."

"Any time. Day. Night. Whenever."

"I miss you."

"I'll be there in about eight hours."

"Go back to sleep, Brenna. I'm sorry I woke you."

"Zach-" Brenna glared at the phone when he disconnected. She closed it and put it on her bedside table. Zach had sounded unsettled. Coming to a decision, she threw back the bed sheets. She hurriedly made her bed with the help of the streetlight that filtered into her room, grabbed her work clothes and put them in her backpack. She made sure her schoolbag was by her door with her clothes for Sunday and her school uniform in it. She debated what to do next and finally woke her sister.

"What's wrong?" Danielle reached out to turn her lamp on, a shadowy figure in the glow of streetlight.

"Leave it off." Brenna brushed her hand away. "I need you to cover for me. Tell Mum I went into work early. But wait until she wakes up. Say I just missed her and then text me with the time I supposedly left."

"What are you going to do?"

"I'll tell you later."

Danielle yawned and sat up. "You can't wander the streets on your own. Especially not on a weekend."

It was odd to have her sister sound worried about

her, but since their parents had threatened to separate them, their relationship had been changing. "I'll be fine."

"Text me when you get where you're going?"

"Okay."

She hurried back to her room, grabbed her backpack and headed for the back door. She paused and listened. The house was quiet. She let herself out the door then locked it. Hurrying away from the house she kept glancing over her shoulder to make sure she wasn't discovered. She hoped her mum didn't notice until at least six. Being a Saturday there was a good chance she'd sleep in longer. Brenna aimed for the nearest main road, pulled out her phone and dialled Jordan's number.

"Brenna? What's wrong?"

"I'm not sure. When did you and Haley leave Zach's place?"

"About three or four hours ago. Not sure. What's the time now?"

"Just after four."

"What's going on, Brenna?"

"I'm probably being overkill, but I had a call from Zach. He sounded... I don't know... unsettled I guess is the best I can describe it. I'm going to catch a taxi and go see him, but you're closer. I was wondering if you could check him."

"Where are you?" As soon as Brenna told him where she was headed, he said, "I'll get Haley to drop me off at Zach's and then pick you up. It'll be quicker than waiting for a taxi."

"Thank you." She smiled slightly when Jordan hung up. Some things didn't change.

Brenna hurried to the bus shelter she'd told Jordan she was going to. The roads were nearly deserted, the occasional vehicle all that broke the silence. She paced back and forth in front of the shelter, glancing up at each car. A car slowed and a young man poked his head out the window and called out to her. Brenna stepped into the shadows of the shelter and held her breath as she watched the car drive past. She looked around. The streets were empty. She pulled out her phone and checked the time. Surely Haley couldn't be too far away.

When Haley finally pulled up in front of the bus shelter, Brenna hurried to the car. She relaxed as she sank into the seat. "Thanks."

"Any time." Haley glanced over her shoulder before she pulled onto the road.

"Do you know if Zach's okay?"

"No. I dropped Jordan out the front and came straight here."

"Sorry I woke you. I didn't know what to do."

"You did the right thing. Even if it turns out to be a false alarm, we'd rather make sure."

Brenna's phone rang and she checked the display. It was Jordan. "Is he okay?"

"I don't know. He won't answer the door or his phone."

Brenna felt a stab of fear. "Can you hear him? Or see him?"

"Can you ring him? See if he'll answer."

"Okay." Brenna dialled Zach's number the moment Jordan hung up.

"Why'd you call Jordan?"

"Why won't you talk to him?"

"Where are you, Brenna?"

"A few minutes from your place." Brenna waited for Zach to speak. He remained silent. "Are you still there?"

"Yeah."

"Are you going to let Jordan in?"

"No. I need time alone."

"Does that mean you're not going to let me in?" He didn't answer. "Zach?"

"Go home, Brenna."

She was tempted to do exactly that, but something in his voice made her ignore his request. "I guess I'll sit on the doorstep until you let me in."

"Tell Jordan to go home." Zach hung up.

"What's happening?" Haley asked when Brenna put her phone away.

"He won't speak to Jordan. I don't even know if he's going to let me in."

"I guess you'll find out in a few seconds." Haley pulled up in the driveway.

Jordan came out to meet them. He opened Brenna's door. "Did he answer?"

Brenna nodded. "He doesn't want to speak to anyone. He wants to be left alone."

"What are you going to do?" Jordan asked.

Brenna shrugged. "Sit on his doorstep until he lets me in."

"Do you want us to wait with you?"

Brenna shook her head. "I think he'd be more likely to let me in if I'm on my own."

Jordan stepped back so she could get out of the car. "Let me know how he's going?"

"Yeah. I told my sister to tell our mum I went to work early. Do you think Matt will cover for me?"

Jordan nodded. "I'll let him know what's going on."

"I wish I didn't have to go to all this effort to check on Zach. But I know Mum would have said no."

Haley glanced into the back of the car when Lily stirred in her baby seat. "We'd better go before she wakes. Let us know how things are as soon as you can."

"Okay. Thanks for the lift." Brenna stepped out of the way so Jordan could get in the car. She waved as they drove off. As soon as they were out of sight, she reluctantly turned towards the house. Adjusting her backpack, she started forward, pulling out her mobile phone to text her sister. The message was sent, and her phone away, before she arrived on the back doorstep.

Zach opened the door before she could walk up the handful of steps. He leaned against the frame and watched her. Brenna hesitated at the bottom of the stairs.

"Are you going to stand down there all night?"

Brenna shrugged. "You going to invite me in?"

For answer, Zach held out his hand. Brenna came forward and took it. Zach pulled her against him, wrapping his arms around her. Brenna's arms encircled his waist. She felt a shudder go through his body and tried to pull back to ask him what was wrong. His arms tightened around her so she relaxed against him.

"Talk to me, Zach?"

"Later."

"I'm worried," Brenna said softly.

"Don't be."

"Zach–"

"Shh."

Brenna fell silent. Zach moved back a few steps, his arms still around her. As soon as they were out of the doorway, he pushed the door shut.

"Zach–"

This time his lips silenced her. The kiss started out light but then Brenna began to worry things were going too fast. She forced herself to ignore the overwhelming sensations and pressed a hand against Zach's chest. His arms tightened momentarily before he stepped back. She dropped her backpack by the door, her gaze scanning the kitchen.

Three large, black plastic bags were piled against the leg of a kitchen chair. One was half busted open and clothes spilled from it. She looked at Zach, a question in her gaze. He shook his head. Not expecting an answer, Brenna strode from the kitchen. She paused in the doorway of his parents' bedroom.

The wardrobe door was open, drawers were on the

floor and bed, two still in the duchess. Several more large black plastic bags were half filled with clothes and more clothes were scattered across the bed, still on their hangers. Brenna turned to face Zach, who'd followed her. She reached out and took his hand.

"You didn't have to do this straight away."

"Yes. I did. I couldn't stay here otherwise. I still don't think I can."

Brenna's throat ached. She wanted to reach out and hold him, but didn't think it was a good idea. She wanted to cry for him since he didn't look like he was going to shed his own tears. "I'll help you sort this mess out," she said softly.

"You don't need to."

"I want to. Give me a second to ring Jordan and let him know you'll be okay."

Zach handed her his phone. "Use mine. Weren't you complaining recently you were low on credit?"

Brenna shrugged. "I always am." She took his phone and dialled Jordan's number.

He answered immediately. "Zach?"

"Sorry. It's Brenna."

"How is he?"

"We're going to clean out his parent's room."

Jordan swore. "What're you doing that for?"

"Because it's half done."

"Why didn't he ask for help?"

"I don't know. I don't think he wants to stay here."

Jordan was quiet for a long moment. "I'm glad he let you in. Call me if you need me. But keep in mind we're leaving tomorrow."

Jordan was gone before Brenna had a chance to say anything else. She handed the phone to Zach and then with hands on her hips, surveyed the room. She moved to the closest plastic bag. "Do you want to pack all the clothes?"

"Yeah. You have to check the trouser pockets since Mum always put money in them in case Dad left his wallet at home. For some reason he regularly did that."

Brenna started to remove the coat hangers from the clothes on the bed and vaguely folded the clothes before she dropped them in the bag. "Have you had any sleep?"

"Not much."

"Why don't you try and have some?"

Zach picked up a shirt and tipped it off the coat hanger. "I didn't hate him. Well, not enough to wish him dead. He made me angry and I guess I felt something like hate at times, but he was still my father." The shirt hung forgotten in his hand.

Brenna took it from him and pushed it in the bag

she was filling. "I think a lot of people have a confusing relationship with their parents."

"It didn't seem real in hospital. But it suddenly hit me they were gone. The place was quiet and I was alone. There was no one to tell me what to do. Or bash on the door if my music was loud. Fuss over me, ground me, take care of things. I'm going to be responsible for everything." He sat down hard on the bed.

Brenna sat beside him. "Why didn't you let Jordan in?"

"He has to go home tomorrow. I can't keep leaning on him." Zach smiled wryly. "I didn't mean to lean on you either, but I couldn't leave you on the doorstep. Why'd you come?"

"Because I was worried." Brenna linked her fingers in Zach's. "Why don't we close this door and forget about it? You look like you could use some sleep."

"I don't want to be alone. The silence is too heavy."

"I'll sit with you. If you promise to behave."

Zach laughed mirthlessly. "I'm too exhausted to do anything."

Brenna rose to her feet and tugged on Zach's hand until he slowly stood up. They walked hand in hand to his room. Brenna hesitated in the doorway. It looked the same as it had the first time she'd seen it.

There was even another couple of coffee cups left on the desk. She looked up at Zach to see he watched her. "You will behave, won't you?"

Zach smiled slowly and stepped closer. "Behave? What exactly are you asking when you say I have to behave?" Zach's lips brushed against her neck.

Brenna shivered at his light touch. "Zach…"

Zach pulled her against him, moulding his body to hers. "Is this behaving?"

"Zach, please." Brenna's breathing sped up and her heartbeat seemed to want to race along too.

His lips hovered over hers. "Was that please yes or please no?"

Brenna closed her eyes tight and took a deep shuddering breath. "No. I can't… we can't… I'm not…"

Zach's arms tightened around her momentarily. "I'm sorry. I'll stop teasing. Open your eyes. Look at me, Brenna." Zach waited for her eyes to open. "You only have to say stop and I will."

"And what if I forget to say stop?"

"Then we have a problem." Zach smiled fleetingly.

Brenna started to pull away. "Maybe I should–"

"No. Please stay." He stepped over to the bookcase and pulled out a book. He handed it to her. "Read to me?"

Brenna stared at the paperback in her hands. Her voice was hesitant. "Okay."

"Thank you." Zach took her hand and led her to his bed where he turned on the bedside lamp before he lay down. He moved over to make space for her. When she continued to stand up, he patted the bed.

Brenna lay down beside him and opened the book. She started to read, trying to ignore Zach's fingers as they played with her hair. Within minutes the story had captured her attention and she began to relax. It wasn't long before Zach's fingers slowed and then stilled. Brenna read for a little longer before her voice trailed off.

She turned so she could gaze at Zach's face. It was more familiar to her while he slept. He shifted slightly and his arm dropped over her waist. She smiled and reached out to brush his hair back from his face. Seeing how relaxed he was in sleep, made Brenna realise how tense he'd been earlier. She wished there was more she could do. As much as her parents frustrated her, Brenna didn't think she'd be anywhere near as calm as he was.

Her phone rang and she quickly pulled it out and checked the display before she answered quietly. "Hi, Matt."

"I just heard from Jordan. How's our boy doing?"

Brenna stared at Zach for a few seconds. His eyes were still closed and his breathing even. "Finally asleep."

"We were worried going home wasn't the best plan. You want the day off?"

"As long as it's not going to make you shorthanded."

"I'll find someone to help out. You take care of our boy."

"You don't mind covering for me?"

"I don't have kids of my own. Zach and my nephews are my kids. You give me a yell if I can help."

"I will. Thanks, Matt."

"And make sure you take time for yourself too. I'll see you Monday afternoon."

"Actually, my dad's picking me up from there. I'll get Zach to bring me over before he arrives."

"Okay."

"Bye." Brenna stared at Zach after she'd hung up. He looked peaceful. She tried to move away, planning to pack the clothes while he slept. His arm around her waist tightened and she relaxed against him, her own eyes closing.

Chapter Twenty-Two

Brenna slowly woke. Her eyes fluttered open. Zach leaned on one arm and stared down at her. He smiled slightly and Brenna smiled in reply. "How long have you been awake?"

"A while. I've been lying here watching you snore." Zach laughed when Brenna blushed. "Kidding. If you snored, it wasn't while I was awake."

Brenna pushed him away. She tried to get out of bed but Zach wrapped his arm around her waist.

"I'm sorry. I told you teasing was a bad habit of mine. Are you going to forgive me?"

Brenna looked at him warily. "You don't look sorry."

Zach laughed. "Guilty. It's the first time I've made you blush in days. Come on, let's see what there might be in this place for breakfast."

After they had jam on toast, made from bread Zach

found in the freezer, he talked Brenna into going grocery shopping. She walked beside him as he pushed the trolley, feeling odd to be there. She stopped when she saw Travis and Adrian enter the aisle.

"What's wrong?" Zach asked.

Brenna pasted a smile on her face when Adrian waved at her. "That's Travis and the one who waved is Adrian. They invited us to a party at Travis' place tonight."

"And you're only telling me now?"

"I have to go to my dad's tonight."

Zach wrapped his arm around Brenna's waist as Travis and Adrian stopped near them. He silently stared at the two of them and they did the same. He held out his hand. "Zach."

Travis shook his hand. "Travis and this is Adrian." Travis' gaze returned to Brenna. "Are you coming to the party?"

Zach answered. "That'll depend on when my friends leave town. They've been visiting for a couple of weeks and leave later today."

"I can't see things finishing before daybreak," Travis said.

Zach shrugged. "We'll see how we go for time. There's a few parties on tonight and we haven't had a chance to decide if we're going to any of them, let alone which ones."

Travis shrugged as well. "Turn up or not. I probably won't notice. It's usually pretty crowded."

Zach inclined his head. "It was… nice meeting you."

"Likewise," Travis said.

Zach kept his arm around Brenna's waist and pushed the trolley with one hand. He bent his head to just below her ear and pressed his lips there. "Next time, more than a few seconds notice would be good."

Brenna looked up at him as he straightened. Words swirled in her mind, but she didn't speak any of them. She wasn't certain how close Travis and Adrian were and she didn't want them to hear anything she had to say. Instead, she smiled slightly and reached up to cup his cheek with her hand.

Zach returned her smile and then turned his head so he could press his lips to her palm. He chuckled when she withdrew her hand. They turned into the next aisle and Brenna caught a glimpse of Travis watching them.

Once they finished shopping, took the groceries home, put them away and spent some time with Jordan and Haley before they left for Rockhampton,

Brenna had to dress for work. She closed the door to Zach's parents' room after she'd put the bags of clothes from the kitchen in there and turned to face Zach.

"You're not to go in there without me. Or someone else."

"I don't need a babysitter."

Brenna's hands went to her hips. "Too bad."

Zach smiled. "I like it when you forget to worry about what people think." He moved close and his hands wrapped around her waist.

"We have to go. I can't be late."

"I'll drive faster."

"No you won't. Come on, Zach. I don't want to be grounded during the holidays."

Zach swiftly kissed her, grabbed her backpack from the floor and dropped his arm around her shoulders as they walked to the back door. "What have you got in here? It weighs a tonne."

"Stuff." Brenna shrugged while Zach locked the door.

When they pulled up in front of Matt's shop, Zach waited in the car while Brenna ran inside, passing the large fruit bins outside the shop under an awning. A glance showed her dad's car wasn't out the front.

She waited until Matt had finished serving a customer before she thanked him.

"How's our boy?" Matt was a large man with a ready smile and a muscular build from carrying bags and boxes of produce.

Brenna's gaze was drawn outside. "He's sticking around for a bit. But he wouldn't say why."

Matt laughed. "To meet your father?"

"God no!"

Matt checked his watch. "You could say you're finished now if you want to go out there and tell him to head home."

Brenna groaned. "I'm too late." She watched as her dad's car pulled up behind Zach's. "It's not a laughing matter." Brenna glared at Matt.

"Jordan says you're good for Zach. That's all I need to hear. Now get out there and stop cowering."

Brenna sighed heavily. "See you Monday."

Matt nodded. "Have a good weekend."

"I'll try." She sighed again and then smiled when Matt laughed. He was such an easygoing person it was impossible to be shy around him. And he always found something to laugh at. She loved working here. Everyone seemed to walk out smiling when Matt was around. Although her smile faltered as she saw her dad get out of his car and start to walk towards her. Zach got out of his car. Brenna's gaze darted between the two of them.

Zach reached Adam before Brenna did. He held out his hand. "I'm Zach, a friend of Brenna's."

Adam shook his hand and glanced towards Brenna. "Adam. I haven't heard Brenna mention you."

Zach smiled. "My parents used to complain about the same thing."

"Used to?"

Zach nodded, his smile gone.

When he didn't answer, Brenna moved near him and put her hand in his. "Zach-"

Zach squeezed Brenna's hand and interrupted her words. "I wanted to ask you if I could take Brenna to a party tonight. It's one of her schoolmate's. She didn't think you'd let her go and wasn't going to ask. But if you aren't given a chance to think about it, of course you can't say yes."

"How did you meet Brenna?" Adam asked.

Zach looked down at her and smiled. "Random chance."

Brenna lightly dug her nails into his hand to let him know she wasn't amused when he repeated her comments from when he was in hospital. She could have sworn he was sleeping when she'd said that. "I ran into Zach at the hospital when I was there visiting a friend. I talked to him for ages."

"Why were you at the hospital?" Adam asked Zach.

"Some kids in a stolen car ran into the one I was in. Anyway, I realise you don't know me, but if you wanted to talk to Brenna's boss, Matt, he's known me since I was about five-years-old." Zach gestured towards the shop.

"I want to talk to him." Adam looked at Brenna. "We should know who you're working for."

Brenna opened her mouth to protest, but Zach squeezed her hand harder than before. She glared at him.

"I'll introduce you," Zach said.

As soon as introductions were over and Matt had made enough complimentary remarks about Brenna's work to make her blush, Zach spoke.

"Uncle Matt, Adam's worried about Brenna going to a party with me when he doesn't know me. Try not to scare him off with stories of what I got up to as a kid." Zach grinned.

Matt laughed.

"Uncle?" Adam glanced between Zach and Matt.

Matt shook his head. "Not really. Him and one of my nephews are best friends. They have been forever. And I wouldn't worry about Brenna going somewhere with Zach. He's always been level headed and not one for following the crowd. Which is a good thing with the direction some kids take in the name of following their mates. He was top in his class last year and I bet he makes up those months he's had off uni and gets back in the top of his classes there too. He's going to make a great vet one day. Although I don't think my dog will agree after the time him and Jordan wrapped her up like she was a mummy. Must have been some major accident she was supposed to have suffered. What were you? Nine? Ten?"

Zach grinned and shrugged. "Probably."

"The time off uni? Is that because of the car accident?" When Zach nodded, Adam asked, "Were you driving at the time?"

Zach shook his head, but before he could answer, Matt spoke. "He was lucky he wasn't or he'd have been killed instead of his parents."

Adam stared at Zach. "You didn't mention that."

"It's not something I like to talk about. Besides, people think you're going for the sympathy vote. I don't want you to let Brenna go to the party because you feel sorry for me. People suffer worse misfortunes all the time."

Adam continued to stare at Zach for several more seconds before he turned to Brenna. His gaze momentarily rested on her hand still in Zach's and she had to force herself not to drop it guiltily. "We'll go back out to the car and let Matt finish up closing." He turned to Matt. "It was good to meet you and see where Brenna works."

Matt grinned. "Any time. Brenna's one of my best workers. If I had a half dozen like her I wouldn't have to work at all. I could retire."

Zach laughed. "You wouldn't be able to stay away for more than a day. How many times has Aunt Susie had to confiscate your phone when you're on holidays?"

Matt laughed. "Point taken." He turned to Brenna. "I'll see you Monday."

"Okay." Brenna followed her dad to the car, Zach still at her side.

Adam looked from one to the other. "Brenna isn't allowed to have a boyfriend until she's seventeen."

"Dad, I-"

"She told me. That's why we're keeping things low key."

"I find that hard to believe. I was a teenager once." Adam glanced at their hands again.

"I'm not telling you this to gain your sympathy, I just want you to understand where I'm coming from. My parents died a couple of months ago. What I need more than a relationship is friends." Zach smiled suddenly. "You might find it hard to believe, but Brenna's very relaxing to be around."

"I do find it hard to believe." Adam looked sceptical.

Zach shrugged. "If you can recall your teenage years, you probably remember behaving differently around friends than your parents." He laughed softly. "You probably still do."

Adam smiled and nodded. "That's an accurate enough comment I guess. But it doesn't change the fact Brenna's grounded."

"That's at Mum's place. Am I grounded when I'm at your place too?"

"Most of my friends whose parents are divorced say each parent has different rules. What Brenna was trying to ask is if that will be the case with you and her mother."

"How old are you?"

Zach chuckled. "Eighteen. My parents were old enough to be my grandparents. I was raised on classical music, opera, theatre and the ballet. I even went through the tortures of a piano teacher when I was younger. There were a few arguments involved until my teacher promised to teach me a modern song for every classical song I learned to play proficiently."

"Ballet!" Brenna giggled.

Zach rolled his eyes. "Yep, but I'll deny it if you ever tell anyone." He turned to Adam. "I was raised around older people and expected to behave a certain way. So people often think I'm older."

Adam nodded thoughtfully. "How late will the party go?"

"Probably pretty late, but we can leave at eleven. I need to get a fairly early night anyway. Sunday morning I want to work on a paper for uni."

"Please Dad? You've dragged me away from all my friends, I don't know anyone out your way."

"You'll leave at eleven?"

"Whatever time you set," Zach said.

"Do you drink?"

"Not when I'm driving."

Zach might not want to use sympathy, but she was willing to try anything. "The kids who ran into his parents' car were drunk."

"I'm sorry." Adam looked uncomfortable.

"I'm not the only one who's lost someone to a drunk driver. As I said earlier, I'm not looking for sympathy."

Adam turned to Brenna. "You can go to the party on the condition that neither of you drink alcohol, you leave at eleven, head straight home and tomorrow you help unpack boxes without complaints."

Brenna grinned and threw her arms around her dad. "You're the best."

Adam returned her hug. "Only because you're getting your own way. You'll probably hate me again by tomorrow night."

"I promise to wait at least until Monday." Brenna continued to grin at her dad as she let him go.

Adam smiled. "I'll believe that when I see it." He turned to Zach. "And drive carefully."

"Of course." Zach held out his hand. "It was nice meeting you. I hope you'll let me visit Brenna sometimes when she's at your place."

"Let's get through tonight first." Adam shook his hand.

Chapter Twenty-Three

Brenna nearly danced to the car. She waved to her dad who stood and watched as she hopped in. As soon as they pulled onto the street, Brenna turned to Zach. "I seriously don't believe he agreed. You're a miracle worker. But I guess when you told him you weren't interested in being my boyfriend that helped."

"When did I say that?"

"I heard you!"

Zach grinned. "I said I needed friends more than a relationship. I didn't say I wasn't interested in a relationship at all."

Brenna frowned as she tried to recall his words. "Are you certain?"

Zach laughed. "Of course I am. I was very careful with how I worded everything."

"What about the low key part?"

"We're not having sex, so as far as I'm concerned, that makes things low key."

Brenna suddenly couldn't think what to say. She stared at Zach, glad his gaze was on the road. She almost groaned when his gaze fell on her for a few seconds before returning to the road.

"Tell me what you're thinking," Zach said.

"You first."

Zach laughed. "I won't hear another word out of you for the rest of the day if I tell you what I'm thinking."

"I guess that's the risk you're going to have to take if you want me to tell you."

"I wish you didn't want to keep things low key." Zach glanced at Brenna. "So what's the silence risk factor?"

Brenna stared straight ahead for a moment. She closed her eyes and reminded herself she'd already shared thoughts with Zach she'd never shared with another person. The butterflies in her stomach had different thoughts about the situation. She ignored them. "You tell my dad we're keeping things low key and you're looking for friends rather than a relationship. You ask me to continue to wear your grandma's rings and then tell me it's because it's safer, but you're not at the hospital anymore and you haven't asked for them back. One minute you tell me not to visit and the next you're kissing me senseless. You tell me you want sex, yet I know you often take a casual view of it. I'm confused. Completely and utterly confused." She opened her eyes as soon as she stopped speaking and looked at him.

Zach parked in front of the garage behind his house. He turned off the engine and faced Brenna. "Join the club." He took her hand in his and threaded his fingers through hers. "I never look for more than a casual relationship. But I seem to lose sight of that with you."

"Why? I've seen pictures of the girls you normally hang out with. I look nothing like them."

Zach ran his knuckles across her cheek and then sank his fingers into her hair. "You might not be beautiful in a classic sense, but a different hairstyle the correct clothes and holding yourself like you believe you're someone important and you could hold your own with any runway model."

"In other words a completely new me."

"No. You just need to believe in yourself. The rest is to help you with that. But it's not your looks that drew me to you. It was your voice I fell for first and then your personality. I never saw you for ages. And then I thought you were the angel you sounded like."

"I think you've been watching too much ballet to be making comments like that."

Zach laughed. "Maybe, but that doesn't change the fact you're gorgeous and the sound of your voice makes me want you. You could wear overalls and I'd still be able to see past them."

"God no!"

"What?"

"I don't have anything to wear tonight."

"Is that all?"

"All! It's a disaster. I've got my work clothes and the ones I was wearing earlier. I can't go to a party in either of them." Brenna's voice rose as she spoke.

Zach eyed her up and down. "What size do you wear?"

"What?"

"Your size in clothing."

"Don't tell me you've got girl's clothes stashed in the back of your wardrobe along with your leotard."

Zach grinned. "I never did ballet. Just watched it. But have you seen where some of those male ballet dancers get to put their hands on their partners?"

Brenna slowly shook her head. "That's not what you're meant to focus on when you're at the ballet."

"Now you tell me." He chuckled. "Are you willing to put yourself in my hands?"

"I don't know." Brenna watched him warily.

"Well, not quite my hands. Trust me?"

Brenna hesitated. Zach looked serious and Brenna had a feeling her answer gained importance by the second. She nodded. "Okay."

Zach leaned forward and kissed her. It started out gentle but soon changed when her lips parted. Seconds spun into minutes until Zach pulled away. He rested his forehead against hers, his breath coming fast. Brenna realised that at some stage she'd wrapped her arms around his neck. She slowly slid her hands away from him, fascinated by the contours of his body under her hands. When Zach groaned, her gaze raced to his.

Zach captured one of her hands. "Don't torture me."

"Oh." The word came out so soft it was barely a sound. "Sorry."

Zach smiled wryly. "I'm not. Well, not yet anyway." He sat back in his seat and pulled out his phone. When he finished finding the number he looked for in his address book, he pressed the talk button and took Brenna's hand as he put the phone to his ear. His thumb made lazy circles that his gaze followed.

Brenna watched his face, fascinated by his

absorption. His gaze met hers and he smiled. Then he looked away and spoke into the phone.

"You busy?" He paused as he listened to the other person. "I have a temporary project you'll love."

"Not Betts?" Brenna whispered.

Zach laughed. "No, I haven't been ignoring you. I've been in a coma."

Brenna heard the shrill 'what' as she watched Zach hold the phone from his ear.

"No I'm not shitting you… they're dead, and don't screech again. My ear couldn't handle it… a makeover… of course… absolutely… I know… you're the genius when it comes to these things… will do. See you shortly." He closed his phone and put it away.

"Not Betts," Brenna said firmly.

"I thought you said you trust me."

Brenna sighed. "Let's get it over with then."

* * *

Brenna stared at herself in Betts' full-length mirror. She shook her head. Her hair bounced around her, the slight wave that was now in it made it move gracefully.

Betts stood behind her and grabbed her shoulders,

pulling them back slightly. "Stand properly. You're ruining the effect. Again."

"You're a miracle worker."

"Not me. Even I need a good base to work from. Now remember to stand properly. A pity I don't have something that would dig into you when you don't keep your shoulders back." Betts frowned thoughtfully.

"I'll remember," Brenna hurriedly assured her.

"Are you certain? I'm sure I could figure something out."

"No. I mean yes. I'll remember."

"Okay then. Let's find Zach and see if we can make him speechless."

Brenna followed Betts through the house she lived in with her parents. It sprawled into separate wings so it seemed like she had her own private apartment. Zach was in her lounge room using her computer. He looked up as they entered the room. The moment his gaze fell on Brenna, he rose to his feet and walked towards her. The ping of the messenger windows he had open were ignored.

"Posture," Betts said from beside Brenna.

She quickly pulled her shoulders back, not wanting Betts to follow through on her threat. She looked at Zach who'd changed his clothes. She guessed he'd returned home while Betts had been busy transforming her.

"Looks like my goal was met," Betts said.

Zach grinned. "You've outdone yourself, Betts."

"Of course. Now don't let her slouch. I'm relying on you to remind her."

Zach nodded. "Sure thing."

"You two get out of here. It's just after seven and I'm sure you're both starving. Never go to a party on an empty stomach."

"Oh, I don't think I could eat," Brenna protested.

"You will," Betts ordered her.

Zach laughed and hugged Betts. "Thank you."

"Yeah well, don't disappear so long again. We thought you'd been abducted by aliens or something." She turned to Brenna. "Anytime you need help, give me a call. You've got my number now. And Kelsey is exactly your size so I can always borrow more clothes from her again."

"Thank you," Brenna said. She was enveloped in Betts' arms.

"Now get out of here. Both of you. A masterpiece must be shown."

"Give me a minute." Zach returned to the computer, typed in each messenger window he'd opened and then closed it before signing out. He took

Brenna's hand and with a grin at Betts, walked to the door. As soon as they were in the car, Zach smiled at her. "What did I tell you? You want to give a runway a try?"

"No! I think I'd fall off the edge. I'm so nervous."

"Don't be. How do you feel about the way you look?"

"Good."

"Then that's all you have to worry about."

"But-" Brenna started to argue.

"No buts. Forget about everyone else's opinion."

"Even yours?"

"Yes. If I don't like you the way you are, then I'm not worth having around either."

Brenna hesitated. "Do you?"

"Do you think I'd go to all this trouble for someone I didn't like? Now let's get out of here before I'm tempted to ruin your makeup."

"Betts lent me lipstick for when I need to touch it up. I mean-" Brenna broke off when Zach chuckled.

"Hold that thought. We're going to get something to eat. Any preferences?"

"Something that won't come straight back up."

Zach chuckled. "You'll be fine. I'll be beside you the whole time."

"I keep thinking Travis has something planned."

"Then let's get our stories straight. Where did we meet?"

"Can we try and stick as close to the truth as possible? Otherwise I'll forget something."

"Sure."

"I ran into you at the hospital when Travis got his arm put in plaster." Brenna turned to Zach when he started to laugh. "What?"

"Does that mean I should thank him for being the cause of us meeting?" Zach glanced over his shoulder, then changed lanes.

"I don't think that'd go down well."

Zach grinned. "Exactly."

Brenna frowned. "Maybe we should hold off on comments like that until we see how he's going to treat us."

Zach's grin faded. "I don't care what he says to me, but I'm not going to have him upset you."

"Why?"

"Why, what?"

Brenna persisted. "Why will it bother you if he upsets me?"

"Because I couldn't care less what he thinks, but you do."

"Well, not so much what Travis thinks, but what everyone else will think."

"I keep telling you their opinions aren't important."

"They probably aren't, but I still can't help caring."

Zach pulled up in front of a take-away shop and they went in to order food. Once it was ready, they ate at one of the scarred timber tables out the front and finished sorting out their story before they walked back to the car. Zach opened the door for her and stood there, his hands on her waist.

"Remember that thought I ask you to hold?"

Brenna frowned. When Zach's lips met hers, she realised what he was talking about. She gave herself up to sensation, thinking things couldn't get out of hand while they stood bathed in the bright lights at the front of the shop. When Zach finally pulled back slightly, Brenna glanced around. She'd completely lost track of her surroundings and wondered if Zach had too. She looked up at him, torn between finding out and the embarrassment of asking.

"Hop in the car before I attempt to convince you to forget low key." When Brenna hesitated, Zach smiled. "Unless you're planning on forgetting about it."

Brenna shook her head and slid into the front seat of the car. She pulled her lipstick out of the small bag Betts had lent her and repaired her makeup. Zach slid into the driver's seat as she put it away.

Other than Brenna giving Zach directions on how to find Travis' place, the drive was quiet. By the time they managed to park several houses away from the party, Brenna had begun to wonder if Zach was annoyed about something.

"Are you sure you want to go to the party?"

Zach turned to face Brenna. "You don't have to be worried about what they'll think."

"That isn't it, although I'll probably start to panic about it soon."

"Than what's wrong?"

Brenna shrugged. "I don't want you to feel like you have to go to the party."

Zach smiled. "Let's show him what he lost."

Brenna smiled wryly. "I don't think he's going to be too devastated."

"Trust me. He will."

Chapter Twenty-Four

They walked hand in hand to the front door of Travis' home, the music greeting them before they'd gone far. Zach tugged Brenna behind him as he made a path through the crowd.

"Brenna! Brenna, is that you?"

Brenna looked towards the person calling and saw it was Ellen followed by Jessica. "What are you doing here? Couldn't you get in to see your dentist?"

Ellen laughed. "I heard you were coming. I thought you might need a bit of support. But you look wonderful. I hope he goes green. I found out he was seeing someone behind your back the last couple of weeks you were together."

Brenna smiled. "I hate to completely ruin my standing as the wronged party, but I met Zach the day Travis broke his arm."

"Way back around the start of August?" When

Brenna nodded, Ellen laughed. "Oh, what a great story. Can I spread it? Please?"

"You might as well give in. You know Ellen will hassle you until you do," Jessica said.

Brenna looked hesitantly at Zach. She mightn't have been dating him, but she had been trying to think of a way to break up with Travis.

Zach smiled at Brenna before he turned to Ellen. "We might have met then, but Brenna didn't go behind Travis' back. She broke things off with him first." He draped his arm around Brenna's shoulders.

It reminded Brenna of how Betts had told her to hold herself. She met Zach's gaze and saw amusement in his eyes. She couldn't resist smiling at him. She blinked at the sudden flash of light and looked in the direction it had come from. One of her classmates with a camera waved at her, a large grin on her face.

And that was the last moment of peace the two of them had. People Brenna barely knew came over to talk to her and be introduced to Zach. They were asked endless questions about how they met and which school Zach went to. Brenna enjoyed the expressions on people's faces when she told them he was at uni. She knew it was shallow, but it still felt good.

Zach bent his head so his mouth was near her ear. "It's nearly eleven. We should go."

Brenna nodded. She watched as Zach expertly dismissed the crowd that were hanging around and walked beside him to the front door. They'd nearly reached it when Brenna saw Travis and Adrian bearing down on them.

"When did you get here?" Travis asked. "I was beginning to think you hadn't turned up."

"We've been here ages. We're just about to go."

"But it's not eleven yet. The night's barely begun."

Zach gazed down at Brenna and slowly smiled at her before he turned back to Travis. "I know. That's why we're leaving now."

Travis glared at someone who tried to smother a laugh as they listened in on the conversation. "You're wasting your time leaving early. She's hopeless in bed."

When Brenna would have angrily answered, Zach tightened his grip on her hand and pulled her close.

"I don't know what you're basing that assumption on since I know you weren't her first." Zach stared at Travis, daring him to disagree.

"Anyone can be easily tricked into thinking they're the first," Travis argued.

Embarrassed by the conversation, Brenna tried to

think of a way to end it, but all she could think of was the people standing around listening and watching.

Zach laughed. "I wouldn't say that. Some things just can't be replicated. Anyway, I've got better things to do than stand here talking. Thanks for the invite. It's not often I have time to attend high school parties these days."

Brenna heard laughter behind them as they left Travis' place. From the abrupt end to the laughter, she guessed Travis hadn't taken it well. She couldn't help smiling as she replayed the expression on Travis' face at Zach's parting words. As she slid into the front seat of the car, her smile disappeared as she thought about what else Zach had said.

"Now what are you thinking?" Zach started the car.

Brenna shook her head.

There was silence in the car for a few minutes while Zach drove through the streets, heading for the nearest major road. "You know I could always pull over and sit on the side of the road until you answer."

"You wouldn't! I have to go straight home."

"I know." Zach started to slow down.

"Zach!"

"Tell me what's wrong."

"Everyone's going to be talking about us at school on Monday."

"I thought that was the idea."

"No… yes… but not… they'll all be thinking we're… that you and I are…"

"Having sex?"

"Yes."

"It doesn't matter what they think. They would have thought that when you were with Travis. And you can bet he was the one who told them."

"No one said anything."

Zach chuckled. "Why would they? And if they hinted at it, you probably wouldn't have noticed because you wouldn't have expected it."

"I knew I shouldn't have said anything to you. You always laugh at me."

"No I don't. Well, not in a nasty way. I laugh at Jordan too. Take it as a compliment. I like to be amused by life." He reached out and took hold of her hand. "Don't let that stop you from sharing your thoughts with me."

"I'd feel better if you used both hands to drive."

Zach glanced at her with a grin. "I wouldn't." His thumb moved back and forth on her skin.

"Zach-"

"Will you still be unpacking in the afternoon?"

"What?" The sudden change in topic made Brenna frown.

"Your father said you had to help unpack boxes tomorrow."

"Yes." Brenna drew the word out.

"I'll come over around one and help."

"I thought you had a paper to write."

"I'm doing that in the morning. By then I'll need a break." Zach let go of her hand and reached into the back seat to hand her an A4 sized envelope. "I nearly forgot. Derrick left this at my place for you."

"What is it?"

"I don't know. There's a torch in the glove box."

Brenna took out the torch and shone the narrow beam on the pages she pulled from the envelope. Derrick had scrawled 'worst case scenario' across the top of the first one. He'd printed up bus and train timetables. "Oh!"

"What?"

"I could still go to the same school even if I had to move to Dad's place next year. Between the commuter train and a couple of buses, I'd still get to school on time. Although I'd spend half my day travelling. I don't see why they can't let me stay where I am."

"Have you asked your father why he wants you to live with him?"

"No."

"Why?"

"Because…" Brenna frowned.

"You might as well finish that sentence. I could add several different endings and not all of them nice."

"Because I didn't think of it. I was focused on finding a way to stay at Mum's."

"Finding out his reason might give you the info you need to get out of moving."

"Do you think?"

"It's a possibility."

"Okay." Brenna returned all the pages to the envelope and turned so she could tuck it in her backpack on the back seat.

Zach reached out and took her hand when she was still again. Brenna closed her eyes and smiled slightly. All up, it had been a good night. She replayed scenes in her mind. The way Zach had looked, how it had felt to have his arm around her, how good it was to have both arms wrapped around her when they'd danced pressed against each other and all the people who'd wanted to meet him. She'd never been the centre of so much positive attention before. Even when she'd been with Travis, the attention had been directed at him rather than her. She wasn't sure what made it different this time, but had a feeling it was the way Zach handled the attention. He didn't bask in it the way Travis did. When Zach squeezed her hand, she opened her eyes.

"I was worried you'd gone to sleep. I need you to direct me to your father's home."

Brenna pulled out the referdex and looked up her dad's street by the light of the torch. The rest of the drive passed too quickly and they pulled up in front of the house. It was lowset, red brick and only a few years old. Brenna turned off the torch and shut the referdex. She started to remove the ring she'd worn to the party.

Zach took her hand. "Let me."

Brenna looked up at him. His face was in shadows, the streetlight not reaching far enough into the car. She felt the ring slide off and then slide back on again. She looked down at her hand and held it near the window so she could use the streetlight to look at it. Her mouth dropped open. It was a narrow band with diamonds on either side of a sapphire that were all set at the same height as the band. She looked over to Zach.

He smiled and got out of the car. Brenna grabbed her backpack and opened the door before he reached it. She stood in front of him, annoyed he didn't say anything.

"Are you going to explain?" Brenna asked.

"This one won't get caught on things at work."

"I never wore yours except when I was at school, so that's never been an issue."

"I know. But it'll make a handy excuse."

"Zach-"

"We can't stand out the front of your father's house all night. He's waiting for you."

"Fine. But why have you gone to the trouble of getting me a ring?"

"Does your father have the internet?"

"Why?"

"Let me know when you find out the meaning for sapphires. And I need my necklace."

Brenna reached up and undid the catch. She dropped the necklace and wedding ring into Zach's hand. She rubbed absently at her neck. It felt bare after wearing the necklace for so long. "I don't need to find the meaning of diamonds as well?"

Zach smiled. "I'll walk you to your door. I don't want your father to have to drag you inside." Zach knocked on the door when they reached it.

Adam opened it almost immediately. He looked from one to the other and his gaze stopped on

Brenna. "I usually manage to forget most times you're not a little girl anymore."

"Dad!"

Zach laughed. "I'm glad I'm not the only one who causes her to use that irritated voice."

"Lately I seem to be an expert at causing that tone," Adam said dryly. He checked his watch. "Thanks for bringing her home on time."

"Thanks for letting me take her to the party. I hope you don't mind, I volunteered to help unpack boxes tomorrow afternoon. I didn't think it fair I got out of the chore after getting to enjoy Brenna's company at the party."

"I'd be an idiot to turn down the offer." Adam glanced at the box strewn lounge room behind him. "As you can see, there's a lot that needs to be done. As well as furniture to buy."

Zach held out his hand, which Adam took. "I'll see you tomorrow." He turned to Brenna and winked slightly, his back to Adam. "Thank you. It was a good night." With a grin, he stepped outside.

Brenna watched him as he sauntered to his car and drove off. She reluctantly shut the door and turned to face Adam. "Thanks, Dad."

He smiled. "I think I might actually like that boy. Providing it isn't all an act for me."

"He's more polite around you, but he isn't completely irresponsible when he's out of your sight either."

"I guess that's good." Adam started to turn away. "Dad?"

"Yeah?" He faced her again.

"Why do you want me to move in with you?"

Chapter Twenty-Five

Adam ran a hand through his hair that was a shade lighter than Brenna's. "I thought you weren't going to hate me again until Monday. If we get into an argument you won't last that long."

"I'm not going to argue about living with you. I want to know why. Can we forget about the yes or no part for a minute?"

"Why."

Brenna nodded. "Yeah."

"Can't you ask your mother?"

Brenna shook her head. "You're the one who wants me to live with you. Why? And why me and not Danielle? Or did you put our names in a hat and draw them out?"

"Not quite. Are you sure you can't ask your mother?"

"Come on, Dad. Or don't you have a real reason?

Are we something else you're trying to split up evenly?"

"It's not a simple answer. And I know whichever option we take isn't going to be perfect. Is it so hard to understand I might want both of you to live with me? But your mother does too."

"Why me?"

"Because you were the one that didn't have as many things to be interrupted by the move. Not quite drawing your name out of the hat, but we thought the move would be easiest for you. What brought on all these questions?"

"It was something Zach said."

"I'm starting to like that boy more and more."

Brenna smiled. "I'm glad. 'Cause I really like him too."

"I still think you're too young to have a boyfriend."

Brenna rolled her eyes. "Dad!"

"Although you look very grown up in that dress and with your hair like that. I haven't seen that dress before, have I?"

Brenna shook her head. "I borrowed it from a friend."

Adam chuckled. "I take it you weren't game to go home in case your mother disagreed with my decision."

Brenna shrugged. She looked around the room, trying to think of an argument free topic. "So where's my bedroom?"

Adam led the way and opened the door of a room that contained her bag and a mattress on the floor. "Maybe we could buy some furniture tomorrow. I've got to go into work for a few hours in the morning because we're behind schedule, but I'm free the rest of the day."

Brenna dropped her backpack in her room. "Can Zach come too?"

"I was hoping just the two of us could go."

"Come on, Dad." Brenna shook her head. "You, me, shopping, decisions? I think we'll need a referee."

Adam laughed. "I'll think about it. Now you better get some sleep."

Sleep was going to be impossible. She'd wonder all night about the meaning of sapphires. "Do you have the internet?"

Adam nodded. "Why?"

"Can I have ten minutes to check something?" When it looked like her dad would object, she pleaded, "Please? It won't take long. I just want to check something someone said to me tonight. It'll take me ages to sleep if I don't. I'll keep wondering."

"Ten minutes and then I don't want to hear another argument."

Brenna grinned and threw her arms around her dad for the second time that day. "So where is it?"

Adam showed her the room he was using as a study and turned on the light. His computer was on his desk, an empty bookcase stood against one wall and a pile of boxes towered nearby. "Ten minutes."

"I'll start timing as soon as the computer's finished turning on." Brenna pressed in the button and the computer hummed to life.

"Is that a new ring?"

Brenna's gaze was drawn to the ring Zach had given her. "It's not that new." It wasn't really a lie. She'd owned it more than a few minutes.

Adam nodded. "You have a toothbrush in the bathroom and the yellow towel is yours." He started to move away from the doorway.

"Dad." Brenna waited until he faced her. "I realised today is the first time I've seen you smile in years. And laugh. Why did you stay if you hated being with us?"

"I never hated being there. Relationships are complicated, Bren. Maybe you should talk about things like this with your mother." Adam ran his fingers through his hair. "She's better at explaining."

"How can she tell me why you stayed? It's not like

she can read your mind. Or is it that she tells you what you're meant to think?"

"Brenna." There was a warning in Adam's voice.

Brenna sighed. "Okay. Fine. I'll quit before we have an argument. See? I can act like an adult." She smiled to show she wasn't angry. But she was. She wasn't sure why and didn't want to examine her reasons while her dad stood there.

Adam nodded. "Night, Bren. And be in bed before I return to the study."

Brenna nodded as her dad left the doorway. She sat at the desk and opened a browser. A few minutes later, she smiled as she read another short article on the meaning of sapphires. For good measure, she looked up the meaning of diamonds too. Taking her phone from the bag Betts had lent her, she sent Zach a text.

Sapphire: loyalty, fidelity, truth, faithfulness. Diamonds: indestructible, pure, enduring.

Brenna turned the computer off, grabbed her pyjamas, used the bathroom then shut herself in her bedroom. She dropped onto the mattress and looked at her phone. There was no message. She checked her message had been sent. Then she checked her coverage. Dropping the phone on the floor beside her bed, she got up to turn the light off. She'd just got comfortable when her phone rang.

She smiled when she saw it was Zach's home number. "Are you going to explain now?"

Zach chuckled. "No hello?"

"After I've finished dying of curiosity."

"The way you came to visit me every chance you could meant a lot to me. I'm offering you the same loyalty. Not as repayment, but because I want to." When Brenna said nothing, Zach asked, "You still there?"

"Yes," Brenna whispered.

"No more questions?"

"No."

"Then what happened to my hello?"

Brenna couldn't resist smiling. "Hello, Zach."

"I miss you already."

"Me too."

Zach chuckled.

Brenna laughed also. "There's no one listening this time."

"I'll let you get some sleep."

"Wait a minute. Dad wants me to go shopping for furniture with him. He's thinking about letting you come along. I told him we might need a referee."

"Tell him if he needs it, I can bring Derrick's trailer. It's five by seven."

"Okay. Not that I know what you're talking about after the word trailer."

"He'll know. Night, Ren."

"Night." Brenna put her phone on the floor again, still smiling. She'd barely moved her hand away when a message came through. She picked it up and read the message Zach had sent from his mobile phone.

Me too.

Brenna glared at the screen. What was he trying to tell her? She'd just finished referring to their phone conversation from when Travis had tried to listen in. What exactly had he said when she'd told him 'me too' when he'd said he missed her? Brenna frowned. It was something about it being a common reply when someone said 'love you' on the phone. She typed four question marks and sent them. The wait for a reply took forever. Then it came in the form of a wink.

"Argh." *Ring me!* She sent the words and waited. The phone didn't even ring once before she picked it up. "Do you enjoy sending cryptic messages?"

"Absolutely."

"Why?"

Zach laughed. "Because when you're annoyed you

forget to be embarrassed. I like hearing what you think."

"Even if it's only me telling you what a bastard you can be?"

"Even then. So, is that what you're thinking?"

She hesitated. "Maybe."

"I guess if you're not really interested in discussing this now, I could let you sleep."

"Don't you dare hang up."

"Then talk to me."

"What did you mean by your message?"

"What do you think I meant?"

"Zach!"

There was a moment of silence before he answered. "I wasn't talking about missing you."

It was Brenna's turn to go quiet. Love? As in romantic love or best friend love? Why couldn't he be clearer?

"What are you thinking, Ren?"

"Why can't you be clearer?"

Zach chuckled. "And you are?"

"It's late at night and I'm sitting on a mattress in the dark whispering to you. I am so not in the mood for games."

"What are you wearing?"

"What?"

"Just trying to picture the scenario correctly."

"Yeah, sure."

Zach laughed. "Will you accept curious?"

"Maybe."

"And?"

Brenna grinned. "And what?"

"You were going to tell me what you're wearing."

"Dream on."

"Oh, I will."

"Zach!"

Zach laughed softly. "Night, Ren."

"Wait. You didn't answer me."

"Love ya." Zach hung up before Brenna had the chance to say anything.

She stared at her phone and wondered if she'd heard correctly. Once again she placed the phone on the floor beside the mattress. Lying down she ran her fingers over the ring he'd given her, smiled and rolled onto her side. Her eyes closed as she replayed the call in her mind.

* * *

With every item Brenna took from the boxes in the kitchen and put away, she checked the clock on the wall. As soon as the clock had reached midday, the hands had slowed. It was nearly one and Brenna hoped Zach would be on time. She didn't think she could wait an extra minute. She checked in the box that sat on the table and, finding it empty, pushed all the newspaper that had been used for packing back into it. She put it along the wall with the other empty boxes and carried the next one to the table.

Before she'd finished unwrapping another item, a knock sounded at the front door. She slid the plate out of the newspaper it had been wrapped in, placed it on the table and raced towards the door. "I've got it," she told her dad as she passed the study where he rose from his desk.

Brenna flung the door open and grinned up at Zach. His lips slowly curved into a smile and he stepped inside, closing the door behind him. He stared down at her and Brenna felt heat wash through her as he continued to gaze at her. She reached out to take his hand and took a step closer. Zach glanced past her for a second and when his gaze returned to her, it had lost its intensity.

"What've you been doing today?"

Brenna frowned, trying to understand his sudden change. "Unpacking."

Zach looked past her. "Adam." He smiled. "I hope you don't mind me tagging along."

Brenna spun to see her dad had followed her into the lounge room. Zach's behaviour now made sense.

"If Brenna's anything like her mother when it comes to shopping I'll probably be glad of an extra pair of hands to help bring it all home. Were you able to get the trailer?"

Zach nodded. "Did you want to take my car to save taking the trailer off and on? You can always drive if you don't feel comfortable being chauffeured."

"You drive. If you're ready to leave, I'll turn off my computer and grab my wallet and phone."

Brenna needed a few minutes alone with Zach before they were stuck shopping with her dad. "I've got one more box to unpack in the kitchen. Can I do that first?"

Adam nodded. "Give me a yell when you're ready. I'll be in the study."

"Okay." Brenna dragged Zach to the kitchen with her. "You did say you'd help unpack, didn't you?" Her mouth went dry as she met Zach's gaze.

One hand went to the small of her back, the other to the nape of her neck. He pulled her close, his lips a breath away from hers.

"Zach," Brenna whispered. "What if-" His lips cut off her words and she forgot all about everything else. Her hands entwined around his neck and her lips parted as she savoured the kiss. She reluctantly pulled back, wishing they didn't need to stop. "I thought one o'clock would never arrive."

"I missed you too." Zach curved his hand along her jaw so his thumb could run back and forth along her cheekbone. "My bed felt empty." He laughed softly when Brenna's cheeks flushed.

Brenna moved back a little more. "We'd better finish unpacking this box before my dad decides to see what's taking so long."

"Don't run. You're the one setting the pace. I might make a few unsubtle comments, but I don't want you to feel pressured. Okay?"

Brenna nodded. "Okay."

Zach picked up the plate sitting on the table. "Where does this go?"

In less than a quarter of an hour, they were in Zach's car, Brenna in the back. He drove them to the shops Adam had decided they needed to visit and in the end it took two trailer loads to get the beds, chests of drawers, duchesses, lounge, coffee table and a desk for Brenna back to the house.

Chapter Twenty-Six

Once everything was inside and vaguely in place, they headed for the kitchen. Adam took a bottle of light beer from the fridge and then looked hesitantly at Zach.

Zach grinned. "Are you kicking me out during the next few hours? Because if you are there won't be any need to offer me one."

Adam handed the bottle to Zach and took another one out for himself. "Thanks for helping with the furniture. You're welcome to stay for dinner. It'll probably be take-away. There's not a lot in the pantry and fridge yet."

"Mind if I look?" Zach asked.

Adam shrugged. "Go for it."

After a quick search, Zach turned to Adam. "How does homemade pizza sound? Pineapple, ham, salami and olives."

"I love pizza," Brenna said.

"Sounds good, but you don't need to," Adam said.

"If you want to put your empty boxes in the trailer, Ren and I can take care of dinner. There's a tarp in the boot of the car to tie over them so they don't fall out. I can drop them at the dump tomorrow." Zach tossed his keys to Adam.

"Thanks." Adam caught the keys in mid air, grabbed a couple of boxes and headed out of the kitchen.

The moment Adam was gone from sight, Zach pulled Brenna close and kissed her. "I've been wanting to do that for hours."

"Me too."

Zach chuckled. "Interesting choice of words."

Brenna smiled. "There's no cryptic message in my words."

Zach lightly kissed her before he turned to the pantry and took out flour and oil. "You want to get a tray?"

Brenna stared at him a moment longer before hunting for a tray and finding only a rectangular one. "We don't have a round one. Will that be a problem?"

Zach shook his head. "No." He took out a mixing bowl he'd put away earlier and tipped ingredients into it.

"What's wrong with measuring them? I'm sure we've got a measuring cup somewhere." Brenna placed the tray on the bench.

Zach glanced towards Adam who entered the kitchen. Adam's gaze momentarily rested on them before he grabbed more empty boxes and headed outside. Zach waited until they were alone before he answered. "No need. Estimating's fine. We're making pizza, not performing brain surgery."

"Okay, but if it doesn't taste good, it's your fault."

"And if it does taste good?"

Brenna grinned. "Then I was head chef."

Brenna and Zach put the pizza in the oven about the same time Adam finished taking out the boxes.

Dinner was eaten at the kitchen table and Brenna was surprised the meal passed without arguments. She couldn't recall the last time she'd sat down with one of her parents for a peaceful meal. And not only peaceful, but one that included laughter and conversation. Real conversation, not arguments.

Adam pushed back from the table. "If you decide you don't want to be a vet, you could make pizzas for a living."

Zach grinned. "I do that part time already."

Adam looked surprised and for a moment it seemed he'd say something to Zach, but he turned to Brenna instead. "You want me to give you a lift home tonight or are you willing to get up really early tomorrow? Eventually you can catch the train, but I haven't had time to look into it. I meant to do it today."

Brenna hesitated. She had an envelope filled with that information. But the last thing she wanted to do was catch the train if she didn't have to. It was going to take ages. She looked at Zach for inspiration.

"Why don't I give Ren a lift home tonight? I'm already going in that direction. It's about fifteen minutes from my place when there's no traffic. It seems pointless us both driving there."

"You'll take her straight home?"

"Of course."

"Hello? I'm sitting at the table too," Brenna said.

Adam chuckled. "Okay Bren, what would you like to do?"

"I know what I don't want to do. I don't want to get up any earlier in the morning than I have to."

Adam nodded. "Are you happy for Zach to give you a lift home?" Adam smiled when Brenna laughed at his words. "I guess that's a yes."

"Yes."

"Ring me as soon as you get home. I won't be impressed if you're late."

"Okay." Brenna's gaze fell on the dirty dishes. "Since we cooked, does that mean we don't have to clean?"

"Only because I don't want you home late," Adam said. "Now go get your gear together."

As Brenna rose from the table, Zach started to gather up crockery. It didn't take long for Brenna to place the things she'd borrowed from Betts in a plastic bag, put the handful of stuff she'd scattered around her room in her backpack and grab her schoolbag. When she returned to the kitchen, Adam was washing dishes while Zach dried them.

Adam wiped his hands on the corner of the tea towel Zach held and moved over to Brenna. "I'll pick you up Sunday week. You and Danielle are spending the second week of the holidays here."

"Okay."

"No arguments?"

Brenna shrugged. "I didn't have too bad a time."

"You were barely here," Adam pointed out.

Brenna smiled. "I'll still be able to go out with friends, won't I?"

"More than likely."

"Then it shouldn't be too bad."

"This from the girl who wasn't moving. At all."

"Ahh, weren't we leaving that topic until after Monday?"

Adam nodded. "Straight home now." He dropped a kiss on her cheek, his arms wrapping around her momentarily.

"Okay."

Zach took Brenna's schoolbag and they all headed to the front door. Adam stood in the open doorway as they walked towards Zach's car.

They were halfway there when Brenna dashed back to her dad and threw her arms around him. "I do love you. Even when I absolutely hate you."

"I know."

Brenna ran back to the car where Zach held the door open. She dropped her backpack on the floor and slid into the seat. The plastic bag for Betts went in the back. She waved to her dad as Zach pulled onto the street. "Why do I feel guilty for leaving?"

"Did you ask Adam why he wants you to move in?"

"Yeah." Brenna recounted the conversation.

"I'm not surprised you feel guilty."

"I don't want to be. I'm worried I might give in and live with him."

"No matter where you end up living, we'll work it

out. It's not so far away. Only half an hour on a good run."

"More than an hour in traffic."

"Then I guess we'll have to avoid peak hour traffic."

Brenna was silent a few minutes. "You don't have to see me to my door when you drop me at Mum's."

"You want my father to haunt me because I'm not living up to the standards he taught me?"

"I don't want you to feel like you have to meet my mum."

"I managed to survive meeting your father. How much worse can meeting your mother be?"

"Much, much worse."

"Should I wear a bullet proof vest?"

"Don't complain if you end up running for your life. I warned you."

"Thank you. But I'm sure I'll survive. Now, I nearly forgot to pass along a message from Haley. She said you should join a club or something."

"I wouldn't have a clue what activity to do or club to join. If I'd been interested in clubs or stuff, I'd have joined one already."

"What are you planning to do for a career?"

"Good question. Next one."

"Then what about uni? You need to figure it out

soon. You've only got a bit more than a year before you finish high school."

"Do you think I don't know? And you're not the only one who's pointed it out. But I wouldn't have a clue. How did you know you wanted to be a vet?"

Zach shrugged. "I'm not sure. I originally considered being a doctor. Then I saw a program on TV about vets. I was fascinated."

"I only wish. The closer the time gets, the more things I look at and think, yeah that looks okay. But it's only ever okay. There's nothing I can imagine myself doing for more than a handful of years without wanting to run screaming from boredom."

"You could start off with a BA and change when you figure out what you want to do."

Brenna shook her head. "My parents aren't paying for uni unless I have a clear plan and know what I want to do at the end."

"Then I guess you take a year off study and work full time while you consider your options."

"Not like I have much choice." Brenna fell silent as they pulled up in front of her home. "Are you sure I can't convince you not to meet my mum?"

"No. Now stop procrastinating."

"Anyone in particular you want me to invite to your funeral?"

Zach laughed.

"I'm not joking." She picked up her backpack and got out of the car. Zach followed with her schoolbag. Brenna opened the front door with her key and managed to suppress her groan when she saw her mum sitting in the lounge room.

As soon as Sandra's gaze fell on Zach standing behind Brenna, she strode to the door. "Who's this and what are you doing home? You're meant to be at your father's another night."

"He forgot to find out train times."

"So why didn't he bring you home? You still haven't told me who this is."

Zach held out his hand. "Zach Reed."

Sandra ignored his outstretched hand. "That doesn't explain why you're bringing my daughter home."

Zach dropped his hand. "I spent the afternoon with Adam and Brenna. Since I live over this way, it seemed pointless for both of us to drive here."

"Pointless! So he lets Brenna come home with a stranger instead. That lazy bastard. If he thinks he can avoid his duties because I'm not there to keep him in line, then he can think again."

"Mum, I have to ring Dad and let him know I'm home. Can I come inside?"

Sandra nodded. "But he's not." She pointed at Zach.

Danielle came into the lounge room. "Who's that?"

Sandra spun to face her youngest daughter. "What are you doing out of bed?"

"I couldn't sleep with all the noise."

"Get back to bed. Now!"

Danielle left the room grumbling.

Brenna turned to Zach and held out her hand for her schoolbag. "Thanks for the lift home."

Zach grinned. "I'll talk to you later." He glanced towards Sandra. "Nice meeting you."

Sandra's answer was a glare, hands on her hips as she continued to stand guard at the door.

Brenna watched as he headed to his car.

"That better not be the boy you want to date. He's too old for you."

Brenna closed the door and turned to face her mum. "He's only two years older than me."

"Is he the one you want for a boyfriend? The one you can't wait until you're seventeen to be with?"

"Mum!"

"Don't think that because your father lets you do something I will. You're too young to have a boyfriend."

"So how old were you when you had your first boyfriend?"

"That has nothing to do with the present."

"Fifteen? Fourteen?"

"Brenna!"

"Twelve?"

"Enough. This conversation is over."

"That's always your answer." Brenna strode to the phone and rang Adam.

"You're late."

"No I'm not. Mum wouldn't let me in the house. She had to give Zach the third degree."

Sandra held out her hand. "Give me the phone."

"She wants to talk to you," Brenna said to her dad.

He sighed heavily. "Put her on."

Brenna handed over the phone and picked up her schoolbag she'd dropped on the floor when she dialled the number. She entered her room to find her sister sprawled on her bed.

"What are you doing in here?"

"Who was that? He's absolutely gorgeous. Don't tell me he's your boyfriend."

Brenna couldn't hold back her grin. "I'm not allowed a boyfriend until I'm seventeen, remember?"

"That's so unfair. I'm prettier than you and I don't have someone who looks like him interested in me."

"Probably because you're too bossy."

"I am not!"

Brenna shrugged. "I've got to get ready for bed. If I'm awake when Mum gets off the phone she'll probably yell at me some more."

"I suppose I should go to bed too. I don't want to be grounded during the school holidays." Danielle paused at the door. "What's it like at Dad's place?"

"Okay."

"Bren!"

Brenna shrugged. "I don't know. Quieter than here I guess." They both looked towards the bedroom door as Sandra's raised voice filtered through to them.

"That wouldn't take much. Night."

"Night, Dani."

Brenna hurriedly got ready for bed, not wanting to be about when her mum got off the phone. She set her alarm and turned off her bedside lamp. She was nearly asleep when her phone rang, vibrating on her bedside table. She checked the display.

"Hello, Zach."

"You want that list now?"

"List?"

"Of who I want at my funeral."

Brenna laughed softly. "I warned you."

"I'd email it to you, but I don't have your address."

"I'll text it to you."

"And your messenger?"

"They're the same."

"Do you want a lift to school in the morning?"

"Yes."

"Meet you at the bus stop?"

Brenna wished he could pick her up from home. "Okay."

"Night."

"Night."

"Love ya." Zach hung up before Brenna could answer.

She smiled as she typed in her email address and sent it to Zach. A few seconds later, he sent his email address. Brenna stared wistfully at her laptop where it sat closed on her desk. She was tempted to go online and see if Zach was too. There was only a week left until the school holidays and with the mood her mum was in, it wouldn't take much to end up grounded. Sighing, she lay down. She'd have to be happy with seeing him tomorrow.

Chapter Twenty-Seven

Between work, school and trying to spend every spare minute with Zach, the week passed quickly. Brenna glanced around as she walked beside Danielle. School was finished and two weeks of holidays stretched ahead of her. She couldn't help smiling. There was more noise than could usually be expected on a Friday as plans were made and cries and exclamations of appreciation for the holidays hung in the air.

Brenna turned when her name was called. She spotted Zach. "Come on, Dani. Zach's here."

"So."

"Come on." Brenna grabbed her sister's arm and pushed her way through the press of bodies that had been headed for the buses lined up waiting for them. She let go of her sister when they reached Zach.

He stepped away from his car, wrapped his arms

around her waist and looked down at her with a smile. "Miss me?" He asked softly.

"Always." Brenna's eyes closed as his lips met hers. She was brought back to earth by someone whistling.

Zach's lips brushed along her cheek and stopped near her ear. "Ignore them."

"We can't stand here all day."

"You want to go somewhere more private and continue this?"

Danielle interrupted. "You didn't have to drag me over here if all you were going to do was kiss him."

Brenna ignored her sister and answered Zach. "Nice try."

Zach laughed softly. He leaned back slightly from her, his voice no longer a whisper. "I'm moving into Mike's old room today. He finally moved in with his girlfriend. Want to help?"

"When did you decide that?"

"This morning. Derrick asked me earlier in the week. I talked to the solicitor today. I'll rent out the house. I can't stay there."

Brenna nodded in understanding. "What do you still need to do?"

"Not much." Zach grinned. "I've decided I need a queen-sized bed." He leaned in close again so he could whisper in her ear. "Although I'll be sad to get rid of mine. I have a very fond memory of it."

"Can I come too?" Danielle asked.

"I want you to tell Mum I went out with friends from school and I'll be home before dark."

"No. You want me to cover for you, I get to come."

"And how do you think you can do that?" Brenna glared at her sister.

"If I can get her to say yes, can I come too?"

"I don't mind," Zach said.

Brenna sighed. "I guess."

"Yes!" Danielle victory punched the air as she pulled out her mobile phone. She rang her mum and moved away from them as she talked.

"Are you sure?" Brenna asked Zach, who still had his arms around her.

"It won't take long to pick out a bed and by the time we get back to Derrick's, him and Brent will probably be there."

"If anyone can talk Mum in to letting us go it'd be Danielle. She gets along with Mum so much better than I do."

Danielle rejoined them and held her phone out to Brenna. "Mum wants to talk to you about the two of us going into the city to go window shopping."

Brenna took the phone. "Yeah?"

"You'll stay together and be home before dark. Understood?"

"Yeah."

"You don't sound very positive about it."

"I guess hanging out with my baby sister is better than sitting around the house being bored out of my brain."

"And no fighting with her."

"Okay."

"And you'll clean up your room after dinner or you won't be going anywhere tomorrow."

"Any other orders?"

"Don't take that tone with me, Brenna."

"Danielle wants to talk to you." Brenna handed the phone back to her sister who moved away from them. Brenna closed her eyes, sighing heavily.

"Need me to take your mind off the phone call?"

Brenna opened her eyes and grinned at Zach. "Don't you think of anything else?"

Zach returned her grin. "I think of... lots of things."

"But all with the same theme."

Before Zach had a chance to reply, Danielle interrupted. "What did you think you were doing?

You nearly ruined all my pleading. Would you rather go home?"

Zach opened the front passenger door. "Time to go." He shook his head when Brenna would've said something to her sister. "I'd like to have something to sleep on tonight."

Brenna glanced at the trailer. "I was wondering why you'd brought the trailer with you."

"Now you know. Let's go try out some beds." Zach laughed when Brenna rolled her eyes.

When they arrived at the furniture store, Zach and Brenna held hands as they wandered about. Danielle walked beside them and regularly interrupted their conversations.

"That bed looks nice." Danielle pointed to a chunky timber one.

"What do you think?" Zach turned to Brenna who shrugged.

Zach pulled Brenna onto the bed and she squealed as she landed beside him. He grinned. "We have to test them out."

Danielle dropped onto the bed too. "There were three in the bed and the little one said…"

"Only three? And I thought it started with a lot more than that," Zach said.

Brenna ignored the rest of her sister's song and

turned her head so her mouth was near Zach's ear. "There better not be."

"Jealous?"

"Maybe."

"What do you think of this bed?"

"I don't know. It's the only one we've tried."

Zach laughed and hopped off the bed, pulling her with him. "Let's test some more then."

They finally settled on a bed with a black metal frame and a bed head in a wrought iron style. Once it was tied in the trailer and they'd visited the department store to use the gift voucher from Brenna to buy linen, Zach headed to Derrick's place. He was correct and both Derrick and Brent were home, playing a game on the playstation. They stopped long enough to help set up the bed. As soon as that was done, they returned to their game, taking Danielle with them.

Zach locked the bedroom door and turned to watch Brenna who stood by the bed. She nervously took a step back when Zach took one forward.

"I didn't think this door locked."

"It didn't. I changed it earlier today."

"Oh."

Zach smiled. "As much as I'd like to say it's because I'm optimistic, the main reason is the parties. I don't want people wandering in and out of my room. It's an external door lock." Zach placed his hands on her shoulders. "Relax."

"I'm sorry."

"About what?"

Brenna's gaze darted towards the bed. "Ahh… about…"

Zach sat on the edge of the bed and patted the mattress. "Come here."

Brenna sat gingerly beside him. She squealed when he put his arms around her and pulled her onto the pillows. "What-"

"Lay beside me and talk."

"What about?"

"Anything." Zach kept his arms around her, his chin resting on her head.

Brenna wriggled until she was more comfortable, his chest against her back as she lay towards her side. "Do you need help cleaning out your parent's room?" She felt Zach's arms tense before he relaxed again.

"No. I'm picking Grandma up Monday morning. She's going to sort through everything. She'll know if anything needs to be kept."

"Can you afford to live here?"

"Yeah."

"Are you sure?"

"My father was planning for his retirement, Ren. He has… had all sorts of investments. Even with paying for uni they were still going to be able to retire on time."

"Then why did he always nag about how much money he had to waste on you?"

"My father was the type of person who always needed something to complain about."

"Sounds a bit like my mum."

"She's an amateur in comparison. But give her a couple more decades and she might be more accomplished."

Brenna laughed. "Please no." Her smile disappeared and she tensed as Zach's hand moved up and down her arm.

"Ren. Relax. I promise not to take things too far. Let's make some new memories for this bed."

She couldn't help smiling. "Okay." She turned to face him. His lips met hers and she eagerly kissed him, her hands mimicked his in their explorations. Time seemed to cease to exist and when there was a knock on the bedroom door, it took a bit for them to notice.

"Yeah?" Zach called out.

"Dani says they have to get home before dark. You ready to go Brenna?" Derrick asked.

"Give me a minute," Brenna said.

"Don't be too long or I'll be knocking on the door again. And if you want more driving time, I can take you home."

Brenna listened as Derrick walked away from the door. She looked up at Zach who leaned over her. One of his hands rested high on her thigh and she tugged the skirt of her uniform down.

Zach smiled and his lips brushed against hers. "I like this bed better."

Brenna couldn't resist laughing. "You would."

"I guess we should get you home before dark."

"Yeah. I don't want to be grounded."

"No. I want you at a party Derrick's throwing here tomorrow night."

"I can't promise anything."

"Try."

Brenna nodded before she rolled off the bed and stood up. She looked back to see Zach stand up beside her as he buttoned his shirt. She felt her cheeks heat and turned away when Zach chuckled. He grabbed her hand and turned her to face him.

He kissed her gently. "I love you, Ren."

"Me too," she whispered.

Zach smiled and kissed her hungrily. They broke apart when there was another knock on the door. "Yeah. We're coming."

"Be quick about it then," Derrick said.

Brenna straightened her uniform and brushed at some of the creases. She looked up and saw Zach watching her. "Aren't you going to finish doing up your buttons?" She ran her fingers down the four buttons that were still undone, resting her hand against his chest when she reached the fourth one. She felt him tense beneath her palm and met his gaze. Her mouth went dry at the intensity of it. "Zach…"

He closed his eyes for a moment then said huskily, "We'd better go before I forget all about my promise and convince you to change your mind." He strode to the door and opened it, doing up another couple of buttons.

They waited for Brent to walk past, giving them a quick grin as he headed for the kitchen.

Derrick turned towards them as they entered the lounge room. "I was about to come hassle you again."

"Let's go then," Zach said.

"It might be better if you stayed here. Not a good male to female ratio when it comes to a paranoid mother. You'll survive if you don't get to go in the car," Derrick said.

"I don't have to drive home," Brenna said.

Zach shook his head. "You need to clock up some

hours or you'll never get your licence. Do you think you'll be able to come over tomorrow?"

Brenna shrugged. "Who knows."

"Maybe I can come over there instead."

Brenna laughed. "And maybe the world will end."

Derrick placed a hand on Danielle's back. "Come on, Dani. Let's head to the car and put the learner magnets on. At least then we can hit the horn if they take too long saying goodbye."

When they were alone in the lounge room, Zach held Brenna close. One hand stroked her back and the other cradled her head. "I wish your mother wasn't so difficult to deal with."

"Tell me about it." She wrapped her arms around his waist.

"So, what do you think are the chances of you being able to come to the party?"

"How close are we to hell freezing over?"

Zach chuckled. "Will you ask anyway?"

"I'll try." Brenna smiled when the car horn sounded. "I guess they're getting impatient. I should–" her words were cut off by Zach's kiss and she forgot what she was going to say. When he pulled back, she gazed up at him. "I could always run away again."

Zach shook his head.

"You'd let me stay here, wouldn't you?"

"Of course I would, but think of another plan."

Brenna sighed. "Okay." She reluctantly stepped back. She stared at him a moment longer and cupped his cheek with her hand. Zach turned his head and pressed his lips to her palm and she shivered. "I'll ask her."

Brenna grabbed her schoolbag and hurried out to the car, sliding into the driver's seat. "Sorry." She tossed her bag onto the back seat near Danielle.

Derrick laughed. "You were quicker than I expected."

"Quicker than I would have been," Danielle said.

"Oh, shut up." Brenna turned the key in the ignition.

Chapter Twenty-Eight

As soon as they pulled up in their driveway, Brenna groaned at the sight of her mum coming out of the house towards them. She stopped, with hands on her hips, as she waited for them to get out of the car.

"Hope you've got a will written." Reaching for her schoolbag, Brenna rummaged for her logbook and handed it to Derrick.

"Yep, and my tetanus shots are up to date too." As soon as he filled it in, Derrick handed the logbook back.

Danielle giggled. "We met you while we were out window shopping in the city."

Derrick nodded and got out of the car. Brenna hurried to join him.

"Who are you?" Sandra turned to Brenna. "How many of them are there? Are you going to come home with a different boy each time you go out? And you can't tell me this one isn't too old for you."

"If you'd give me a chance to introduce myself, you'd know I'm Derrick. I'm twenty-one and far too old for your daughters."

"Then why are you hanging around with them?"

"Brenna knows my cousin."

"The one who was here last weekend?"

Derrick shook his head. "No, that's his best friend."

"I don't care who you are. You stay away from my girls. I don't know you and I'm not interested in knowing you or having my girls know you."

"Lady, you need to relax. What are you doing tomorrow night?"

"I beg your pardon?"

"You look like you could do with a night out. I'm not busy, so what do you say?"

"That you're far too young for me."

"I only asked you out for the evening. I wasn't inviting you to bed. Would it change your mind if I said I was gay?"

"Are you?"

"That doesn't answer my question."

Sandra shook her head and turned to Brenna and Danielle, who followed the conversation avidly. "Inside you two."

"I'll see you later. Bren. Dani." Derrick grinned at them.

Brenna didn't move until Danielle grabbed her hand and tugged her towards the house. As soon as they were inside, she turned to her sister. "I wanted to see what happens."

"Ring him later and ask. I thought he had a party at his place tomorrow night." Danielle frowned. "I hope he's not taking Mum there."

They both looked towards the door when their mum stepped inside. "Dinner's nearly ready. Get cleaned up." She walked towards the kitchen without yelling at them.

They looked at each other in amazement. Danielle ran forward. "Mum. There's a party tomorrow night. Can we go? We're celebrating the start of the school holidays."

"Both of you?" Sandra looked preoccupied.

"Yes," Danielle replied before Brenna could speak. "Okay."

"We were thinking of going into the city first and catching up with friends. They asked if we wanted to sleep at their place after the party," Danielle said.

"As long as you stay together," Sandra said.

Brenna opened her mouth to speak, but Danielle pinched her. She lost her opportunity as Sandra turned away and headed to the kitchen. "You weren't invited to the party," she hissed at her sister.

Danielle grinned. "But at least I'm getting you there."

"You can't come."

Danielle shrugged. "Then I guess you won't be going either." She grinned smugly. "I've never been to a real party before. Don't be mean."

"You always get to do things before I do."

"So? What's more important? Making me wait to go to a real party or you getting to go there?"

Brenna sighed. Her sister was right. She had no choice but to put up with Danielle. "Just stay out of my way."

"Definitely."

Brenna headed to her room where she rang Derrick. She didn't bother with greetings. "What did you do to my mum?"

Derrick laughed. "Confused her. Gave her a lot to think about."

"Is she going out with you tomorrow night?"

"No, but I didn't think she would."

"What would you have done if she'd said yes?"

"Taken her out."

"But–"

"How about you say thank you for defusing the situation?"

"You did more than that. She's walking around like her brain's gone on holiday. She agreed to let us go out tomorrow, to the party and sleep over. She didn't even ask a million questions about who and where. What did you talk about when we went inside?"

"That isn't your business, Bren."

"But it must have been something major for her to let us go without a fuss."

"Have you ever asked your mum why she has all the rules she does and tries to monitor everything you do?"

"No."

"Think about asking her. But don't do it when you're having an argument because she probably won't discuss it with you."

"Did she tell you?"

"A little."

"How did you manage to get it out of her?"

"If you're curious, talk to your mum."

"You're so frustrating."

"Yep."

"Oh, when you told Mum you were gay-"

"I didn't tell her I was, I asked if that'd change the situation."

"Are you?"

"No." Derrick laughed. "I'll see you tomorrow night."

"Okay." Brenna ended the call and sat on her bed. Sometimes life was confusing. Last week her dad was laughing. This week her mum was letting her go to a party without interrogating her for hours on end.

* * *

Brenna glared at her phone as the music pressed in around her. She looked around for her sister and spotted her in a corner talking to a guy who appeared about ten years older. She pushed through the crowd and waved the phone under Danielle's nose.

"I'll be back soon," Danielle called out as Brenna dragged her through the crowd.

Brenna answered the phone as they stepped outside. "Yes, Mum." She couldn't keep the annoyance out of her voice.

"Let me talk to your sister."

Brenna handed the phone to Danielle.

"Yeah… no… we'll be going to bed soon. Are you going to ring all night and keep us awake? Sorry… okay." Danielle ended the call and handed the phone back to Brenna. "She said we're to ring when we're going to bed. And not to be up all night."

"She won't believe we're going to bed with all this noise," Brenna said.

"So we walk down the road and then ring. In about an hour. It'll be a bit after midnight by then," Danielle said.

"I'm so sick of this. She's been ringing us randomly all day. I'm surprised she hasn't tracked us down and dragged us home."

Zach stepped outside. "I was wondering where you'd got to." He draped his arm around Brenna's shoulders.

Brenna shrugged his arm off and handed her phone to her sister. "Here, you deal with her." She stalked inside and pushed her way through the crowd. She hovered outside the kitchen door, waiting to get through the crowd to the drinks.

A young man drinking from a plastic cup and leaning against the hallway wall gestured towards the doorway. "If you're trying to get a drink it might be a wait. A hoard just descended. A very thirsty one by the look of it."

The young man beside him shoved a beer bottle under her nose. "Want a drink? I grabbed two when I saw them coming."

Brenna took a mouthful and grimaced. She held it out to him with a shake of her head.

"Try this. You might like something sweeter." The one with the plastic cup handed her his drink and took the beer.

She took a tentative mouthful. "Much better." She grinned at the young man who'd given her his drink.

"Are you here with anyone?" he asked.

"Yeah." Zach reached Brenna's side and put his arm around her.

"Hey, Zach."

Zach nodded and turned to Brenna. "What are you drinking?"

"Anything and everything." She drained her cup and handed it to him.

Zach sniffed the cup. "Come on."

"But I want another one of those." Brenna glared at Zach's back as he held onto her hand, tugging her through the crowd.

He unlocked his bedroom door and waited until Danielle joined them. He closed and locked the door behind them, shutting out most of the noise, before he handed Brenna's phone to her.

"What am I meant to do with this?"

"We're going to ring Mum and tell her we're going to bed," Danielle said.

"Why should I waste the credit on my phone? Why don't we use yours?" Brenna put a hand on her hip.

"Because you work and I don't," Danielle argued.

"Here. Use mine." Zach held out his phone.

Brenna shook her head. "No. I don't want her to have your number." Brenna moved towards the bed and stumbled. "Whoops." She giggled.

"Just make the bloody phone call, Ren."

"Fine." She sat on the bed and dialled her home number. The phone was answered nearly instantly. "Mum."

"What's wrong?"

"We're going to sleep. We're sick of you ringing every few minutes and ruining our night."

"Brenna! Give me the phone." Danielle snatched the phone. "Don't listen to her Mum. She's being obnoxious. I'm tired. She wanted to stay up, but I reminded her we're meant to be glued together." Danielle moved away from them.

Brenna looked up at Zach. "I want another one of those drinks."

Zach shook his head. "They're stronger than they taste."

"You're not my father. I want another one of those drinks."

Zach watched her for a few more seconds before his lips slowly curved into a smile. "I'm definitely not. Sure, if you want to learn things the hard way, I'll get you another drink."

Danielle handed Brenna's phone back to her. "Are you trying to get us grounded?"

"Yeah well, she shouldn't go out of her way to annoy me." Brenna slid her phone in her pocket and stood up. She swayed and grabbed Zach for balance. "Are we going to get my drink now?"

Zach nodded and unlocked the door. He relocked it as soon as they were out. "This way." He led them to Derrick and pushed Danielle in front of him. "Look out for her, will you?"

"Where will you be?"

"Helping Ren get drunk."

"Zach–"

"Don't look at me. Talk to Ren."

Brenna stared defiantly at Derrick.

"There's Panadol in the bathroom cabinet." He pulled Danielle closer. "Come on, kid, let's see what we can do to keep you amused."

"I'm not a kid," Danielle complained.

"Derrick." Zach waited until his friend turned back to him. "See she has somewhere safe to sleep?" When Derrick nodded, Zach guided Brenna to where the drinks were, pushing through the crowds. He made the requested drink and handed it to her.

"Only one? And what about for yourself?"

Zach made another two drinks and handed another to Brenna. With an arm about her waist, he guided her through the crowd to his room. Once they were inside, with the door locked, Zach put the two extra drinks on his bedside drawers.

Brenna drank half her drink in one go.

"Slow down, Ren."

Brenna looked pointedly at him, drank the rest of her drink and handed the empty cup to him.

Zach put the empty cup next to the full ones. He watched her for a couple of seconds and then laughed. "Are you going to poke your tongue out at me and say 'so there' before you scull the rest of the drinks?"

"I'm sick of being told what to do."

"Really?" Zach stepped forward, resting his hands on her hips. "I'm sorry you're not having a good time."

Brenna shrugged. "It's not your fault." She locked her hands behind his head and pulled him forward. "You want to improve the night for me?" She kissed him hungrily and he kissed her back until she began to unbutton his shirt.

He placed a hand over the one that was working on his buttons. "What are you thinking, Ren?"

With a glare she pulled away from him, sat on the edge of the bed and reached for another one of the drinks. She watched him as she drank it. "Don't look at me like that."

"Like what?"

"Like you're laughing at me."

Zach chuckled. "And what if I am?" He sat beside her.

"Then you can stop."

"Last time I got drunk I did something stupid."

"So. Maybe sh… shtupidity's the answer." Brenna reached for the last cup, but Zach beat her to it.

"This one was mine, remember?" He took a mouthful.

She was sick of everyone telling her what she could and couldn't do. "Then I'm going to get an…nother one." She stood up, stumbling.

Zach returned his cup to the bedside drawers and reached out to steady her.

Brenna pushed at his hands. "I'm fine."

"I'm not."

"What's wrong?" She squinted up at him.

For answer, Zach's lips met hers. Brenna's arms

twined around his neck and she pressed herself against him.

Chapter Twenty-Nine

Brenna groaned and her hands went to her head. It seemed ready to explode. She felt someone tug one of her hands and she opened her eyes to see Zach lean over her. She took the tablets he pressed into her hand, sitting up to swallow them down with the glass of water he held out. She hoped the Panadol would kick in quickly.

She froze, suddenly aware she was naked and the sheet had dropped to her lap. She pulled it up and looked at Zach. The sheet covered most of him, but his chest was bare. Alarm raced through her. She wished she could pull the sheet back to see if he was as naked as she was. She tried hard to recall the night. The last thing she remembered was undoing his shirt.

"Zach…"

"What?"

"Oh quit smirking."

Zach laughed. "What do you want to know, Ren?"

Brenna glared at him. "You know perfectly well what I want to know."

"You only have to ask."

Brenna pulled the sheet away from him to reveal black, cotton boxers. Some of the alarm evaporated.

"I had to wear something when I got your Panadol and water."

"Just tell me. What did we do?"

Zach kissed her lightly. "Nothing, Ren. When we–"

"If."

"When we make love I want you to recall every single second of it."

"What happened to my clothes?"

"You rather enthusiastically scattered them around the room. Along with mine."

Brenna dropped back against the pillow and pulled the sheet over her head with a groan. She ignored Zach's chuckle.

"Are you going to come out of hiding any time soon?"

"Nope."

Zach tugged at the sheet. "You were very sweet."

"Sweetly stupid. Aren't you going to tell me I told you so?"

Zach shook his head. "I'm sure you don't need me to point out the obvious."

There was a knock on the bedroom door. "Bren? Are you in there?"

"Yeah, Dani."

"Mum's ringing back in a couple of minutes. She wanted to talk to you, but I told her you were sleeping. She said to wake you because she's ringing back."

"I need my clothes," Brenna whispered.

"They're mostly on the floor," Zach said with a sweep of his arm.

"Get them for me," she hissed.

Zach chuckled as he got out of bed and started gathering clothes, throwing them on the bed around her.

"Are you going to let me in?" Danielle knocked on the door again. "She'll be ringing soon."

"In a minute." Brenna frantically pulled her clothes on while trying to stay covered by the sheet. She glared at Zach who continued to watch her as he pulled on his jeans. He smiled when she frowned at him. She heard her sister's phone ring and as soon as she was dressed, threw back the sheets. Zach unlocked the door and let Danielle in.

"Sure, Mum, she's right here." Danielle held the phone out to Brenna.

"Yeah."

"Why isn't your phone on?"

Her gaze was drawn to the bedside drawers where her phone sat. "Probably ran out of charge from all the phone calls yesterday."

There was a short pause before Sandra demanded, "When will you be home?"

"When we get there."

"Don't take that tone with me, Brenna."

"I've just woken up. I haven't had breakfast." Brenna swallowed as the thought of food made her queasy. "I wouldn't have a clue what time I'll be ready to leave."

"I want you home for lunch."

"That's only an hour away."

"You couldn't give me a time."

"Five."

"Three at the latest."

Brenna started to protest.

"Don't argue with me Brenna, or you can come home now."

"Fine. Three. Danielle wants to talk to you." Brenna ignored her sister shaking her head and handed the phone over. She dropped back on the bed, pulling a pillow over her head. She felt the bed sink slightly beside her. And then the pillow was tugged from her hands.

Zach grinned at her. "I turned your phone off in case your mum rang and you answered it while you were drunk."

"Thanks."

"Do you want breakfast?"

"I don't even want to think about food. Let me die in peace. I'm never drinking again in my life."

Zach laughed softly. "Until next time."

"Nope. Never."

"You'll forget how bad it is. Just next time, don't drink so much all at once."

"It was nice while I was drinking them."

Zach twisted a lock of her hair through his fingers. "Why don't you sleep a bit longer? I'll wake you in a couple of hours."

"What will you do while I'm sleeping?"

Zach lay beside her and slid his arm under her neck. "Sleep." He set the alarm on his phone and put it on the bedside drawers.

Brenna shifted until she was comfortable. Her eyes closed again and she felt Zach stroke her hair. "Think my head will be normal then?"

"Possibly."

"I hope so." She opened her eyes to meet his gaze. "I'm sorry I ruined your night."

Zach grinned. "Not even close." He laughed softly and ran a finger along her cheekbone. "Go to sleep."

She closed her eyes, wishing the heat in her cheeks would hurry and fade.

* * *

The first week of the holidays passed quickly. Brenna worked most mornings and hung out with Zach in the afternoon. Zach worked several evenings and the other evenings tried to catch up with his classes. He also put all the things he was keeping from his parents' house in storage and the house in the hands of a real estate agent. It took two days to find a tenant. He took some of the kitchenware and the table and chairs with him to Derrick's place, as well as his desk and bookcase for his room and a handful of other things.

There was a party Friday night that Brenna wasn't allowed to go to and she was tempted to sneak out so she could. Since she had permission to go out with Zach Sunday, she decided not to risk it. Although she wasn't too sure how much fun the day would be. She was finally going motorbike riding with Zach in the forestry. He'd arranged with her dad to drop her over there afterwards. Danielle wouldn't be staying with them until Tuesday as she was sleeping at a friend's place. Brenna was relieved since she didn't want her sister tagging along.

On Sunday, Brenna rose early and reached the bus stop before Zach. She dropped her backpack, bag of clothes and denim jacket onto the seat and sat beside them. He pulled up minutes later, three motorbikes in the trailer. Derrick got out of the front seat and sat in the back with Brent, leaving the door open for Brenna.

Zach popped the boot and got out of the car to put her bag in there. As soon as that was done, he greeted her with a kiss. "Looking forward to the day?"

"No. I still think you're going to change your mind about having me on your bike."

"We'll see."

"Are you two coming or are you going to maul each other all morning?" Brent called out.

"I'd rather stand here than get on a motorbike again." Brenna eyed the trailer's contents.

Zach smiled. "Come on. Time to go." He guided her to the car and closed the door once she was in. When Zach was in the driver's seat, he said, "We've got to get fuel before we leave Brisbane."

Brenna nodded as she buckled up. There wasn't much traffic on the road this early and it didn't take long before they were at a service station on the north side. Brent and Derrick went into the shop to buy soft drinks and Brenna got out of the car to ask Zach how the party had been Friday night.

"Brenna!"

Brenna looked at the next petrol bowser and nearly groaned. Travis beckoned Adrian over to finish filling the car and then headed towards her. She continued to walk to Zach who now filled the jerry cans. He glanced up to see what she wanted and then followed the direction she looked in.

"Travis," Zach said by way of greeting.

"Zach." Travis looked at the motorbikes in the trailer. "Where are you headed?"

"Forestry."

"We're going to my uncle's place. You're welcome to come. A lot better than the forestry. He has jumps and decent tracks."

Zach shrugged. "There's another car heading out there with us. Your uncle probably doesn't want another five bikes on his place."

"He won't mind."

"I'll ask the others. It's not just up to me."

Travis glanced at Brenna. "Bren knows where the place is. Come out if you want." He shrugged.

Zach finished filling the jerry cans and hung up the nozzle. "Okay. We might see you there."

With a nod and another glance at Brenna, Travis sauntered back to Adrian.

Zach put the jerry cans in the trailer and tied them in. "What do you think?"

"I don't know."

"You have first say in the matter."

"Why?"

Zach smiled. "Because he's your ex. You might not want to be anywhere near him."

"I see him every day at school. I'm not angry with him anymore. But I wouldn't say we're friends either."

"Who's the dark haired girl in his car?"

"Adrian's car. And it looks like the one he was cheating on me with."

"Who was that you were talking to?" Derrick asked when he and Brent arrived back at the car.

Zach looked at Brenna who shrugged. The thought flitted through her mind that this was her chance to show Travis she wasn't a rag doll. "I don't care. And I do like Ben, Travis' uncle, and wouldn't mind seeing him again. I'm not about to avoid people

I like so I don't have to see Travis. But if you stack the bike with me on the back, I'll never forgive you."

Zach grinned. "I wouldn't think about it." He turned to Derrick and Brent and explained the offer.

"Sounds good." Derrick looked at Brenna. "Are you sure you don't mind?"

Brenna shook her head. "It's fine."

"I'll give the others a ring." Brent pulled his phone out and moved away from the bowsers.

"I'll pay for the petrol. Coming, Ren?"

When Zach and Brenna returned to the car, it was to find the rest of Derrick's friends were going to the forestry while they'd go to Ben's place. Brenna had second thoughts as they came closer. Not to mention third and fourth. What if she was just as hopeless a passenger for Zach as she'd been for Travis? Then there'd be no doubt it was her and not Travis that was the problem.

Zach reached out and took her hand as they turned off the highway. "You okay?"

Brenna nodded. "Yeah. Just not looking forward to being on a motorbike."

"You'll love it."

"Sure," Brenna said dryly.

Derrick laughed. "Give it a chance, Brenna. You might be surprised. From all I've heard, your Travis strikes me as the sort of person who's only interested in making sure he has a good time."

"He's not mine," Brenna protested. "Turn here, Zach." She pointed to the road ahead of them before she turned in the seat to talk to Derrick. "His new girlfriend is well and truly welcome to him."

"Just don't give up on getting on the motorbike. If Zach's hopeless at taking you for a ride, you're welcome to ride with me."

Brenna smiled at Derrick's offer. "Thanks, but the deal I made with Zach didn't include anything other than hopping on with him."

"But you've got to give it a fair chance or it doesn't count," Zach said.

"I will."

Brenna's dread skyrocketed when they arrived at the property and she saw Ben take a jump on his motorbike. She glanced over to where Adrian and Travis were pulling on their gear.

Adrian came over to greet them first. "Hey Bren, you should've come camping with us this week. We took the motorbikes. It was great."

"I noticed Travis had his cast off." Brenna wondered if she should ask how they accomplished that.

Adrian grinned. "Hacksaw blade. I only nicked him once."

Brenna laughed. "I guess it could've been worse. Adrian, this is Derrick and Brent, you've met Zach."

Adrian came forward to shake their hands. "Travis is getting Kelly out of the car and then he'll be over."

They all looked at the car where Travis talked to the girl they'd seen at the service station. They were too far away to hear what was said. She shook her head. Then they saw her speak before she returned to painting her nails. Travis walked towards them without her.

Chapter Thirty

"Are the others coming?" Travis asked when he reached them.

Derrick shook his head. "No. They decided they still wanted to go to the forestry."

Brenna went through the introductions again.

"You could probably sit with Kelly and watch us," Travis said.

"She's going on my bike." Zach draped an arm around Brenna's shoulders and pulled her against him.

Travis laughed sharply. "You're wasting your time. Take it from me. She's a rag doll."

Ben rode up beside them, turned off his motorbike and pulled off his helmet. He was in his late twenties with sandy blond hair and a friendly grin. "How you all doing?"

Brenna once again went through the

introductions. Ben held out his hand and each of them stepped forward and shook it.

"Make yourselves at home. Any accidents, they're your problem. I don't want to know about them. You're riding at your own risk."

"No drama," Derrick said while the rest nodded.

"There probably will be an accident." Travis looked pointedly at Brenna. "Zach's taking Brenna on the back of his bike."

"She probably needs some more time on a bike," Ben suggested.

"Yeah!" Travis smirked. "Like a decade or two."

Brenna tried not to glare at Travis. She didn't want him to know his comment bothered her. There was no way she dared fall off the bike today. Travis would never let her hear the end of it. And he'd probably tell the entire school.

"We've got plenty of time," Derrick said. "She's welcome on any of our bikes."

"Next you'll be telling me you'd let her ride one on her own," Travis said.

"If she wanted to." Zach turned to Brenna. "What do you say, Ren? Want to take my bike for a spin?"

"I'll think about it." Brenna didn't believe he really meant it. She recognised the amusement in his eyes.

"Let's get these bikes off the trailer," Derrick said. "We're wasting daylight."

"That's not a problem." Travis grinned at his uncle. "We strap lights on our helmets. They work reasonably well."

"No they don't," Brenna said.

"What's life without a thrill or two?" Travis stared at Brenna as he asked the question.

"I'll catch you out there." Ben pulled his helmet on and kick started his motorbike. He turned it before he accelerated and took off for the jumps again.

"Are you going to give us a hand to get the bikes off, Ren?"

Brenna nodded. Anything was preferable to standing around talking to Travis. Now all she had to hope was that she didn't cause Zach to have an accident like she nearly had for Travis the one and only time she'd been on the back of his motorbike.

"What can I do?" Brenna watched as Zach wheeled his motorbike off the trailer.

Brent tossed one of the ratchet straps to her. "Roll this up."

Brenna rolled up the straps while the last motorbike was taken off the trailer, the tanks were filled and they pulled on their motorbike jackets and scuffed boots. She grabbed her denim jacket from the car. If she was going to come off the bike, she wanted as much protection as possible.

Zach handed her a pair of black gloves. "Better to be safe than sorry." He grinned at her.

"I really hope it's a waste of time wearing them." Brenna pulled them on, surprised they were the correct size.

Zach shrugged. "We'll be out here a few hours. If we're lucky the only thing they'll do is stop your hands getting sunburned." He handed her a helmet.

"Gee, Zach. I feel so much better after that pep talk."

Zach laughed and caught her around the waist. His lips met hers briefly. "Did that make you feel better than the pep talk?"

"I'm not sure. Maybe we should try it again."

"You're just trying to postpone the ride."

"What are my chances?"

"Good, but only temporarily." The next kiss was anything but brief.

"Come on you two. You can do that later," Derrick called out.

Zach grinned. "I told you it'd only be temporary. Now, I want you to be as close to me as those gloves are to your hands. All you have to do is hold on tight and be my shadow. Think you can do that?"

"I don't know."

"Of course you do. Did you ever play the mirror game when you were a kid?"

"Mirror game?"

"Yeah. One person is the mirror and stands in front of the other and they have to copy whatever the other person does."

"Yeah." Brenna drew the word out.

"Be my mirror."

"A mirror, great! Is that a step up from being your shadow? Or was I demoted?"

"Helmet on. We're out of here."

"But–"

"You made the deal, time to pay up." Zach pulled on his helmet and gloves.

With one last glare, Brenna donned her helmet. She watched as Zach got on his motorbike and started it. He patted the seat behind him as he looked at her. Brenna reluctantly threw her leg over the seat and slid close. She pushed the visor down on the helmet before she wrapped her arms around him, her legs on either side of his. Zach's hand covered hers for a moment and squeezed reassuringly.

"Hold on and don't let go." Zach pushed his visor down and slowly rode the bike to the tracks.

Brenna held on like they were going a hundred

times faster. As soon as they reached the track, Zach sped up slightly. They wound their way through gum trees and open spaces, dust drifting on the air behind them as they followed the circuit. By the end of the first lap, Brenna started to relax. Zach didn't go anywhere near as fast as Travis had ridden and she had no trouble mirroring him. After about an hour, he stopped and pushed his visor up.

He turned his head so she could hear him. "Ready to hit the track a little harder?"

Brenna slid her visor back. "No."

Zach grinned. "You certain?"

"Not too hard."

"Keep doing what you're doing. Maybe you didn't want to be wrapped this close to Travis." Zach winked before he pushed his visor down. Brenna closed her own.

This time he took off a little faster. By the end of the next hour, Brenna wasn't sure if she should be scared or thrilled. There were moments when she wanted to throw her head back and yell from sheer excitement. At other times, she wanted to close her eyes and pray, even though she wasn't certain exactly how to go about it.

Zach pulled up next to the car and pushed his visor back. "Want to grab a drink? Something to eat?"

She pushed her visor up before she answered. "Yeah." She hopped off the motorbike as soon as he turned it off and her legs nearly gave out on her.

Zach grabbed her forearm and held her steady. "You right?"

Brenna nodded. "I've been sitting too long." She pulled her arm away so she could remove her helmet.

Zach took it, hung it from the handlebars, putting his on the other side before he hopped off. He grabbed a blanket and an esky from the boot and headed for a shady tree.

"What did you think?" Zach asked as soon as they were sitting on the blanket.

Brenna couldn't resist smiling. "Well…"

"Can you understand the fascination now?"

Brenna smiled as she realised what made him ask the question. "I can't believe you heard everything I said to you in the hospital."

Zach chuckled. "I love the sound of your voice. I could listen to you for hours." Their gazes met and held. "Your voice kept dragging me back."

"What's for lunch?" Derrick called as he and Brent walked towards them, interrupting the moment.

Zach took the lid off the esky. "Cold pizza or chicken and salad sandwiches."

"Cold pizza?" Brenna peered in the esky to make sure she'd heard correct.

"You want some?" Zach removed a slice from a freezer bag and held it out to her.

Brenna shook her head and grabbed one of the sandwiches instead. As the four of them had lunch, and she listened to the guys talk about the track, Brenna's attention strayed to where Travis stood at Adrian's car and spoke to Kelly who hadn't moved from the front seat. It looked like they were arguing. Zach's hand dropped onto her thigh and her gaze was drawn to him. He smiled slightly before he turned back to Derrick who spoke to him.

Her attention stayed on Zach, the conversation fading to a low hum as she tuned it out. He laughed at something Derrick said and shrugged. Brenna noticed his hair was a little longer and probably needed a trim. His jacket was unzipped to show the plain t-shirt he wore underneath. Her gaze was drawn to his hand resting on her thigh and she thought of how they felt when they roamed her body. Their warmth and strength and the way he sometimes ran them lightly over her skin. Brenna looked up to his face to find his gaze on her. He smiled.

"What?" Brenna asked.

"Derrick asked how your day is so far."

"Oh." Brenna turned to Derrick. "Not bad."

Derrick grinned. "Let me know if you want to go for a ride with me. I'm a better rider than Zach."

"My grandma can ride a bike better than you," Zach teased.

Brent laughed. "Now that's something I wouldn't mind seeing."

"I can't picture Marian on a motorbike," Brenna said.

Zach grinned. "Years ago. Grandad had one. I don't know that she ever rode it by herself, but it wouldn't surprise me."

"Here comes the poser," Brent said under his breath.

Brenna looked up to see Travis walk towards them. Zach's hand moved back and forth slightly on her thigh. She rested her hand over his and he stilled. She met Zach's gaze, a question in hers. The only answer she received was a slight smile before he turned towards Travis.

"I take it Kelly isn't into motorbikes," Zach said.

Travis shrugged. "She prefers to watch." He crouched beside the blanket. "After lunch Ben, Adrian and myself are going to have a race on the track. Anyone interested?"

"Count me out," Derrick said. He looked at Zach. "I can take Brenna for a ride if you want to go."

Zach turned to Brenna. "Your call."

"I don't mind either way."

"Are you going to let her dictate what you can do?" Travis asked incredulously.

"Not that it's any of your business, but we came here together, we'll decide together what we do." Zach stared coldly at Travis.

Travis rose to his feet. "About half an hour if any of you are interested. We'll start over there." He pointed to the part of the track they'd start at, before he sauntered to his motorbike.

Derrick rose to his feet. "Everyone finished with the esky?"

Zach grabbed out soft drinks for him and Brenna. "Now I am."

"I'll put it in the boot." Derrick picked it up and walked towards the car.

"I'll fuel up the bikes." Brent followed Derrick.

As soon as they were alone, Zach turned to Brenna. "Would you mind if I joined their race?"

Chapter Thirty-One

Brenna shook her head. "I honestly won't mind. But are you okay?"

"What do you mean?"

"I don't know. When Travis came over... you were... I thought..." she gestured with her hands, unable to find the right words.

"Every time I see him I want to punch him in the face."

Brenna looked surprised. "Why?"

"Because he hurt you when he cheated on you."

"I'm over that now."

"You sure?"

"Yeah."

Zach reached out and tucked a loose strand of her hair behind her ear before he ran his knuckles across her cheekbone. Then he cupped her cheek with his hand. "I still want to make him hurt as much as you were hurt."

"He worries about what people think of him. Always likes to be seen as better than everyone else."

Zach grinned. "Then I guess I'm going to have to race him after all and make sure I beat him."

"He always comes second. Ben first, but he's been riding for decades and knows the track really well. There are two jumps at the end close together that if you don't time it right you'll come off. Even Ben has a couple of times. But don't push it. I'd rather you came last than get hurt."

Zach kissed her before he spoke. "I haven't seen anything from Travis to impress me."

"He's been taking it easy."

"So've I."

"Don't use me as an excuse when I can see you're itching to get out there."

Zach laughed. "You're never an excuse. I'd survive if you didn't want me to join their race."

"But you'd wonder if you could have beaten him."

Zach shrugged. "Probably."

"I'll watch."

"Derrick can take you for a ride."

Brenna shook her head. "I'd rather watch. I haven't seen you ride yet. I'm curious."

"In that case, my phone's in the front of the car. Do you want to record the end of the race for me?"

Brenna laughed. "Evil!"

Zach grinned. "Yep. But I can see you really like the idea too."

Brenna shrugged and tried unsuccessfully not to smile. "Maybe."

Zach rose to his feet, holding out his hand. "I'd better get organised if I don't want to miss out." He pulled her to her feet and picked up the blanket.

Brenna shaded her eyes with her hand as she watched Brent put the jerry cans in the trailer. "Just don't get hurt or I'm going to be pissed off with you."

"There's a cap in the car."

"Did you hear me?"

"Yep, and you've got nothing to be worried about."

"I hope not."

Zach put the blanket in the boot, handed Brenna his phone from the front of the car and held up a black cap. When she nodded, he popped it on her head with a smile. "Are you going to give me a kiss for luck?"

"The way you're talking it sounds like you don't think you need luck."

"Then kiss me because you want to."

Brenna wrapped her arms around his neck. "I thought you were in a hurry so you didn't miss the start of the race."

"I can catch up."

Brenna's lips lightly touched Zach's. Then she deepened the kiss when his arms went around her. Her eyes closed and she clung tightly. She reluctantly broke their kiss. "You should go before they start without you," she said softly.

Zach kissed her again. "If we're going to continue this after the race I'll get to the end before Ben."

Brenna laughed. "Sure. Millions are begging for my kisses."

"Well they'll have to keep begging because I don't share."

"Me neither."

"Hurry up, Zach," Brent called from where he sat on his motorbike.

"Meet you at the finish line." Zach grinned as he reluctantly let her go and got on his bike.

Derrick came to stand beside Brenna. "Do you want a ride?"

"Maybe later. I want to see this race."

"So where's the best vantage point?"

"Come on."

Brenna stood beside Derrick and watched as the

five riders took off in a cloud of dust. "Why aren't you out there?"

Derrick shrugged. "I know where I place against Brent and Zach. I often beat Brent, but never Zach. I couldn't care less how I do against the others. Besides, I'll have an idea with how Zach does. I'm just not overly competitive on a bike." He grinned. "Actually, I'm not overly competitive about most things."

"Who taught Zach to ride?"

"My dad. I would've been about eleven and he took us all out on the weekends with an eighty. It was great. When Mum was sick, she insisted we keep going. Even back then Zach was always the better rider. If he came off, he hopped back on and pushed it even harder."

Brenna watched as the five of them reached the halfway point. Ben was nearly a metre in the lead. Zach, Travis and Brent were keeping pace with each other while Adrian brought up the rear. "They look to be fairly evenly matched."

Derrick laughed. "They're playing with him. They should be up the front with Ben."

Travis was in between Brent and Zach. Brenna held her breath as Zach's back wheel seemed to wash out on the edge. He lost ground momentarily and then was up beside Travis again. She pulled out his phone and put it on the setting to record the race. Brent and Zach looked towards each other for a split second. Zach nodded first and then Brent.

"All right. Now we'll see how they do."

"What do you mean?" Brenna held the phone steady.

"They've decided to quit playing with him." Derrick had no sooner spoken when Zach and Brent shot ahead. The gap between them and Ben narrowed and Travis tried to catch up with them.

"Come on," Brenna muttered under her breath as Travis came level with Zach's rear wheel. Then Zach pulled ahead again, slightly in front of Brent. The last two jumps were coming closer. Ben took them and Zach followed, mimicking his actions exactly. Brent lost ground on the jumps while Travis gained. He was halfway along Zach's bike. Not for long. Then Zach was alongside Ben's rear tyre, the end of the race in sight. Brenna had to force herself to stay still when all she wanted to do was jump up and down and yell encouragement. Then the race was finished, Ben first, Zach not far behind him, Brent and Travis neck and neck and Adrian last as usual.

Brenna stopped recording and put the phone in her pocket as Zach rode over to where they stood. He pulled his helmet off, his eyes bright and a grin on his face. Brenna couldn't resist grinning back as he hopped off the motorbike and pulled her against him.

"What do you reckon? Ready to take some jumps with me?"

Brenna shook her head, still smiling. "You've got to be joking."

"It'll make you feel alive."

"If I don't die from a heart attack first."

Zach laughed before his lips met hers. Brenna clung to him, her senses going into overdrive. His hand slid under her jacket and the world receded, becoming a place that only contained the two of them.

"Get a room."

Brenna looked over to see Travis near them. She didn't have a clue how long he'd been standing there.

"Have you got one we can borrow?" Zach asked.

Travis grunted. He glared at Brenna for a second before he turned to Zach. "How about a rematch? You and me."

Zach shook his head. "Maybe later. I'm not leaving Brenna standing around all day waiting for me."

"She doesn't mind." Travis turned to Brenna. "Do you?"

"Actually, I do." She had told him several times before that she hated waiting around while he rode his motorbike. She'd always suspected he'd never listened. Either that or he hadn't believed she could expect him to give up his fun to entertain her.

Ben joined them. He held out his hand to Zach who shook it. "Good race. For a minute there I thought you had me. Anytime you want to have a rematch let me know." He turned to the group in general. Brent and Adrian had wandered over to join them. "What do you guys say we go down to the creek? The day's certainly warmed up enough."

"Sounds good," Derrick said.

At the same time, Brenna spoke, "I don't have swimmers with me."

"Brenna's an ice queen. She wouldn't be caught dead skinny dipping," Travis said.

"I'm wearing my jeans in," Brent told her.

"Only because he doesn't believe in underwear," Derrick said.

Brenna wrinkled her nose. "Too much info."

"What do you say?" Zach asked. "Wear your jeans and t-shirt in? You'll dry quick enough once you're out. Either that, or I'll go faster on the bike. That'd dry you."

"How thoughtful of you," Brenna said dryly.

Zach laughed. "Swim?"

Brenna nodded. "I guess so."

"Last one to the gate has to open and shut it," Ben said.

"We'll go last. It'll be easier for me to get the gate rather than someone else hopping off their bike," Brenna said.

"Is Kelly coming?" Adrian asked Travis.

He shrugged. "Who knows? She's sulked most of the day."

"I'll see if I can talk her into coming. It'd be rude to go off and leave her." Derrick strode towards Adrian's car before Travis had a chance to say anything.

When Travis started to follow Derrick, Zach said, "You don't have to worry about him stealing her on you. He doesn't invade other people's territories."

"Unlike some." Travis stared at Zach pointedly.

Zach smiled slightly. "You're welcome to think that if you like. It doesn't bother me. I know the truth." With an arm still around Brenna, he draped his other one around Brent's shoulders. "Let's get the bikes. I can hear the water calling my name."

"It's probably the voices in your head." Brent grinned.

When Brenna climbed on the back of Zach's bike, she was surprised to see Kelly climb on behind Derrick, Ben's spare helmet on her head. Kelly gingerly put her hands on Derrick's waist and he pulled her forward, clasping them in front of him. Brenna glanced towards Travis to see how he was taking the situation. She guessed not too well with how he took off on his bike.

He was waiting at the gate for them when they arrived. Brenna hopped off Zach's motorbike, unhooked the chain that wrapped around the gate and pushed it open.

Ben lifted his visor up and stared at Travis. "Hey!" When Travis turned towards him, Ben said, "No scaring the cows. Take it easy this time." He looked around at everyone. "That goes for all of you." He smiled. "I wouldn't want one of them to panic and run in front of you because my money would have to be on the cow." He pushed his visor down and rode into the paddock.

As soon as everyone was through, Brenna closed the gate and hooked the chain around. She climbed on the motorbike, wrapping her arms around Zach. They were the last ones to arrive at the creek. Zach left his jacket and t-shirt on the seat of the motorbike and his boots on the ground. Brenna dropped her jacket on top of his gear and kicked off her sneakers. She put both her and Zach's phone in the pocket of her jacket.

Zach took her hand and they walked down to the

creek where everyone was already in the water. Even Kelly, who was wearing a skimpy bikini that had been under her clothes, was in the water laughing at something Brent had said. Brenna guessed she'd been told they might go swimming. She wished she'd brought her swimmers along, but she hadn't expected to need them. As they reached the creek, Ben climbed out, grabbed the rope hanging in a gumtree at the water's edge and swung out into the middle of the creek. He tucked his legs up and dropped into the water, sending a splash that reached them on the bank.

Zach glanced from the rope to Brenna. "Do you mind?"

She shook her head with a grin. "Go for it. I'll follow you."

"You use a rope swing?"

She hit him lightly on the arm. "Hey! I'm a Queenslander. I was practically raised in creeks in the summer. And what decent swimming hole doesn't have a rope swing?"

Zach tugged her forward, his hand in hers. "You go first." He caught the rope and held it for her. He kissed her as she took it.

Brenna grabbed high on the rope and jumped up so she could sit on the knot at the end. She swung out over the creek and let go, holding her breath as she plummeted into the water. She swam to the surface, her head coming out in time to see Zach swing out and drop into the water. She tread water and briefly closed her eyes as the splash cascaded over her. He was grinning when his head broke the surface.

Zach swam over to tread water near her. "How strong's the rope?"

"Why?" Brenna asked cautiously.

"Swing out together?" When Brenna hesitated, he winked. "I promise not to land on you… hard."

Brenna laughed. "Okay, why not?"

The rest of the afternoon passed rapidly and the last of the sunshine found them lying in the grass drying off. After about ten minutes, Zach tugged gently at Brenna's hair. She opened her eyes and looked at him.

"Let's ride. We'll dry soon enough."

Brent groaned when he heard Zach's words. "Don't want to think about moving. Let me die in peace."

Derrick, who was talking to Kelly, laughed as he glanced at his friend. "You knew we were going riding today. It's your fault you got in after midnight. No sympathy."

"If I had the energy I'd show you what you can do with your lack of sympathy." Brent yawned.

"What do you say, Ren?" Zach leaned over her.

Chapter Thirty-Two

Brenna's thought processes stopped as she looked up at him, his face centimetres from hers. She lifted her head from the grass so her lips could meet his. Her hands reached out to curve around him and run along the hard plains of his back. His skin felt warm even though there were now more shadows than sunlight. There was a moment of surprise in Zach's eyes and then he was kissing her back, his chest pressed against hers.

"Do we need to throw you pair in the creek to cool off?" Derrick asked.

"Need a hand?" Travis asked.

Zach pulled back slightly and laughed softly. "Was that your answer?"

"What was the question again?"

"Ride?"

Brenna worried at her bottom lip with her teeth.

Seconds later, Zach lightly nipped at it. Brenna drew her breath in sharply. "Zach."

"You're a major distraction," Zach said softly.

"Sorry."

"I'm not." He pressed his lips to her forehead. "Creek or bike?"

"What?"

"I need a different distraction."

"Oh. Bike I guess."

As soon as Zach was on his feet, he pulled Brenna to hers and looked around. "Anyone else coming?"

Brent groaned, but like everyone else, he rose to his feet. Within minutes, they were all dressed and on the motorbikes. Kelly was again behind Derrick after having refused to hop on behind Travis. Brenna guessed Travis would be ditching her soon. He didn't tolerate people who disagreed with him.

The rest of the afternoon was spent riding around the track and when the sun was only a splash of colour on the clouds, they pulled up beside the cars. Travis came over to talk to them. "I thought you said you'd race again later."

Zach shrugged. "I guess we ran out of daylight."

"That's not a problem. I can get the headlamps. Or do you think it was a fluke earlier?"

"They aren't bright enough," Brenna protested.

"He's been over the track enough times today that if he's a decent rider he should be able to ride it blindfolded," Travis sneered.

"Give me ten minutes to talk it over with Brenna. She might have other plans for the evening."

"Yeah right. Something boring and nowhere near a bed. You were full of shit when you hinted you'd slept with her."

"And yet I believe you made a similar statement."

"I only said she was hopeless in bed. She freezes up if you try to do more than kiss her."

Zach glanced at Brenna and smiled warmly at her. "I've never encountered that problem." He looked back to Travis. "Ten minutes. Take it or leave it."

"Ten minutes then." Travis stalked to his car.

Brent and Derrick moved away from them and Brenna was glad of the privacy. She looked at Zach. He seemed miles from his usual relaxed pose.

"Are you all right?"

"Yeah," Zach muttered.

"You seem…" words failed her.

"Like I want to deck him?"

"Do you?"

"He's such an insensitive bastard."

"And you've never been one?"

Zach laughed. "At times. I just don't go out of my

way to constantly be one. Will it bother you if I race him?"

"I don't want you to get hurt. The lights aren't very bright." Her eyes narrowed. "You want to, don't you?"

Zach shrugged. "Yeah."

"And not just to rub his nose in another win. You like the danger of racing through the dark with hardly any light on a track you've only spent a day on."

Zach grinned. "Yep."

Brenna shook her head, poking him in the chest with a finger. "If you end up in a coma again I'm not sitting at your bedside."

"Yes you would."

"Maybe."

Zach wrapped his arms around her. "Kiss for luck?"

Brenna willingly gave in to his request and was reluctant to break contact with him. And not just because of the heat that raced through her. She didn't want him to ride his bike in the dark.

When Zach hopped on his bike, Derrick and Brent came to stand with her. Derrick dropped his arm across her shoulders. "Same viewing place?"

"I guess."

"He'll be right." Brent clapped her lightly on the

back as they walked to where Adrian and Ben stood. "If anyone was taking bets I'd back him."

"Bets?" Ben brightened. "Twenty bucks? My money's on Travis."

Brent held out his hand. "Done."

"I'll run and turn on the spotlight. It hits the finish line. We need to make sure we can see who's the winner." Ben strode towards his house. The verandah lights of the sprawling low set house cast dim pools of light into the yard. A few minutes later spotlights cut through the gloom, one landing where the cars were parked, the other on the finish line.

Zach and Travis started before he was back. Brenna strained her eyes to see them. All she was able to see were lights bobbing above the ground, speeding around the track, the sounds of the motorbikes loud on the night air.

Ben joined them again. "Can we see who's in the lead?"

Brenna shook her head. "I wouldn't have a clue."

"Zach is. I can tell by the height of his headlamp from the ground. He hunches over the handlebars more than Travis and leans further into the turns," Brent said.

Kelly walked over to stand beside Derrick. "What's happening?"

"Zach and Travis are trying to kill each other." Brenna clasped her hands tightly at chest height, barely remembering to breathe.

"I didn't realise it was going to be so boring here." Kelly moved nearer Derrick who still had his arm draped casually around Brenna's shoulders.

Derrick moved closer to Brenna, and she suppressed a grin. Taking pity on him, she moved to his other side supposedly to talk to Kelly. "Yeah, unless you like motorbikes, there isn't much to do."

"Swimming was fun." Kelly looked past Brenna to Derrick. "Don't you think?"

Derrick's answer was a shrug.

"Here they come," Ben exclaimed.

Brenna pulled out Zach's phone and prepared to record the end of the race. She saw the light from the headlamps rise up in the air and guessed they must have hit the last jumps. Her heartbeat sped up as she watched the lights come towards her. One was definitely well in front of the other. Then they rode through the pool of light the spotlight cast and Brenna nearly yelled in excitement. Zach was in front, Travis a good metre behind him.

As soon as Zach stopped not far from them, Brenna raced over to him, shoving his phone in her pocket. Her lips met his the moment his helmet was off and her hands clung to him. "Don't ever expect me to stand by and watch you do anything like that again."

Zach grinned. "You could always join me next time."

"Not likely."

Ben came over to clap him on the back. "You have to come out again. I always appreciate a challenge."

"Sure."

"Any weekend. You don't even need to tag along with my nephew." Ben glanced at Travis who was throwing his helmet in the back of the car along with his gear. Kelly was sulkily sitting in the front seat again. "Although he's usually out here most weekends."

"Thanks."

Ben grinned. "We're having a camp here next weekend. Anyone's welcome. Bring your bikes. I'll be shifting the cattle from the far paddock and we'll be camping over there. A few are bringing four-wheel-drives. Great country up there. No need to let me know. Come along and bring whatever you need for the weekend. Tents, food, alcohol, cooking gear. There's plenty of firewood here. People will start arriving Friday night. If you can't make it the whole weekend, pop out for the day. There's even a few staying until Monday."

"We'll think about it." Zach held out his hand. "Thanks for having us."

"Good to have another experienced rider about." Ben grinned. "Keeps me on my toes. And next time I'll know to bet on you." He sauntered back towards his house.

At Zach's confused expression, Brenna said, "He lost twenty dollars to Brent."

"Ahh." Zach pulled off his glove and curved his hand around the back of her neck. "Want to drive home?"

"What? No! There's a trailer on the car."

"So?"

"I–"

"I'll drive to the highway and then it's basically a straight line from there."

"Maybe."

Zach kissed her briefly. "I'll take that as a yes." He let her go and she stepped back so he could start the motorbike and ride it over to the car. Brent and Derrick were putting their motorbikes on the trailer and it wasn't long before they were leaving. Travis had left before them, without saying goodbye.

While they were headed for the highway, Brenna sat beside Zach, staring at him by the light of the dash, a half smile on her face. The day had been a lot better than she'd expected it to be. And it had been nice to see Travis lose. Twice. Her smile widened as Zach glanced at her.

He reached out and took her hand, placing it on his thigh before covering it with his.

Chapter Thirty-Three

The days of the second week of the school holidays seemed to pass as quickly as those of the first week. Zach and Brenna spent as much time as possible together and Thursday lunch, Zach gave Brenna a lift to her mum's since she had to work that afternoon as well as Friday morning. She was returning to her dad's place Friday night and he'd agreed to let Zach take her to a party first. She just hadn't explained it was at Derrick's place.

After work Friday, Brenna, who was still annoyed by a conversation with her mum from the previous night, found herself in her mum's room. She was determined to get an answer to the question Sandra always turned aside. And since she was on the phone, it seemed the perfect opportunity. It took longer than she expected.

"What are you doing?"

Brenna spun to face Sandra and held out the driver's license she'd taken from Sandra's handbag. "You were seventeen when you had me. Why didn't you tell us?"

Sandra took her driver's license. "It's none of your business."

"Of course it is. You always say you're twenty-one again when anyone asks. Is this why?"

"Mostly."

"Is that why you and Dad got married?"

"Brenna this has nothing to do with you. Stay out of what doesn't concern you."

"But it does concern me. It's why you want to lock me away and not let me have a life. Isn't it?"

"You're a kid. It's my job to set boundaries and make sure you stay within them."

"Did your mum set boundaries for you?"

"We're not having this conversation. Now get out of my room and stay out."

"She did, didn't she? And you still fell pregnant. So where was I conceived? In the back of a car?"

Sandra pointed towards the door. "Get! Out! Now!"

"I'm not you. Just because you had me at seventeen doesn't mean I'm going to do the same."

"Out!"

"Why don't you ever talk about being a kid? I wouldn't even have known you'd moved out of home at seventeen if you hadn't accidentally said something one day."

"Do you want to be grounded for the rest of the school holidays?"

"I might as well be when I'm at your place. You don't let me do anything."

"One more word out of you and you're grounded."

Brenna glared at her mum. "Go ahead. I go to Dad's later today."

"And you'll be grounded there too."

"Maybe I'll show you I'm not you by moving out of home when I'm sixteen. Think then you might understand I'm me?" Brenna slammed the bedroom door behind her. She ignored her mum calling after her to come back and shut her own bedroom door and locked it.

Sandra pounded on the door. "Unlock this door now before I get a screwdriver to open it."

"Why should I? You can tell your lies just as easily through the door."

There was silence on the other side and Brenna was tempted to open the door to see if her mum was still there. She jumped when her phone rang. The display read 'Dad'.

"What?"

"What are you doing, Brenna?"

"Wondering what else the two of you have lied about."

"What's going on now? Your mother said you were talking about running away again."

"How old are you? And don't give me that stupid twenty-one again line."

"Tell me what's going on, Bren."

"I know Mum's thirty-three. So how old are you?"

"The same."

"Did you ever consider aborting me?"

"No!"

"Not even once?"

"I couldn't even think about it."

"But Mum did?"

"Why don't you talk to your mother about this?" She sat on the edge of her bed. "She told me it's none of my business."

"Then stop asking questions about it."

"Is this why Mum's parents have nothing to do with us?"

"Brenna."

She ignored the warning in her dad's voice. "I'm not planning on making the same mistake as you and

Mum. The last thing I want to do is have a kid. Not for another decade. If ever."

"Life doesn't always go according to plan."

"Just because you had me young doesn't mean I'm going to do the same."

Adam laughed. "No, but you're the most impetuous. Your sister weighs things up before she does them."

"So do I."

"Not always. Especially not when you're angry."

"Then considering how angry you and Mum always make me I should've been pregnant at thirteen."

"That's enough, Brenna."

"Is that what happened with you and Mum? A rebellion gone wrong?"

"You carrying on like this isn't reassuring us you're not going to end up in the same boat."

"I'm not going to have sex until there's a contraceptive that's one hundred percent effective."

"Well, I guess that's one question we can stop wondering about for a while. But you're still not having a boyfriend until you're seventeen."

"Considering it only takes nine months, I'd still have the chance to have a kid when I'm seventeen. If that's the theory behind the rule, it's seriously flawed."

"Brenna. Enough. Should I pick you up now?"

"I'm going over to Zach's place."

"No you're not. I agreed he could pick you up at six."

"I'm really pissed off at you two right now. I want to hang out with friends and calm down. Otherwise, I'm likely to do something stupid in rebellion. And we all know how well rebellions pan out in our family."

Adam was silent for a moment. "I still expect you to leave the party by eleven."

"Only if you clear it with Mum so I don't have to argue with her about going early."

"I'll ring her now. And Brenna, don't make me regret letting you go to the party tonight."

"You won't." She hung up and quickly threw some things in her backpack. The landline rang and she waited a few minutes before she headed for the front door.

"Get back here now, Brenna. I don't care what your father says. When you're here, you're under my rules." Sandra spoke into the phone again. "I'm not interested in what you have to say. You've ruined enough of my life without ruining our kids' lives too."

Brenna stepped outside and closed the front door

quietly behind her. She knew she'd only have a few minutes before her mum came looking for her. She ran down the street and headed towards the main road. She pulled her phone out as she ran, dialling Zach's number.

"What's up, Ren?"

"Are you busy?"

"I'm at work. A last minute shift."

"Oh."

"Problems?"

"Not exactly."

"I finish work in an hour. Do you want me to pick you up then instead of later?"

"What's the address of your work?" When Zach told her, she said. "I might even meet you there. Give me a call before you leave work if I haven't turned up."

"Okay. Talk to you later."

Brenna reached the bus stop and was relieved to see a bus pull up. Not caring where it headed, she boarded and was relieved to find it was going to the city. She could get to anywhere much easier from the city.

By the time she reached the city, Brenna decided it made more sense to catch a bus to Zach's place. She sent him a text to let him know. She arrived about ten minutes before he did but Derrick was there to let her in. They were putting things like the playstation in Derrick's bedroom in preparation for the party. Brenna helped while she waited for Zach to arrive. She couldn't stop thinking about what she'd learned. Her parents would have been her age when they fell pregnant.

When Zach stepped into the kitchen, Brenna was busy pulling plastic cups out of their packaging and stacking them on the bench. Before Brenna could greet him, Derrick was in front of Zach, turning him by the shoulders and heading him down the hallway. Brenna stared after them, wondering what was going on.

Was Derrick annoyed she'd turned up early and unannounced? He hadn't seemed bothered. Before she could think of another explanation, Zach was in the kitchen and wrapping his arms around her.

"What's wrong?"

Brenna shook her head. "Later. Just hold me."

Zach's arms tightened around her. "For as long as you want."

"Does that mean you'd let me stay here tonight if it was for that long?"

Zach laughed softly. "Do your parents know where I live?"

"No. Would the answer be no if they did?"

"Nah, I just wanted to know if I'd have to leave town before your mother came after me with a knife to castrate me."

"She wouldn't do that."

"Are you sure?"

"Well… maybe."

"That's what I thought." Zach removed one arm from around her. He put his hand in the front pocket of his jeans and pulled out two keys. One was purple and the other silver. He dropped the purple key in her hand. "Front door." The silver key joined it. "My door."

Brenna stared at the purple key. "What did Derrick want when you came home?"

"To give me a front door key for you."

Brenna pulled out the key ring that held the keys to her parents' places and Zach's home that was now rented. She added the two keys to her collection. "Thanks."

"Well we can't have you sitting on the doorstep if no one's home and you need somewhere to go. Are you ready to talk now?"

Brenna gestured towards the cups she was stacking. "What-"

"Forget them. Come on. My room." Zach led the

way to his room and picked up Brenna's backpack she'd left at his door. He unlocked it, dropped the backpack on the floor inside his room and locked the door again. He kept hold of Brenna's hand, leading her to his bed.

She stretched out, resting her head on the pillow, his arm behind her neck. Minutes passed before she hesitantly started to tell Zach about her day. When she finished, she lay quietly beside him and waited to hear what he had to say.

"I guess that explains why your mother wasn't happy to see me the night I dropped you home."

"Why couldn't they have told me?"

"Maybe she's embarrassed."

"Are you sticking up for her?"

Zach shook his head. "Just trying to figure her out."

"It sounds like you're sticking up for her."

Zach rolled so he leaned above her. "I think with the mood you're in, you'd find a problem with whatever I said."

"I would not."

"Ren…"

She stared up at him, worried by his tone and expression. She reached up to run her fingers across his lips. She grew more worried when he barely seemed to notice. "What's wrong?"

"I went out to visit... that is I thought I should... I know they had to have their funeral... shit, I'm babbling like an idiot." Zach rolled away to lay on his back, an arm across his forehead.

Brenna leaned over him so she could meet his gaze. "I'd have come with you."

"I wanted to go alone. It felt right. At least it did until I got there."

"You did that before work?"

"Yeah, I know. Stupid, huh?"

Brenna smiled. "Maybe."

"Thanks," he said dryly.

"You asked."

"I also drove past the house on the way here."

"Why?"

"They were on my mind."

"How long did you live there?"

"All my life."

"Does it feel strange having someone else live there?"

"Not as strange as being there alone."

"I could've moved in with you. Separate rooms though."

Zach took his arm away from his forehead and pressed his hand against the back of her head to bring her closer. "What would I do without you? You make me smile when I don't think it's possible."

"You're there for me too."

"Always." His lips met hers and all conversation ended.

The room was filled with lengthening shadows when Derrick knocked on the bedroom door. When Zach finally answered, he said through the closed door, "Are you pair joining us tonight or you having a private party?"

Zach tossed one of the pillows from his bed at the door. It hit with a soft thud.

Derrick laughed. "Bathroom's free if you want it."

They listened to his footsteps recede. Zach smiled slightly. "So… we having our own private party or joining everyone else?"

It took Brenna a few seconds to gather her thoughts so she could answer. "Probably best to join everyone else."

"Yeah. I guess you're right. Anyway, after all the talk of getting pregnant young, I think I want you on the pill as well as using a condom."

"And what if I'm not ready for years?"

"Do you really think that?" Zach pressed his finger against her lips when she opened her mouth. "Answer honestly. And if you're looking for inspiration for your answer, think back over the past couple of hours."

Brenna blushed, but continued to meet his gaze. "What happened to no pressure?"

"Slightly shredded, but still about." Zach smiled. "Want to take that shower now?"

"Let me know when it's my turn."

"You don't want to do your part to help conserve water?"

"Nice try."

Zach laughed. "You can go first."

"Then you'll have to move. I can't go anywhere when you're lying on me." She pushed lightly against his bare chest.

"If you're certain…"

"Not at all. But I think we both need a shower."

Zach swiftly kissed her before he rose from the bed, holding out his hand to pull her up. "Do you think you can avoid the alcohol tonight? One of your parents out for my blood is more than enough to cope with."

Brenna grinned. "I'm not making any promises."

Chapter Thirty-Four

By the time they'd both showered and dressed, people were starting to arrive. Brenna recognised some of the faces from last time. And she nearly died of embarrassment when one of them remembered her.

"Hey, it's the girl with the sweet tooth. Want me to get you a drink?"

Brenna shook her head, grateful Zach had his arm wrapped around her waist.

"Don't tell me the morning after scared you off. They're much better when you don't drink a gallon of them. Trust me!"

"He's doing a law degree, so I'd take that last comment with a bucket load of salt," his friend, who'd offered her a beer last time, said. His gaze fell on Zach. "I don't see you around much anymore."

Zach shrugged. "Life's busy." He turned to Brenna. "This is Mason and the wanna be lawyer is Kyle."

"Wanna be!" Kyle grinned. "And who's gonna help you when someone tries to sue you because their prize winning pet dies?"

"Me of course." Betts joined their group in time to hear the last comment.

"Guess I'll have to represent the prize winning pet then." Kyle shrugged.

"Great friend you are," Zach said to Kyle after greeting Betts.

"It'd just be business."

"I won't be stabbing any friends in the back in the name of business." Betts dropped her arm around Zach's shoulders. "Don't worry, I'll look out for you."

"Thanks, Betts. Glad to know who my true friends are." Zach look pointedly at Kyle.

"Well, if your girlfriend there would smile at me like she did last time and promise to go out to dinner with me, I'd represent you for free."

"I'd have to check my diary, but I believe it's pretty full for the next decade." Brenna wanted to take back the words as soon as she'd said them. A million times she'd thought of comebacks she never voiced. She couldn't believe this time she'd actually spoken one at a party where she barely knew anyone.

Kyle laughed and theatrically clutched his heart. "I feel like I've been mortally wounded."

"Now that I'd believe if you had a heart to beat in there, tin man." Betts drained the last of the drink she held. "I need another drink. Anyone coming?"

Kyle and Mason both looked at their nearly empty glasses and joined her. Brenna turned to Zach when they were alone.

"Just one drink?"

"Your choice, Ren."

Brenna hesitated before she nodded.

"Same as last time?"

"I don't know. Maybe you could surprise me."

"How about something sweet, but without the kick of a donkey?"

"Okay."

It took them nearly fifteen minutes to make their way to the kitchen for Brenna's drink. People kept stopping Zach to talk to him. The rest of the night was the same. The only time they weren't interrupted was when they were dancing.

When Brenna got into Zach's car just before eleven o'clock, she smiled over at him. "Did you know everyone at the party?"

Zach shrugged. "Possibly." A knock on his car window made him turn his head. He set the ignition to accessories and pushed the button for the electric window.

Brenna recognised Tracey. She had to force herself not to stare. She was even better looking in life than in a photo.

"Zach, honey. You aren't leaving already are you? Oh, you have your little friend with you." Tracey smiled insincerely and waggled her fingers at Brenna in greeting. "Are you dropping her home? I'll be here when you get back."

"Don't bother waiting around for me," Zach said.

"I won't be waiting, but I'll still be here. Come and see me when you get back. It's been a while since we caught up. We had some good times."

"See you, Tracey." Zach pressed the button and the window started to rise.

"Later." Tracey smiled, waving breezily as she walked towards the front door.

Brenna stared after Tracey, doubts hitting her as she watched.

Zach started the car and pulled out onto the road. "What are you thinking?"

She opened her mouth to say and then closed it again. She sighed at all the words she couldn't speak. Eventually she managed to say something, just not the words she desperately wanted to voice. "She's very beautiful."

"It's only skin deep. Come on, Brenna. Talk to me.

I can practically hear all the words you're holding back."

"She… she was offering you sex, wasn't she?"

"Yeah."

"What… why…"

Zach pulled over onto the side of the road and turned to Brenna. "I'm not interested in her or any of her offers. She could strip naked in front of me and I wouldn't touch her."

"Yeah, right."

"I wouldn't touch her. I wouldn't hurt you like that." Zach grinned. "I'd look. I've never claimed to be a saint. I just wouldn't touch."

"But she's beautiful and interesting and you've even said you prefer casual relationships."

Zach reached out and took her hand. "My head and heart don't always agree. I'm letting my heart make this decision. You don't have to worry about Tracey, or anyone else."

"Why?"

"Why what?"

"Why me?"

"How many hours have you got?"

"None. Dad's expecting me."

"Then I guess we'll have to leave this discussion for another time."

Brenna nodded. Zach pulled out onto the road, the two of them falling silent.

When they were closer to her dad's house, she broke the silence. "I had a good night. Thanks for taking me back to Dad's tonight so I could go."

"I'm glad you wanted to go. I like spending time with you."

She was relieved he didn't seem to be brooding on their earlier words. "I was surprised the day ended better than it started. The earlier part of the day was enough to give me nightmares."

"I hope your dreams will be better now."

"Ahh… maybe."

Zach laughed softly. "Does that mean I might feature in them?" When she didn't answer, he laughed again. "Cat got your tongue, Ren?"

"Oh, stop teasing me."

"I might as well. It's not bright enough to see if I've made you blush."

Brenna ignored the heat in her cheeks. "I rarely do anymore."

"Guess that means I need to make more of an effort." Zach reached out and took her hand. He placed it on his thigh, resting his over hers.

Brenna sighed heavily as they pulled up in front of

her dad's house. Her hand tightened on his thigh. "I don't want the night to end."

"I wish you could have stayed with me, Ren."

"Then take me home with you."

Zach reached out to cup her cheek. "I wish I could. But you don't want to be in trouble with both your parents, do you?" Zach smiled when Brenna didn't answer. "Come on. I'll walk you to your door. We don't need to make your father wonder what we're up to."

They walked hand in hand to the front door. Before they reached it, the door swung open. Adam stood there.

"Thanks for bringing her home." Adam continued to block the doorway.

"Thanks for letting her come to the party."

"Time for bed, Brenna. Early morning tomorrow. You girls can help me in the yard."

"Can't Zach come in for a bit?"

Adam grinned. "He can always come back tomorrow morning."

Brenna rolled her eyes. "Please-" she stopped and looked up at Zach when he touched her back lightly.

"I'll see you in the morning. I'll bring some movies we can watch once the yard's been done. Any objections to action?"

"Only if you bring along a soppy one to follow it."

Zach groaned theatrically. "Only if you don't complain when I fall asleep during it."

"What's happening?" Danielle appeared behind Adam.

"Bed, young lady." Adam turned to face her.

"All the noise woke me." Danielle held up her hands when Adam continued to look at her. "Okay, okay. I'm going."

Zach took Brenna's right hand and smiled slightly. "Sweet dreams."

Brenna grinned. "You too. I'll see you in the morning."

*　*　*

Brenna lay on the floor beside Zach, her head on a cushion she'd pulled from the couch. Zach sat against the couch, his fingers absently playing with strands of her hair. Danielle was sprawled in a beanbag chair, while Adam was in an armchair. He'd started out watching Brenna and Zach more than the movie, but by a quarter of the way through, he was as caught up in the action as the rest of them.

When the credits came up on screen, Brenna

turned her head to look up at Zach. "Ready for an afternoon nap now?"

Zach groaned dramatically. "Are you sure you don't want to do something other than watch the next movie?"

"What is it?" Adam asked.

Zach picked up the case that sat near him and tossed it to Adam. He laughed at Adam's tone when he read the title.

Adam rose to his feet. "Unlike some, I can't laze around all afternoon. I'll leave you kids to it."

"Can you put the movie on before you go, Dad? I don't want to move for a week. Can't we pay someone to do the lawn?" Brenna stretched and then groaned. "Maybe I should make that two weeks."

When Adam had left the lounge room, Zach bent forward to whisper. "You want me to give you a massage?"

"You know how to give a proper one?" Brenna's voice was equally soft so her sister couldn't hear.

"Isn't it just hands wandering all over your body with a bit more pressure?"

"Not quite."

"Sounds good to me though. What do you think?"

"I don't think much at all when you start talking like that. My brain takes a holiday."

Zach laughed. "Interesting."

"What are you two whispering about?" Danielle demanded.

"Nothing," Brenna said hurriedly. "Okay, quiet now. The movie's starting."

The movies were followed by an early dinner and then Brenna and Zach went into her room and lay on the bed to talk. Brenna wished she could have locked her door, but her dad had said the door could be shut as long as it was left unlocked.

As they spoke, their words grew further apart until they drifted off to sleep. Brenna's heart felt like it leapt through her chest when Adam demanded, "What's going on?"

Brenna tried to focus on her dad, but the light seemed too bright after having her eyes closed for… she peered at her alarm clock. She couldn't believe it had been so long. "We must've fallen asleep. We were talking…"

Zach sat up, pulling his arm from behind Brenna's neck. "I'm sorry Adam. I guess you wore us out with all the yard work this morning."

"In that case it must be time for you to go home, Zach."

"Dad-" Brenna began, her voice bordering on a wail.

"No arguments, Brenna. As soon as he's finished waking up properly he can leave. I expect that shouldn't be more than five minutes."

"Night, Ren," Zach said when Brenna would have argued again.

"Zach-"

Zach smiled as he said, "Sweet dreams."

Brenna glared at Adam before she turned to Zach. "I'll walk you to your car."

When they reached the car, Brenna stepped close to Zach. He grasped her hands when she would have wrapped her arms around him. She frowned when he smiled at her.

"I'd like you to come over to my place tomorrow. So don't go upsetting your father."

"We weren't doing anything. He acted like we were criminals or something."

"We weren't doing anything this time. Please? No fighting with him?"

Brenna sighed heavily. "Fine."

"You don't want to spend the day with me tomorrow?"

"Of course I do. I just hate being treated like a little kid. It's like they blame me that they had me when they were so young. Or like I'm going to do the same thing. There's no way I'm having a kid so young."

"Is that the only reason you're keeping things low key?"

"No."

"And I'm guessing you're not going to discuss those reasons with me."

Brenna shrugged. "You'll probably think I'm being stupid."

"Never." Zach glanced towards the house. "I'd better go before Adam's out here dragging you inside. Text me if I can pick you up tomorrow."

Brenna nodded. Her gaze dropped to Zach's lips, wishing she could kiss him goodbye. She guessed that wouldn't be a good idea, in case her dad was watching.

Zach smiled. He pressed two of his fingers against her lips momentarily. "Sweet dreams, Ren."

"You too."

"Oh, I will." His smile became a grin.

Chapter Thirty-Five

Brenna walked back to the front door and stood there to watch Zach drive off. She stepped inside to find Adam in the lounge room. His expression was serious and he'd obviously waited for her.

"Sit down, Brenna."

Brenna sat in the armchair furthest from him. "I'm tired."

"This won't take long. I'm concerned about you and Zach."

"There's nothing to be concerned about."

"I find you asleep together on your bed, of course I'm going to wonder what's going on."

"We told you already, we were talking. Actually, Zach was complaining about the stray cats in his neighbourhood and that got him started on getting animals fixed. Talking about veterinary procedures is not in the slightest bit romantic. No wonder I fell asleep."

"So he's not your boyfriend?"

"Do I look like the sort of girl someone like him would be interested in? You should see some of the girls who call him. They could be models."

"There's nothing wrong with you, Brenna. Any fellow would be lucky to have you as his girlfriend."

"You've got to say that, you're my dad."

"I don't want you to ruin your life."

"Are you saying having me ruined yours?"

"Of course not!"

"Then what are you trying to say?"

Adam ran his hand through his hair and looked away. "You really should have this conversation with your mother. I'm no good at discussing these things."

"Actually, you're better at these conversations than Mum. She tells me what I have to do and how and then yells when I disagree. At least you listen."

"It's been harder for your mother than me. I've got my family. She only had me. It's difficult when your family refuses to acknowledge your existence. You couldn't understand what she went through."

"When no one listens to me I feel like I don't exist. Like my feelings and thoughts are unimportant."

Silence filled the room as Adam stared at his hands

that were now clasped in front of him. "I won't make you move. But I'd like you to spend part of your holidays with me. You and Danielle."

Brenna was speechless. She stared at her dad, words floating around in her head. Disjointed words that would have made no sense if she'd spoken them.

"Isn't that what you wanted?" Adam stared at her when she continued to remain silent.

"To choose. That's all I want."

"Then what do you choose?"

"I'm not sure. It's quieter here. I can't seem to talk to Mum without us arguing. I still want to stay at the same school, and work at Matt's shop. Why couldn't you have got somewhere closer?"

"I thought it'd be nice not to have to travel so far to work every day."

"Why did you never talk to me before?" Brenna frowned when Adam looked away. "It's because of Mum, isn't it?"

"Now Brenna, she–"

"I don't want you making excuses for her. I want to know why. We never bothered asking you if we could do something because we knew you'd check with Mum. It was always easiest to go straight to her because she never bothered to check with you. And when we asked you things at the dinner table, she'd answer. We stopped talking to you. I only realised that recently. We were kids when it started. But you were an adult. Why did you let her do it?"

Adam shook his head. "Brenna, it's really none of–"

"No! Don't tell me that. It is my business. You wrote us off. You didn't bother with us. You went to work, came home, argued with Mum and went to bed. Unless you drove off angrily. Why did you let her isolate you? We don't know you and you let her do that."

"It's complicated."

"That's always your answer."

"What do you want me to say, Brenna? That I'm weak and let your mother walk all over me because it was easiest?"

"Yes! If that's the truth."

"Guilt."

"Huh?"

"Guilt. It was my fault she was pregnant. She had plans to go to uni. She was going to be a doctor. I ruined it for her."

"How?"

"You'll have to ask your mother."

"She wanted to abort me and you wouldn't let her."

"I'm not discussing that part with you. You'll have to talk to your mother if you want to know."

"She won't say anything. But I know I'm right."

"This wasn't exactly the talk I'd planned to have with you."

Brenna grinned. "At least we managed to talk without arguing. Well, without major arguments. That's more than Mum and I can do."

"We didn't get anything resolved though."

"Can I go somewhere with Zach tomorrow?"

"Where?"

Brenna shrugged. "I don't know. It doesn't really matter. Hang out with friends. See a movie. Just out."

"I don't know, Brenna. I think you're spending too much time with him."

"I like to spend time with him."

"And that's what concerns me. I think you like spending time with him a little too much. I think I'm going to have to say no."

"Dad! That's so unfair. What do you think we're going to do?"

"I remember being eighteen. I know perfectly well what you can get up to."

"What do you want me to do? Promise I won't have sex if I go out with him tomorrow?"

"But would you keep your word?"

"Of course I would."

"But it's not just tomorrow you want to hang out with him."

"Fine. Until the end of grade eleven. I promise I won't have sex until the end of grade eleven if you let me regularly see Zach." Brenna shook her head. "I seriously can't believe I'm having this conversation with you."

"How do I know I can trust you? That you're not saying it to get your own way?"

Anger rushed through her. "What do you want me to do? Get medical proof? You want a letter from my doctor?"

"Brenna."

She glared at her dad, ignoring the warning tone. "Maybe if you hadn't written us off for so many years you'd know whether or not you could trust me."

Adam stared at her for long silent seconds. "I'm going to trust you. You break my trust and that's it. I won't believe another word you say. Do you understand?"

Brenna nodded. "Does that mean I can go out with Zach tomorrow?" Adam hesitated and Brenna spoke again in case he was still thinking no. "It's the last day of the school holidays. Please."

"Okay. But he's to bring you here and you and your sister will catch the train to school on Monday."

"Thank you."

"You're to be home by eight since you have school the next day."

"Okay." Brenna rose to her feet.

"We'll have this conversation again when you finish school this year."

Brenna smiled, slightly embarrassed. "If we have to. Night, Dad."

Adam rose to his feet. "Night, Brenna."

Brenna hugged her dad before she left the room. She glanced back at him as she reached the doorway. For a second she thought he looked like he might cry. The impression was gone as quickly as it came and Brenna mentally shook her head before she headed to her room. She grabbed her pyjamas, used the bathroom and climbed into bed. With only the bedside lamp on, she sent a text to Zach so he knew to pick her up in the morning.

The phone rang seconds later. Brenna smiled when she saw Zach's name on the display. "Hey."

"How long are you allowed out tomorrow?"

"I have to be home by eight."

"Great! Any thoughts on what you want to do?"

"Not really. What were you thinking?"

"We could take the bikes out to Ben's. He's having that camp there this weekend."

Brenna groaned. "Don't tell me you want to go to that."

"Only if you'll join me. On the bike too."

"I'll think about it."

"Fair enough."

"So how did you convince Adam to let you out tomorrow? He seemed a little upset with us."

"Ahh… well…"

Zach laughed. "Why do I get the feeling the talk involved a discussion on sex? Or rather on not having it?"

"I promised not to until I finished school this year."

"That's not too far away."

"That doesn't mean… I'm not going to…"

"I know. But I can hope."

"Talking about end of year, there's a dance. I was wondering…" she trailed off. Why would he want to go to a high school dance?

"What were you wondering?"

She took a deep breath. "Would you go to it with me?"

"Of course."

Surprise made her mind temporarily blank, then she said in a rush, "Thank you."

"Should I pick you up with or without the

motorbikes tomorrow? Would your father freak and not let you go if we had them with us?"

"I haven't agreed to go yet."

"But you will, won't you?"

"Maybe. But you probably shouldn't bring the bikes. I'm not sure how well he'd take it."

"Okay. I'll see you around seven. Sweet dreams, Ren."

"You too."

"Love ya."

"Me too." Brenna stared at the phone for several minutes after Zach had hung up. She reached out and turned off the bedside lamp, smiling as she thought back over their conversation. She drifted off to sleep with an image of Zach in her mind.

Chapter Thirty-Six

Brenna stood beside Derrick and watched the motorbikes race across the rough ground. The aim of the race was to avoid being the last person past the checkpoint. The last person was kicked from the race each time the checkpoint was passed. The race had started with twenty-six. Travis had been the last one to be sent off the track and now there were only four riders left. Ben and Zach were in the lead. The other two riders still in the race were friends of Ben's.

Brenna turned to Derrick who stood beside her. "I won't be long. I need a drink. If spring's this hot, summer's going to kill us."

Derrick nodded. "I'll yell if you take too long and it gets down to the last two riders."

"Thanks." She walked towards the car and popped the boot so she could get a soft drink from the esky.

"Your boyfriend thinks he's really good on that bike of his. But he won't beat Ben. No one does."

Brenna turned to face Travis as she closed the boot. "He isn't expecting to beat Ben. He's just having fun."

"Sure! The way he's riding, he's trying to come first."

Brenna opened the can and had a mouthful. She watched Travis as she did. What had she ever seen in him? "Not everyone feels the need to prove themselves every minute of the day."

"You've changed. And not for the better."

"I'm going to argue that. I used to let too many people tell me what I should be doing. I don't do that much anymore. So I'd have to say that's an improvement."

"He won't stick around. You'll bore him."

"That's my problem, not yours."

"You keep telling him no and he's going to find someone who says yes. Why do you think I found Kelly?"

Brenna froze for a moment and her confidence started to evaporate. When Travis grinned triumphantly she forced herself to meet his gaze. "You obviously weren't the right one for me because no just isn't in my vocabulary these days."

"Why you little bitch." Travis took a step forward.

"Brenna! Last two," Derrick called out as he came towards them.

Brenna was relieved to see Derrick. For a split second panic had raced through her. "Get over it, Travis. Anyone would think you're still pining for me." She started to walk towards Derrick who waited for her.

"I wouldn't take you back even if you paid me."

Brenna looked over her shoulder at him with a grin. "Good, because the feeling's mutual." She strode towards Derrick, still grinning.

Derrick draped his arm casually around her shoulders. "You look like the cat that swallowed the canary. And a bowl of cream, probably half a dozen budgies too."

Brenna laughed. "And they were delicious."

Derrick returned her grin. "I take it the poser didn't come off too well in your conversation."

"Not at all." They reached the checkpoint and Brenna stared up the track waiting for the last two riders to come into view. "Is Zach still in the race?"

"Of course. And Ben."

Brent joined them, unzipping his jacket. He ran his hand through his sweat dampened hair. "It's hot out there." He glanced along the track. "Oh good, I haven't missed the end." He'd been sent out of the race before Travis, missing the checkpoint by centimetres.

Brenna offered her soft drink to Brent who took a couple of mouthfuls before he handed it back.

"Here they come!" One of Ben's friends called out as he pointed.

Brenna handed her drink to Derrick and pulled out Zach's phone so she could record the end of the race. She'd be surprised if he beat Ben, but just in case, she wanted proof so Travis couldn't argue the fact. She glanced to her right where Travis stood, scowling. Her lips again curved into a self-satisfied smile before she focused on the race.

Zach and Ben rode next to each other, Ben slightly ahead. Then they were level. Brenna held her breath. At the last moment, Ben pulled ahead, winning by seconds. Those watching yelled in appreciation. Some of them clapped and whistled. Brenna put Zach's phone in her pocket, took her drink off Derrick, noticed it was lighter and moved forward as Zach stopped his motorbike next to Ben. They both pulled off their helmets and grinned at each other as they shook hands.

Brenna was unable to move closer as everyone crowded around excitedly. Zach met her gaze through the crowd. He hopped off his motorbike and pushed through to stand in front of her. He glanced at the drink in her hands.

"Why not. Everyone else has helped themselves." She held out the drink to him.

With a chuckle, Zach downed the last of the drink. He tossed it towards the bin that sat open by a tree not far from them, grinning as it went in.

"Show off." She wrapped her arms around his neck and looked up at him.

"Want to take a ride with me?"

"Well…"

"I'll ride with you if she doesn't want to," one of the women Ben had invited said as she came near them.

Brenna lightly kissed Zach, wanting to tell the woman to back off. "Sure."

"Come on then. Let's get your helmet."

Brenna was no longer terrified they'd come off the motorbike. After all morning, and the last time they'd been here, she felt confident in Zach's abilities and no longer thought she'd cause an accident. The near accident when she was on Travis' motorbike must have been his fault for not letting her slowly get used to it.

After several laps around the track, Zach came to a stop, flipping up his visor as he turned towards her. "Want to learn how to ride?"

"No." The word burst from her as she pushed up her own visor.

Zach grinned. "You sure?"

"Ahh… yeah… I don't know."

"We can take it slow. I can even borrow a smaller bike for you next weekend if you want."

Brenna shook her head. "No. I'm not ready. Maybe one day, but not yet."

"Okay. You let me know when you are." He slid his visor back into place and Brenna did the same before he started around the track again.

When they left around three o'clock, it was amidst many protests and Ben reminding them they were welcome any time. Brenna noticed Travis wasn't one of the people hanging around to say goodbye. As soon as they reached the highway, Brenna took over the driving, glad the traffic was light.

Once the motorbikes were away, the trailer unhooked and the dust of the day washed from them, Brenna and Zach relaxed in his room, sprawled on the bed. Zach tugged down a strap of the sundress Brenna had changed into after her shower and she slid it back into place. With a grin, he tugged it down again.

"What are you doing?"

"Hassling you."

"Why?"

"Do you realise I see you more when you're at your father's place?"

"But it's so far away. And it'll take me forever to get to and from school every day. I'm not changing schools. I wouldn't know anyone at a new school."

"I could give you a lift home in the afternoon."

"I don't know." Brenna frowned.

Zach reached out to smooth her forehead. "Just a thought. You don't even have to commit yourself to moving. You could suggest a trial run."

"Why would you want me to live so far away?"

"No point in having you within touching distance if I can't actually touch."

Brenna shivered as Zach ran his hand along her side at his last word. "That makes sense. At least I can talk to Dad. Which is a surprise."

"The complete opposite to what I had."

"I never want to mention your parents. I always worry it'll make you sad."

Zach smiled wryly. "I think I feel more anger than sorrow when I think about them. And don't ask me to explain that because I wouldn't have a clue and I don't want to figure out why either." His smile widened, becoming more mischievous. "How about you take my mind off them?"

Brenna couldn't help laughing. "You're so predictable." She kissed him, still smiling slightly. Then laughter was forgotten, as well as thoughts.

When Derrick knocked on the bedroom door later, Brenna lay in Zach's arms, dazed. "I know you're both in there. You could answer me."

Brenna heard laughter rumble through Zach's chest where she rested. "You answer him," she whispered.

"What's up?" Zach raised his voice so Derrick would be able to hear him through the door.

"We're ordering Chinese. Interested?" Derrick asked.

Zach looked at Brenna who nodded, her cheek brushing against his chest. "Yeah."

"Anything in particular?"

Zach glanced at Brenna again who shook her head this time. "Nah. Whatever you order." He turned back to Brenna when the sound of footsteps moved away from the door. "Are you ready to drag yourself from bed now?"

Brenna shook her head. "My whole body is mush."

Zach laughed. "It feels okay to me." His hand glided over her skin.

"If you can make me feel like that with just your hands, I'm not going to survive sex." Brenna closed her eyes as she realised what she'd said. "And I can't believe I said that aloud."

"I like to hear what you're thinking."

"Even when I say idiotic things?"

"Keep sharing your thoughts with me and I might even let you read what I've written about you in my diary."

"Is it good or bad?"

Zach grinned. "All good. But it'll probably make you blush so hard you won't stop for a week."

"Maybe I better not read it."

Zach laughed, rolling off the bed to stand beside it. "Come on, we better join the rest of the world. We'll have to head to your father's place once we've eaten."

Brenna joined him beside the bed. "I wish I didn't have to go."

Zach ran his knuckles lightly over her cheekbone. "Me too."

When the food arrived, they sprawled on the lounge room floor and shared the containers. Brenna ignored the wooden chopsticks and automatically picked up the plastic cutlery.

"Where's your sense of adventure?" Zach used chopsticks to hold food at her mouth.

"Being practical." She ate the food offered.

"Tell me about it." Brent also grabbed plastic

cutlery. "I'm more likely to put someone's eye out with those sticks than get food to my mouth."

The meal was filled with teasing and laughter and Brenna reluctantly walked with Zach to his car afterwards. The drive home went far too quickly and they pulled up in front of Adam's house at twenty to eight.

"Do you want me to pick you up and give you a lift to school tomorrow?" Zach asked as they reached the front door.

Brenna shook her head. "I want to see if I can handle getting up early and catch the train without a drama. No good giving something a trial run if I'm not going to do it properly."

"Really?"

"Yeah, really."

Zach grinned. "I hope that means I see you more often."

"Me too." She turned and unlocked the door. She nearly groaned when she saw her dad sitting in the lounge room.

Adam checked his watch. "Time to spare. Nice to see."

"Evening," Zach said.

Adam rose to his feet. "Did you have fun?" When

they nodded in answer, he asked, "So, what did you end up doing?"

Brenna seriously considered making something up, but decided to see how the truth worked. "Motorbike riding."

"You can't ride a bike, Brenna."

"No, but Zach can. I was a passenger."

"You wore a helmet?"

Zach nodded. "Of course. Gloves, jacket, jeans and enclosed shoes as well."

"Zach's been riding since he was eight. Matt's brother taught him."

Adam nodded. "Well, time for you to get ready for bed, Brenna. Have you had anything to eat?"

Brenna nodded before she turned to Zach. She smiled slightly. "Sweet dreams."

"Text me."

Brenna nodded. There were words she wanted to speak, things she wanted to do, but her dad stood behind her and watched. She mouthed the words 'love you' and smiled at the sudden heat in Zach's eyes he instantly masked.

When Zach had left, Brenna turned to Adam. "Can I talk to you?"

"That was going to be my line."

Brenna was suddenly wary of why her dad had

been sitting in the lounge room doing nothing. She had the impression he'd been waiting for her. "What's wrong?" Her words were cautious.

Chapter Thirty-Seven

Adam pointed to the armchair and waited until they were both seated before he spoke. "First, if you're going to do something risky like motorbike riding I want to know about it before the fact. And where you'll be. You can't roam around without letting someone know where you're going. If something had happened, I wouldn't have had a clue where you were. I thought you were going to the movies or something."

Brenna shrugged. "We don't always know what we're going to do until the last minute."

"Then ring or text and let me know at the last minute."

Brenna nodded. "Okay." She waited for him to get to his real reason for the talk. Silence filled the room instead. She wondered where her sister was and how her dad had managed to keep her away from the lounge room when she liked nothing better than being in on everything that was happening. When the silence stretched out even further, Brenna wondered if she should ask her dad what the problem was. She chickened out. If it was this hard for him to speak about it, maybe she'd be better off not knowing.

"Anything else you did today I should know about? Hang gliding? Parachuting?"

Brenna smiled feebly and shook her head. She decided if he wasn't going to say what he wanted, she'd take her turn. "I was talking to Zach today about you and Mum wanting me to move."

"Ahh…"

"You do still want me to move in with you, don't you?"

"Of course I do."

"He said I should give it a trial run. See how I like it before I say no."

"Trial run."

Brenna nodded. "Yeah. Move in here for the last school term and see what I think. You never know, you might be the one saying no by the end of the school year."

Adam chuckled. "And to think I've been sitting

here trying to tell you I was serious when I said you didn't have to move."

Brenna stared at her dad. His words echoed in her head, followed by the image of him sitting there like he was about to tell her someone had died. "You really want me to live here, don't you?"

Adam nodded. "I've already told you that."

"I just thought…" Brenna shrugged. How did you say you felt like you were something else to be divided up? She swallowed hard to try and dislodge the lump in her throat. "It's only a trial, okay?"

Adam nodded again.

"And I'm still going to work part-time and go to the same school."

Adam nodded yet again.

"And we've got to get wireless. I need to be able to use the net in my room."

Adam grinned. "Don't push it."

Brenna returned his grin. "Should I see if Zach can borrow Derrick's trailer again? 'Cause I can't be months without all my stuff."

"Yeah, but maybe we better wait until the weekend when I can help you load up your gear. Your mother isn't really impressed with Zach."

"She doesn't like any males."

"Well…" Adam cleared his throat, looking

uncomfortable. "Maybe you better get ready for bed. You'll have to get up early tomorrow."

Brenna rose to her feet. "Okay." She reached the doorway before she turned back. "You like him, don't you? Zach."

"Yes, but that doesn't change the fact you're not getting serious with any boy until you're seventeen. And you won't be spending as much time with him in future. I think you're getting too involved."

Brenna's first impulse was to yell and tell her dad he couldn't run her life. She barely managed to hold the angry words back. She reminded herself he'd listened to her before. "Would you rather I snuck around behind your back and lied to you about where I am and what I'm doing? You can't police me twenty-four seven and I'm not going to stop seeing him. Doesn't my promise mean anything?"

"I'm more concerned about his view on the subject."

"He didn't seem overly bothered by it."

"What!"

"He–"

"No! What I want to know is what situation brought that particular topic up."

"No situation. He's my friend. My best friend. We

tell each other stuff. Share thoughts. Aren't you meant to be able to tell your best friend everything?"

"I thought Bec was your best friend."

"There's no rule that says I can only have one best friend. And besides, she lives all the way over on the other side of the country." And she was beginning to believe the distance had killed their friendship.

"It's more common for your best friend to be the same sex as you. And don't try telling me he only thinks of you as a friend. I've seen the way he looks at you sometimes."

"When we go anywhere, it's with a group. We went motorbike riding with a group, parties always have a tonne of people at them and even here we aren't alone. You can't lock me away until I'm seventeen. I must be the only person in my whole class, actually in my whole grade and the one below me that isn't allowed to have a boyfriend. And don't give me that stupid bridge line. You know perfectly well I wouldn't jump off a bridge just because everyone else is doing it." Brenna stopped abruptly, her voice having risen. She took a deep breath and tried unsuccessfully to calm down. All she could think was she had to see Zach. As often as possible.

"Brenna-"

"No! Do you trust me?"

"Brenna-"

"It's a simple question. You only need to answer yes or no."

"Don't carry-"

"Yes or no. I thought I could talk to you and that you'd actually listen to me. Was that all an act to convince me to move in?"

Adam stalked across the room, a warning in his voice. "Brenna this is-"

"Yes. Or. No."

"I trust you."

"Then you aren't going to prove it by locking me away until I'm seventeen. I'm not asking to see him every day. If I keep up with schoolwork and everything else, why can't I see him as much as I have been?"

"I think you're getting too involved."

"We aren't." Brenna blocked the images of the day from her mind. "Give me a month. Let me show you I can balance the amount of time I spend with Zach with all the other demands on my time."

Adam stared at her a moment, his forehead creased. "At the end of each month we'll reassess it. If I think you're neglecting everything else then you'll only see him twice a week. Understand?"

"Yes."

Adam sighed. "Get ready for bed, Brenna. It's much later than I'd planned for you to be up. Your sister's already asleep. If you haven't woken her with all your noise."

Brenna could only nod. She knew if she opened her mouth it'd be to argue. Instead she retreated to her bedroom to grab her pyjamas. As soon as she was in bed, she picked up her phone and sent Zach a message. *Trial run.*

He rang seconds later. She noticed he was using his home line. "When?"

Brenna grinned. "Hello, Zach."

He laughed softly. "Hello, Ren. I'd offer to help you pack your gear, but I get the feeling I'd be as welcome as a plague."

"She'd probably welcome the plague before she welcomed you in the house."

"How did your father take it? Happy you're moving in?"

Brenna told Zach about their conversation. It was easier to tell him over the phone. She waited silently for him to digest everything she'd said.

"Best friend, huh?"

"I–" Brenna's mind went blank.

"And here I was thinking I was more than that."

Brenna was finally able to whisper, "You are." She

forced herself to continue. "But you're my best friend too."

There was a moment of silence before Zach replied. "Love you, Ren."

"Me too." She couldn't hold back the smile her lips curved into.

"Are you sure you don't want me to pick you up in the morning?"

Brenna hesitated. "I'll catch the train."

"It's going to be a long day."

Brenna's smile widened at his words. "I know."

"So… you still going to catch the train?"

"Yeah. I'm trying to be sensible here, Zach. You're not helping."

"I'll see you tomorrow afternoon."

"Okay."

"Love ya."

"Me too."

Chapter Thirty-Eight

Brenna was surprised at how quickly the last term of school seemed to go. Every minute of every day seemed to be filled and there never was enough time. Weekdays were consumed by school, work and Zach. Weekends by work and Zach. The weekends she had with her dad she didn't work, the ones spent at her mum's, Matt cooperated and filled her days with work. There were times when Brenna wondered if living with her dad was the right choice. Like when she'd been up late doing assignments or homework and then had to drag herself out of bed to catch the train. Mostly, she found it easier than living with her mum. There were less arguments, he actually listened to what she had to say and usually gave her the opportunity to prove herself before assuming she was going to make the wrong choice.

Then it was the last week of school and Brenna

was counting the days until school was out for the Christmas holidays. She looked forward to weeks of being able to spend more time with Zach.

She smiled as she let herself into Zach's room. He glanced up at her from where he sat at his desk, returning her smile. He turned back to his laptop and typed another couple of lines before he saved his work and turned it off. Then he was at her side, greeting her with a long kiss.

"You look really happy." Zach's arms tightened around her.

Brenna nodded. "I think I've figured out what I want to do."

"Yeah?"

"You know how Matt's been teaching me about ordering, paperwork and stuff?"

"Yeah."

"Well we had a delivery this morning that was nothing like what we ordered. And Matt had a difficult customer, and I mean real difficult, so I said I'd take care of the order since it was only the two of us. No way was I going to deal with the customer. But anyway, I loved it. I got it all sorted and had the correct order there within the hour. Matt said that in some large companies that's all some employees do. Purchasing and making sure the correct orders come in. I went online at Matt's shop and had a look at what business degrees they have at uni and there are tonnes. Even at your uni."

Zach smiled. "Really?"

"Yep." She pulled away to rummage through her handbag. "I printed up a list. I know it's in here somewhere. I think I've got too much crap in my bag." She tipped it onto Zach's bed and pounced on the folded piece of paper, waving it triumphantly. "I knew it was in there somewhere." She unfolded it. "Are you paying attention?" She looked at the bed to see what Zach stared at.

He took a step forward and picked up the card of pills lying amongst the rest of the contents of her handbag. "How long?"

"Umm." Brenna's cheeks heated, something she'd not felt for months. Her contraceptive pills had been the last thing on her mind when she'd dumped the contents of her bag on the bed.

"I take it the pill you've circled is the day your promise runs out."

Brenna could only nod and stare at the circle halfway through the month's supply. "It… I…"

"Talk to me, Ren." He dropped the pills on the bed with the rest of her things and stepped close so he could wrap his arms around her.

"I can't leave them at home. My sister goes through my stuff."

"When did you start?"

"This is the second card."

"Why are you taking the pill?" Zach stared down at her.

The intensity of his gaze left her breathless. "I haven't decided. But… well… I didn't want to be unprepared. Not when…"

"Not when what?"

"Not when I've wanted to forget the promise I made Dad and several times been close to breaking it."

Zach's arms tightened around her. "You certainly know what to say to make it harder for me not to pressure you."

"Sorry."

Zach kissed her. "Don't be. I want you to tell me what you're thinking. Although I'm kinda glad I haven't known sooner. I probably would've forgotten all about helping you keep your promise last weekend. I'm surprised your father hasn't made you promise not to have sex during the school holidays."

Brenna grinned. "I think he's been trying to, but I've been avoiding him."

"Why?"

"Until I make up my mind and after the end of school."

"How will that help?"

"Because if I decide yes, then I'll wait until afterward to talk to him. That way I'll promise not to take things any further than they've gone until my seventeenth birthday. Or something like that. I really don't want to lie to him. He trusts me. And I like the fact he does. It's a nice change."

Zach looked surprised. "You're actually thinking about it seriously."

Brenna nodded. "Yeah."

"And what if he corners you before this promise is over?"

"I'm staying at Ellen's the rest of this week. I've got some early shifts at work and two more exams left that are later in the day."

Zach laughed. "So when will you let me know?"

"When I know?"

"Fair enough. Need a reminder of what you're deciding on?"

Brenna grinned, hitting him lightly on the arm. "Can't you think of anything else?"

"Not when you're in my arms."

"I still sometimes wonder why you feel that way."

"Then stop wondering. Of course I feel that way. I love you, Ren."

"I know, but that's the part I don't always get. Especially when we run into Tracey."

Zach's fingers traced her jaw. "Why would I want a cruel heartless bitch like her when I've got you?" His lips lightly touched hers. "You completely distracted me earlier. I had a question to ask you."

"What?"

"I'm wondering if you plan to keep living with your father."

"Yeah. It's not perfect, but it's way better than living with Mum. We get along a little better when we're not in each other's face too much. And although I miss Danielle sometimes, we don't fight as much either."

"That's good. So… any ideas on what you want to do these holidays?"

Brenna shrugged. "I don't know."

"Let me know your decision so I can plan either going to the beach or barricading us in my room Saturday."

Brenna laughed, finally deciding. She gazed up at him, a smile hovering on her lips. "School officially ends three p.m. Friday." She paused. "And we're not going to the beach."

"Friday." Zach's lips slowly curved into a smile. "I'll be waiting for you."

Brenna's smile became a grin, then it disappeared as she kissed him, her hands pulling him closer.

Free Ebook

Subscribe to Avril's newsletter to receive a free ebook. This ebook is exclusive to those on her mailing list. To find out more about this offer visit: http://www.avrilsabine.com/free-ebook/

*

We value your privacy and will not sell, rent, exchange or loan your email address to third parties. Your information is confidential and you are under no obligation to remain on the mailing list and can unsubscribe at any time.

Acknowledgements

Many thanks to the usual crew. How would I manage without you?

To The Reader

If you enjoyed this book, why not consider leaving a review to help other readers discover it too? Reader engagement is one of the few ways that lets an author know readers want more books in a particular series or genre. So leave a review and tell friends, not only about this book but also about other ones you've enjoyed, so you can continue to enjoy books by your favourite authors for years to come.

Dreams are meant to be lived,

Avril.

About The Author

Avril is an Australian author who lives with her family on acreage in South East Queensland. She writes mostly young adult speculative fiction, but has been known to dabble in other genres. You can find more information about her at her website www.avrilsabine.com where you can also subscribe to her newsletter to be kept informed about new releases, current projects, blog posts and exclusive news.

Titles By Avril Sabine

Stories about strong characters and characters who discover their strengths.

SERIES

Assassins Of The Dead- Young Adult Fantasy/ Paranormal

Book 1: Dark Blade

Book 2: Dragon Touched

Book 3: Society Against Vampires

Book 4: King's Request

Dragon Blood- Young Adult Urban Fantasy (with elements of romance)

(5 book series)

Book 1: Pliethin

Book 2: Wyvern

Book 3: Surety

Book 4: Knight

Book 5: Mage

Dragon Mage- Young Adult Urban Fantasy (with elements of romance)

(Series two of Dragon Blood series)

Book 1: Promise

Dragon Blood Chronicles- Young Adult Urban Fantasy (with elements of romance)

(Companion stand alone series to Dragon Blood)

Book 1: Oath

Book 2: Betrayed

Guardians Of The Round Table- Young Adult Fantasy LitRPG

(Co-written with Storm and Rhys Petersen)

Book 1: Dexterity Fail

Book 2: Goblin Boots

Book 3: Singed Feathers

Book 4: Frog Mage

Book 5: Crystal Mine

Book 6: Cursed Harp

Rosie's Rangers- Young Adult Western Steampunk

(6 book series)

Book 1: Justice

Book 2: Vengeance

Book 3: Treachery

Book 4: Accused

Book 5: Wanted

Book 6: Corruption

Mark Of Kings- Children's Fantasy

(Upper middle grade/preteen)

(4 book series)

Book 1: The Arena

Book 2: The Island

Book 3: The Assassin

Book 4: The King

STAND ALONE SERIES

*Demon Hunters- Young Adult Urban Fantasy/
Horror (with elements of romance)*

Book 1: Blood Sacrifice

Book 2: Retribution

Book 3: Tainted

Book 4: Premonition

Book 5: Cursed

Book 6: Feud

Book 7: Extrication

Plea Of The Damned- Young Adult Urban Fantasy/Paranormal

(6 book series)

Book 1: Forgive Me Lucy

Book 2: Forgive Me Aiden

Book 3: Forgive Me Jena

Book 4: Forgive Me Kobe

Book 5: Forgive Me Marti

Book 6: Forgive Me Dawson

Realms Of The Fae- Young Adult Urban Fantasy (with elements of romance)

The Sword (short story in Like A Girl Anthology)

Heart Of Stone

Book 1: A Debt Owed

Book 2: Marked By The Hunt

Book 3: The Magic Collector

Book 4: An Unexpected Betrayal

Book 5: Imprisoned By Iron

Fairytales Retold (Short Stories)

Snow-White And Rose-Red

The Twelve Brothers

The Light Princess

Beauty And The Beast

Sleeping Beauty

Aschenputtel

The Golden Bird

The Frog Prince

The Death Of Koshchei The Deathless

Myths And Legends Retold (Short Stories)

Ion, Son Of Apollo

Sir Gawain And The Maid With The Narrow Sleeves

Princess Ilse, The Giant's Daughter

YOUNG ADULT NOVELS

Young Adult Fantasy (with elements of romance)

Elf Sight

Earth Bound

Young Adult Urban Fantasy

Stone Warrior (with elements of romance)

The Jungle Inside

Young Adult Contemporary (with elements of romance)

Through Your Eyes

The Ugly Stepsister

Perfect Little Princess

Young Adult Contemporary/Paranormal

Whispers In The Dark (with elements of romance and same sex relationships)

Over Too Soon (with elements of romance)

Young Adult Sci-Fi

Experiment X-One-Six (Urban Sci-Fi/Superheroes)

An Endless Dawn (Post Apocalyptic Sci-Fi)

CHILDREN'S BOOKS

Dragon Lord (Preteen/early teens) (Fantasy)

The Irish Wizard (Upper middle grade) (Urban Fantasy)

SHORT STORIES

Urban Fantasy

Eternally Late

Dealings With Joe

Glimpses (short story in That Moment When
Anthology)

Contemporary

The Brat Next Door

Fantasy LitRPG

(Set in the same world as Guardians Of The Round
Table Series)

Tales Of Inadon 1: The Disc (Co-written with
Storm and Rhys Petersen) (short story in Game On!
Anthology)

Post Apocalyptic Sci-Fi

Compulsive Directive

NONFICTION

A Year Of Weekly Writing Exercises (Creative Writing)

Cooking For Families With Allergies (Cooking) (Co-written with Storm Petersen)

Tell Me A Story, Grandma (Memoir)

For the most up to date details on available titles visit:

www.avrilsabine.com/books/bibliography

Disclaimer

This is a work of fiction. Names, characters, businesses, places, events and incidents are either the products of the author's imagination or used in a fictitious manner. Any resemblance to actual persons, living or dead, or actual events is purely coincidental. The opinions expressed or beliefs held are those of the characters and should not be assumed to be the opinions or beliefs of the author.